Southern Stories

Books by Clark Blaise

A North American Education (1973)

Tribal Justice (1974)

Days and Nights in Calcutta (1977)
(with Bharati Mukherjee)

Lunar Attractions (1979)

Lusts (1983)

Resident Alien (1986)

The Sorrow and the Terror (1987)
(with Bharati Mukherjee)

Man and His World (1992)

I Had a Father (1993)

Here, There and Everywhere:
Lectures on Australian, Canadian, American and Post-Modern Writing (1994)

If I Were Me (1997)

Time Lord:
Sir Sandford Fleming and the Creation of Standard Time (2001)

The Selected Stories of

CLARK BLAISE

Volume One

Southern Stories

With an Introduction by
Fenton Johnson

The Porcupine's Quill

CANADIAN CATALOGUING IN PUBLICATION DATA

Blaise, Clark, 1940–
Southern stories: the selected stories

ISBN 0-88984-219-1 (v. 1)

I. Title.

PS8553.L34S68 2000 C813'.54 C00-932402-X
PR9199.3.B48S68 2000

Canada

Published by The Porcupine's Quill,
68 Main Street, Erin, Ontario NOB 1TO.
Readied for the press by John Metcalf; copy edited by Doris Cowan.
Typeset in Minion, printed on Zephyr Antique laid,
and bound at the Porcupine's Quill Inc.

Represented in Canada by the Literary Press Group.
Trade orders are available from General Distribution Services.

We acknowledge the support of the Ontario Arts Council,
and the Canada Council for the Arts for our publishing program.
The financial support of the Government of Canada
through the Book Publishing Industry Development Program
is also gratefully acknowledged.

1 2 3 4 • 02 01 00

Contents

Introduction

The world is a continuum of borderlands – when Canadian French is so commonly spoken in Maine and Mexican Spanish in California, what meaning has the invisible dotted line? And yet the demarcation of 'here' versus 'there' is among the richest of literary territories, probably because it offers such opportunity to juxtapose the self with the other.

For more than twenty years I have turned to Clark Blaise's writing as I might hire an interpreter in a foreign land – someone to help me understand my own borderlands, the rich and scary places where I am brought up against the shifting construction of identities I call myself. Clark Blaise is of my America and apart from it, at once a Canadian and a U.S. citizen, Yankee and Southerner, native and exile – a global citizen before we invented the phrase to describe the condition.

Blaise's childhood embraced the most radically different of North American subcultures: Canada relying on its European heritage to distinguish and distance itself from the U.S., and an American South fiercely disdaining all that smacked of Yankees and the North. He is a chronicler of paradox – which as any fictionist knows is where the real goods lie – writing fictions of contradiction set in landscapes divided North from South, rich from poor, white from black, insider from outsider. He is the immigrant's legitimate prophet – understanding 'prophet' not as one who foretells the future but as one who (like Isaiah or Jeremiah) offers an unflinching portrait of the realities of the present. In these stories, this encompasses a description – sometimes poignant, often harrowing – of what it means to be an intruder into the sullen culture of the white communities of the South, a culture of defeat, so vastly insecure that its principal source of validation lies in victimizing any and all who are different, foreign, 'other' (even when, as is often the case with African-Americans, the 'other' constitutes a numerical majority).

No landscape offered the prophet richer potential than that of the Old South in its last-gasp days – on the verge of becoming, for the second time in its history, the destination of Northerners seeking the quick buck, except that this time the carpetbaggers would be welcomed with open arms, and for better and worse would settle in to stay. The American South of Clark Blaise's stories – the South in which I grew up – was teetering at the precipice of its century-late tumble into the modern world; on the verge of transforming itself – or, more often, being transformed – from a culture that measured time by generations into one that measures it by the time card and the clock. Blaise writes of that transition from the most peculiar and fascinating perspective – the outsider's timeless time, the immigrant's placeless place.

* * *

The great religious historian Mircea Eliade describes how Judeo-Christian civilization invented linear time. Earlier cultures envisioned time as a circle or spiral or sphere in which history endlessly repeats itself; then the late Jewish prophets initiated the conception of a linear, chronological progress toward apocalypse – the end of time, after which the saved and the damned would dwell in some eternal place, a place outside of time. Taken up by Christianity, that idea achieved its apotheosis in the American experiment. The founding of the U.S. sprang from and requires the notion of perfectibility, of progress ('our most important product') toward some city on a hill which, once attained, will constitute the end of time and the beginning of some new, timeless eternity.

The South of Blaise's stories – rural, poor, obsessed with the fantasy of creating victory wholecloth from the tatters of defeat – still dwelt in something closer to that ancient, circular time. Into this humid, unchanging landscape walks a Northerner of Canadian ancestry, a creature more exotic than even a European because he seems in the face of manifest destiny and good sense to have stubbornly chosen his fate (as a schoolchild I looked at the long horizontal stretch of Canada and wondered why its citizens didn't concede the obvious, throwing in the maple leaf flag and becoming the fifty-first state).

Probably because of his status as outsider, Blaise seems always to have resided in and written from non-linear time. Even as the American publishing mainstream was adhering to chronological, apocalyptic time – the action rising in a strong, consistent line to a dramatic climax, after which the author quickly and gracefully exits – Blaise was writing round, seamless narratives that share more with the Southerner Eudora Welty or the Canadian Alice Munro than with the Mid-Atlantic Seaboard ideal. These stories circle back on themselves – they dwell not in chronological but in circular time, the time not of the railroad engineer but of the priest and the poet. They have their roots in a mythological time, even as one senses the vastness of the change looming on the horizon, and the protagonist's place caught in between. 'I'm still a young man, but many things are gone for good,' says a character in *A North American Education,* straddling in a single sentence the boundary between the Southerner's obsession with memory and the Northerner's obsession with progress. In 'Notes Beyond History' – the title is telling – the anonymous bureaucrat of the New South looks from his eighth-floor office over the (now landscaped and manicured) lake of his childhood and considers how 'not only has the lake been civilized, but so has my memory, leaving only the memory of my memory as it was then ... *change* merely reflects the unacknowledged essence of things. That's what history is all about.' These are stories of people in motion in conflict with people in stasis – immigrant stories written for a nation of immigrants, by a writer who is of and apart from the country of which he writes.

* * *

Reality, Nabokov wrote, is the only word that ought always to be enclosed in quotation marks. Saying the same thing differently, my storytelling father once told me, 'I never met a fact that couldn't be improved with a little exaggeration.' The 'improvement' of which my father spoke is of course art, an improvement that paradoxically renders it more, not less, representative of truth (as distinct from 'reality').

Reading these stories decades after their publication (the earliest was completed in 1958), I'm struck by how they are postmodern well before the term came into vogue, so postmodern they evoke Western fiction's roots in Smollett, Richardson and Sterne. The early stories have enough autobiographical detail to read like a memoir – until some quirk reveals the artist's hand, shaping the raw and disordered clay of experience into truth. As with those eighteenth-century predecessors, the fiction sustains no artificial distinction between reality and imagination; the story *is* the reality, with one critical difference – these protagonists have known the Holocaust and the bomb; they are in full possession of the old wisdom of the fall. Amid the frantic cheerleading of the Age of Reason become the Age of Advertising, they illustrate and illuminate the tragic destiny of human fallibility. To read these stories is to journey into the synapses of memory, to understand how its flawed and warped mirror *is* reality, how we take our affirmations from others to construct identities that are not so much whole and distinct as shifting images in an ongoing, ever-changing collage composed of our responses to the ever-changing world.

An open-ended terror underlies these stories, the sense of something truly awful always on the verge of happening. Even the earliest stories focus on process – there are no neat epiphanies here. The boy falls into the alligator-infested water, but we do not learn his fate; the sheriff (coming, in contravention of his official duties, to wrack violence?) cruises by but does not gain entrance. In a way that's uncomfortably true to life, the characters never entirely comprehend the forces that have been brought to bear upon them.

In his later writing Blaise moves on from this particular geography, but he would continue to explore the themes and techniques first presented here – a fascination with the relationship between time and memory, an affection for the darker side of human encounters in which nothing is what it seems and where men's plans often lead to disastrous consequences they could not have foreseen. 'The Love God', a later story, represents a logical progression in its exchange of the illusions of social realism for the more straightforward illusions of the world of fantasy. A shape-shifting son of a stud stallion becomes a media consultant who lives in suburban Atlanta, until his father returns as a woman to seduce him back to his true vocation, which is to liberate himself and others through sex.

Going beyond the weirdly inflexible logic of the clock, Blaise's premodern postmodern imagination has shape-shifted into magical realism – a transmogrification accomplished in their very different ways by William Faulker, Flannery O'Connor, and Welty. Reynolds Price wrote of Eudora Welty that she was recasting Ovid in Mississippi, but he could easily have extended the observation to a whole raft of Southern writers, among whom Blaise has a legitimate if uneasy place – constructing a reality with the sureness and aplomb of the Southern storyteller, but in the particular and elegant Commonwealth diction of the Canadian.

* * *

I grew up in rural Kentucky, ninth of nine children. None of my two centuries of Kentucky-born ancestors had lived outside my home county; now – in one generation – we are scattered to the corners of the continent. Like most Americans I live between wanderlust and nostalgia; we long to be on the move even as we create and follow with unparalleled devotion the cult of home – with 'home' defined as that imagined and imaginary place where nothing changes. That no such place exists only strengthens its hold on our imaginations, leading us to construct national identity – and with it social, economic, and political policy – around the increasingly untenable illusion of the clapboard house whose happily married inhabitants are as white as their picket fence.

That we are obsessed with home makes perfect sense, of course – those people farthest from any sustainable experience of home romanticize it most – but on the whole U.S. writers are too immersed in the illusion to perceive and write out of its contradictions; our very adjective for citizenship ('American') presumes that we and the continent are coterminous, as if no America exists outside the lower forty-eight states. To understand ourselves fully we must turn to outsiders – to immigrants sufficiently removed from the vastness and power of the U.S. to perceive its illusions, and in writing of them to give us a glimpse of the truth that lies on their other, darker side.

Reading Clark Blaise's stories from the South is like visiting a retrospective of a brilliant painter – one sees in the earliest work the themes that gradually emerge and sharpen. This is the great joy of writing, enough to offset its burdens. Across a lifetime a writer's words, diligently and honestly compiled, allow his essential character to emerge, and as it emerges to shape what comes behind, a symbiosis between art and nature in which the writer shapes the clay that shapes himself. Across these stories the reader has the great privilege of witnessing the writing become as transparent as glass, leaving the writer standing revealed to himself and to the world in his nakedness. In that state of grace he offers a glimpse of the truth, which, if we have the courage to seize it, is the instrument of our freedom.

Fenton Johnson is an assistant professor of creative writing at the University of Arizona, novelist, memoirist, essayist, and author of the forthcoming *Beyond Belief: A Skeptic's Journey.*

A Fish Like a Buzzard

Sellers Landing now. 'Foley, you wake up. See, I poled clear up to ol' man Sellers's.'

'That's good, Escal,' the littler one answered, then closed his eyes and laid his head upon his slim bluish arm. 'I done seen it enough anyhow,' he said.

'Foley, you wake up good now. I ain't been talking on no account. Stay awake. You promised 'fore I'd take you on a gar hunt you'd stay awake.' He lifted the long cypress pole from the muck and flicked it at his brother.

'Quit it, Esc,' Foley whined, but still kept his eyes closed. 'I been awake the whole time.'

'Then act awake. I knowed I shun't have brung you at all. Still a baby, like Ma says.'

'That's a lie,' Foley retorted, and sat upright so quickly he swayed the frogboat, nearly spilling his older brother into the creek.

'*Now* see what you near done? That right there shows you don't know what to do in a boat. Just sit down and shut up.'

'You called me a baby,' Foley defended. 'Ain't no call for that.'

'I said shut up. I don't know which is worst, you sleepin', doin' nothin', or you awake yappin' like a wormy hound.'

'I wisht you'd fall in, plumb in a gator nest,' Foley cried, and still sitting upright added, 'And anyways, if I'm a baby, it don't make you much more'n one yerself.' Content that he had the last word, he nestled his head in his folded arm again and closed his eyes.

Escal wasn't ready to drop the argument. 'You wisht I'd fall in?' He repeated. '*Then* what? You'd set right here cryin' till you got the boat snagged in sawgrass. You'd try to git out but you couldn't. You'd just set and starve till you'd try swimmin' fer it, then some gator or gar'd come along, and snap you like you was nothin' but a minnie.'

'I wouldn't,' Foley cried in anger. His chest heaved against oncoming tears, and his ribs and shoulders looked like they'd pop through his papery skin. 'I'd pole right back past Sellerses', down to Davises', then I'd tie up the boat an' walk home. You ain't as smart as you think. You was afraid to hunt gar alone, that's what.'

Escal laughed, a hard laugh that hurt Foley more than all the previous insults. 'I jist decided it's a whole lot better polin' by myself not listenin' to a passel of lies from you.'

'They ain't lies ...'

'Hush up, Foley. You been lyin' to me, and it don't make it better to say you ain't.'

'They ain't lies,' he screamed again, and then grabbed the tapered end of the cane fishing pole that lay at his side and with a lunge, drove the flat stubby end at his brother's stomach. 'They ain't,' he cried again, and his throat burned with tears and rage. The pole missed, but Escal grabbed it as it rushed by, and, tugging, pulled Foley toward him. For an instant he just stared at his little brother.

Foley sensed his brother was going to hit him – he always hurt something after he looked at it long and hard that way. 'Don't hurt me,' Foley pleaded, but it was too late. Still holding on to the cane pole, perhaps for balance, Escal kicked him, catching him on the chin, snapping his whole upper body backwards as if it were on a swivel.

'Don't you never try that again, you hear, or so help me, I'll stick this pole clean through you,' Escal swore in a voice so tense it lowered like a man's. Foley was too pained and astonished to answer. From his chin a slim line of dull red trickled to the hollow of his chest. He touched it, and smeared it on his stomach where he could see it better. Then he began to rock slowly and whimper.

Escal said nothing for a few minutes, just looking over his brother's head, down the creek. Foley still cried.

'Lookit here at my toenail,' Escal finally said. 'I plumb near ripped it off.' Foley stopped whimpering and peered at the nail. A stark white crease ran diagonally across the nail; beneath it, the quick was red and purply.

'Can't hardly pole, it hurts so bad, but I ain't cryin' 'bout it none,' Escal said.

But it ain't the same, it ain't the same at all, Foley thought. You done that when you kicked me, and it ain't the same as getting kicked. I still got me a right to cry.

He dried his eyes with the back of his hands, and the tears washed grey smudges onto his cheeks. Then he sucked in all the sniffling and crying and spit it into the creek, like his brother always did. He sat quietly and looked ahead, upon the dark water.

Haines Creek was four miles long, counting the distance that wasn't a creek at all but just a widening of the boat-wide aisle between cypress and mangroves, and often the trees were so old and bent that Escal had to stoop beneath the chigger-laden moss. The water was dark green, almost black, and no direct light penetrated to the creek or the forest floor. It was like drifting in a subterranean river. Only when there was a break, a dead or dying cypress that created a small clearing, was the sunlight able to tumble through the shaft and illuminate the water. On the water the intermittent splotches of light gleamed like spotlights. In the sun the water looked to Foley like the air around the projection beam at the movie house in Waycross – dirty and dusty with little particles bouncing every which way, except down like they were supposed to.

Escal poled into a patch of light but kept the pole in the muck, holding the boat fast in the brightness. 'Sun feels good,' he said. 'I was cold back yonder, and my arms was gettin' stiff.'

Foley didn't reply, but instead crawled from the front to the back of the frogboat because the sun felt good on his back. Stopping at the shallow poling ledge, at his brother's feet, he peered into the water at the foreshortened pole, visible for a foot or so until it blended into the deeper, greener shadows of grass and roots. The water dimpled around it, and the dimples drifted downstream and flattened out. Foley reached for the pole and shook it at a tiny sunfish that had been nudging it, perhaps thinking the pole was a slim cypress knee he could bump a barnacle off. The movement of the pole sent the fish reeling back into the muddy shadows. Foley crawled back to the front.

'Sun feels *real* good now, Escal,' he said. Then he closed his eyes and let his head loll on the side of the boat. He faced the sunlight and opened his mouth, as though to swallow the warmth. Escal nudged him with his foot, and Foley opened his eyes.

''Stead of just settin' there gulpin' flies, why don't you fetch some bait?'

'In a spell,' Foley answered. 'We got plenty of time.'

'No, we don't. You gotta do it now,' Escal answered, 'else it won't be dead and smelly when we need it out on the lake.'

'Who wants smelly ol' shiner anyhow?' Foley asked.

'Mind me, Foley,' his brother said in an even voice. 'You asked me if you could come on a gar hunt. I said yes if you'd do like I said. I done this before, an' I know how to do it. If you don't do it my way, I'll pole right back to Sellers's and let you off.' Escal started poling again and the sun disappeared behind the trees.

'I'll stay with you,' Foley answered. 'If you say so, I'll fetch us a couple of shiner. If that's what we need to git us a big ol' gar ...' His voice trailed off and he watched the water part slowly in front of the boat.

'Then mind me. You need lots of bait, and it's gotta be dead and smelly.'

'An' you gotta spread it in front of his mouth an' git him close 'nuff, then club him on the head, ain't that right?' Foley asked, turning his head to face his brother.

'Ain't all that easy. Gotta be strong.'

'But I can hit real hard, honest I can, Escal,' Foley said.

'An you gotta know where to hit, else you break a spear like you was hittin' a tree, and the ol' gar'd just drift off like nothin' more'n a dragonfly lit on him.'

Foley thought a moment. 'They bigger'n that snappin' turtle Doc Banyon pulled out of Lake Harris that took a leg off'n that Yankee girl last summer?'

'Plenty bigger. Them's the biggest thing you ever seed, I'll just bet. Big snapper run only couple hunnert pound. Big gar go twicet that.' He laughed. 'You can't even knock me off the boat with a cane pole, an' I don't even weigh a hunnert pound.'

'You'll see. When it's time, you'll need me,' Foley said.

'Now I've had enough. You jist quit talkin' like that and fetch bait. I ain't fixin' to argue with you no more.'

Foley took a piece of bread from the moist cellophane package that lay under the cane pole. He sprinkled it with a few drops of water, then moulded it into doughballs, a half dozen, the size of marbles.

'Find some light, so's I can see what's down there,' he said.

'Quit your fussin', I done seen some up yonder,' Escal answered.

As Escal poled, Foley slipped the ball onto the hook, and not bothering to use the pole, looped the line about his wrist and dropped the baited hook into the water. As it touched the warm water it looked like a ball of frozen milk; a cloud trailed from it and flecks peeled off as though it were an aspirin tablet. Then a firm white ball remained, securely fastened to the hook, so that only a fish could remove it.

They reached another lighted area, and Escal lay down on the floor of the boat. He stretched his legs until they hurt, because his bones didn't come together right. He lifted the pole into the boat, and the boat didn't drift in the shallow currentless water.

'Watch you don't fetch nothin' we cain't use, Foley,' Escal cautioned.

'I'm fixin' to get me a shiner, but a li'l snapper keeps comin' out after the ball,' he answered.

'Them doughballs is nigger bait, but watch you don't fetch no nigger food, 'cause if you do you can dig the hook out.'

A few seconds later Foley said excitedly, 'I got me a shiner, watch him run.'

'Just haul him in and cut out the sportin'. I ain't got all day to mess with bait.' Escal stood, ready to pole.

'Jist a second. Man, he's big.'

'He's fixin' to get loose, Foley. Listen to me – they ain't hardly got a mouth, they's all the time breakin' away.'

Foley started twisting the line about his hand, then suddenly stopped. 'The snapper, Esc, he done come up and took the shiner.'

Escal bent over and glared at his brother. 'God*damm*it, Foley, I warned you where your messin' around would get you. Give me that line.' He reached for his brother's arm, then looked into the water. A plume of inky blood surrounded the line and on it, instead of a whole shiner, was just its front part and a baby snapping turtle.

'For God's sake, didn't I tell you what would happen? Why can't you mind me just once? And it would be a snapper, too.' He lifted the turtle into the boat and flipped it on its back. It opened its beak and hissed; the rest of the shiner rolled out and ran up the line a few inches.

'Olive Sellers lost a finger feedin' a snapper a little bigger'n this,' Foley noted.

'An' she's plenty smarter than you, so I reckon you'd better figure on losin' two or three 'fore you git that hook out.'

Foley poked a finger at the turtle and again it hissed.

'His tongue wiggles, Escal, jis' look at that. Looks kindly like a worm in there.'

'*Dam*mit, Foley, I don't care what it looks like, jist git that hook out. Anyhow I seen tongues on them big snappers they drug in from the lake last year – them ones that weighed two hunnert and fifty pound – that was thicker 'round than bead snakes.'

'How deep you figger he took it?'

'How should I know? They took to shiners like rats take to babies. Prob'ly all the way.'

'Think it hurts him?'

'I *don't* know.'

'He don't look like he feels it none.'

'He will, less'n you dig that hook out. You're gonna feel it too if you don't hurry up.'

'Can't I just cut the line? Norman Sellers says they got somethin' in 'em that soaks up hooks after a while. Then it don't kill 'em,' Foley said.

'You can't cut the line 'cause we ain't got more hooks,' his brother answered angrily. 'If I knowed you was fixin' to fish like you did, I'd of brung a hunnert hooks.'

'Then what I can I do? I ain't fixin' to dig in there with my fingers just for a hook, an' I don't care what you do.' He examined the turtle more closely. 'Took it in the head, all the way in, back in his gullet, curlin' up.'

The turtle, still on its back, was attempting to right itself. It swayed back and forth along the ridge of its back, and its legs pumped a turtle gallop in the air.

'We can't waste no more time, Foley,' Escal decided. 'An' since you ain't about to git that hook out, there's only one thing left to do, an' that's use this thing for bait.' He reached over and picked it up, holding it by the shell far down by the tail. Stretching the line taut so the turtle could not double back and bite, Escal gave the line a quick snap. The neck popped and the turtle died with a shudder; grey film flashed across its shaky eyes and the legs twitched in midstride. Escal tossed the remains at Foley, and fresh spots of blood spattered on his chest. 'Now play with this an' git the hook out,' Escal ordered. Gradually the creek widened and grew deeper. It was midday when they finally reached the open grey expanse of Lake Harris. Overhead, gulls wisped across the misty sky, and from high in a cypress back in the swamps an owl hooted:

a wet and feathery echo from deep in the throat. Escal once told him it was the sound chickens tried to make after their heads were cut off, and Foley could never hear an owl without thinking of blood, and chickens, and Escal. He was glad to be out of the swamp.

By now he had extracted the hook and bent it back into its original shape. Before they reached the lake he caught two shiners, strung them through the gills, and hung them over the side, as Escal directed, barely in the water. The tub had to hug the shore, as the pole was only six feet long, but the poling itself was easier since the lake floor was hard-packed sand and didn't try to swallow the pole like swamp muck.

'You know where to head?' Foley asked.

'To the coves, where it's shady, but near the pads where there's lots of ducks and bream. That's where they hang out, swimmin' round all day, just waitin' on a duck or frog.'

'An' snakes too, them eats mocc'sins, ain't that right, Escal?'

'Sure, everything. They eat everything – eat you if they had a chancet, but there ain't nothin' they like better'n dead shiner. They spot a shiner floatin' with its belly all swole out with his scales not hardly shinin' no more, an' they jist set by and watch it. I seen 'em, jist paddlin' round like there wasn't nothin' on their minds but how nice the water was.' Foley listened, but didn't look up at his brother. He ain't talking to me anyhow, he thought.

'Then after a while they back up real slow, 'cause they're too big an' heavy to move fast. Then they head straight fer it – that's when you better not be in the way – an' when they're a foot away they jist open up that mouth real wide – even little ones swallow your leg and have room left over – and chomp down. Then they jist coast on by till they stop.'

He lifted the pole and let the boat drift for a few moments. 'Like watchin' a buzzard in the sky, they just coast an' don't hardly move a wing, then they spot somethin' way down, like a dead cow, an' they jist circle down and down, 'cause they know there ain't nothin' can stop 'em, an' the ole cow ain't fixin' to go nowheres anyhow.'

He started poling again, then added, 'Buzzards are just like gar, only they go smoother and faster. I could watch a buzzard all day and never get tired.' Foley looked up into the grey mist, but all he could see were some white gulls.

Ahead lay Buck's Cove, its surface as smooth and black as a fish's back and at the far end where it melted into the shore grew a dense blanket of lily pads. In the middle, spires of a dead cypress shattered the surface like the fingers of a drowning man.

'Plenty of pads, Esc,' Foley said. 'Think maybe one's knockin' 'round by the cypress over yonder?'

'Can't tell till I draw 'em out. He could be anywheres, under them pads, chewin' on worms, or knockin' that stump, or maybe there ain't none in here.'

'Then what?'

'Then maybe I'll rest up. Prob'ly pole over to Sem'nole Island. Then maybe we'd go back.'

'Are we comin' out tomorrow, if we don't see nothin' today?' Foley asked.

'No. If we don't see none today, it means we don't see none tomorrow neither. Means the water's hot and they got plenty of food down below without never comin' up. Ain't nobody gonna see one 'cept maybe some Yankee trollin' deep fer bass with a big ol' half-dead shiner. Then that man's gonna lose his whole Yankee rig right down to the bottom of the lake.' Foley laughed at the thought of a tourist latching on to a gar.

'Man, I sure would like to see that,' Escal continued. 'Probably ol' Norman Sellers hisself guidin' them, an' all of a sudden here goes the Yankee's gear smack out'n his hands straight down so fast he don't even see it. He says to Norman, "What the hell happened? We musta snagged on the bottom." An' ol' Norman looks real serious and says, "Why no, sir, I do believe y'all hooked up with a Lake Harris largemouth like you done seen on the signpost. Why yes indeed. I do believe that's what done it. A shame 'bout your rig – I should have warned you 'bout it."' Foley and Escal both laughed.

'Yeah, that's what ol' Norman'd tell him,' Foley said. 'You can tell 'em anything, they's so dumb'.

Escal poled silently toward the dead cypress. Foley continued talking. 'I seen one chuck a mudfish back,' he said. 'An' I seen one even try and pick up a bead snake ...'

'Hush up, Foley,' Escal interrupted. 'Can't make noise from here on, 'cause they hear it. Jist gotta set and watch. Lemme see them shiners,' he whispered.

Foley lifted them from the water. Their eyes were cloudy, and their scales more chalk than silver, but the gills still heaved.

'Good,' Escal said, then pushed his finger into the red gill lobes until some thick blood dribbled out. He stood, and threw both dead fish as far as he could in the direction of the pads. They landed like tinfoil, bright and weightless. The boys sat and watched.

'Foley,' Escal whispered. 'You fetch some more bait.' He looked into the dark grassy water. 'Plenty of shiner down there. I don't think a gar's fixin' to be first of them other ones.'

Foley slipped another doughball onto the hook and dropped the line into the water while Escal watched the shiners.

'I need me another hook, Escal. This one ain't strong enough after I bent it back. It's fixin' to snap.'

Escal reached for the back pocket of his Levi's and lifted off a small hook that had been placed there, half dangling, half inserted.

'Use this then,' he said.

Foley took it and quickly tied it to the line and baited it with a flesh doughball. He had another one all along, he thought.

In a couple of minutes Foley had caught two more which he strung and dangled in the water. Then they both sat quietly and watched the floating bait.

After a few minutes of silence Escal started talking softly. 'I remember oncet at Rob Boyd's they had a big ol' gar settin' in a flood ditch that took off one o' Rob's cow's legs that crosst over it. Ditch weren't hardly big 'nuff fer him to turn around in. He'd jist been layin' there in the mud, waitin' on chickens an' rats an' snakes, an' maybe Carrie Boyd if she stepped near 'nuff.'

'Then what ol' Rob Boyd do, after the cow?' Foley asked.

'Then Rob and Frank took a chicken an' stuck it on a pulley hook that was plenty sharp, an' tied a heave-rope onto the hook, an' chucked the whole rig into the ditch. Pretty soon the ol' gar comes 'long, chomps on the chicken, an' takes the hook. Frank and Rob, an' even Miz Boyd come out an' heaved that gar out'n the ditch. Then Frank comes out with his axe – plenty sharp you can bet – and goes to work, figgerin' to chop him up, then bury him.'

'Did he chop him up, Escal?'

'Yeah, he chopped him into two pieces, each of them six foot long and throwed away his axe 'fore he was through.' Escal laughed. 'Carrie Boyd says that critter smelt worst than the outhouse in July, so they got some niggers to come out an' haul it away that night.'

'Escal,' Foley asked, 'if an axe don't chop him up, how you 'spect to do it with nothin' but a cypress pole?'

''Cause like I done told you, I know where to hit. I done this before.' He lifted the pole from the water where it had been floating, and showed it to his brother. 'See, right there's a point I whittled myself. Stick it clean through his eye, then up into his head, an' that's all there is to it. That don't mean it ain't hard to hit it right – an' hit it hard enough,' he added.

They sat still a while longer. The sun was hot now, and the mist was clearing. A moccasin eased its way across the cove, with just its ugly spade head above the water. It reached the cypress stump, the halfway point, and braided itself around the knee, coiled in the sun. A kingfisher that had been perched on a higher knee swooped down and pecked it until the snake dropped back into the water and swam away.

The water around the floating shiners swirled slightly. Escal was the first to notice; he stood, and poled a little closer to the bait.

'Somethin's down there, jist waitin', and it ain't no gar. Bet it's a bass, fixin' to strike.' He shook the pole under water in the direction of the swirls, and they disappeared. 'Bass all right. Gars don't run,' he added.

They sat and stared at the shiners. They're pitiful, Foley thought, like the chick Carrie won at the Easter fair that got sicker'n sicker but she still kept it, and slept with it, not letting it go, even though she had a brood hen. Never had he looked at dead fish for so long; he didn't feel good. At his feet, flies buzzed around the carcass of the turtle that was beginning to smell. It didn't float, so Escal hadn't let him throw it in.

'Throw another in,' Escal ordered, and Foley did. It was not dead yet, but could not right itself. Foley wished it could, now that it was free. 'Another one,' and the fourth, less lively than the third, was tossed in. Only his tail fin moved. They waited and soon all the shiners were dead.

Foley laid his head on the side of the boat and looked out over the water. Escal watched the bait and there was total silence. The kingfisher flew over the shiners but showed no interest. Skimming the surface, he dived on a bream instead, clamped it in his bill, then flew back to the cypress stump.

Half an hour passed; the bass returned, but now the fish were too dead to hold any interest, and it passed by. The kingfisher turned to a diet of dragonflies and was hovering over the blossoming lily pads. Foley was thinking how to suggest turning back, because of a headache and because he was tired, and because he felt sick, when he saw the gar, not more than ten feet away, behind the boat. He shook violently at the sight, and immediately Escal asked, 'Where?'

'Behind,' Foley answered in a half whisper he could barely contain.

'Yeah, I see. Lord, he's big. He's seen them shiners, you can bet.'

About two inches of its back and head rose above the surface of the water, and small ripples washed its sides as though it were a long thin floating island of branches and logs. How big, Foley thought, how big and ugly can one thing get? Longer than the boat, maybe twicet as thick as the two of us hugging together. His brother stood, and Foley saw the goose bumps on his shoulders, and saw his muscles twitch. He was breathing hard and fast and his thin bowed legs were trembling. Foley was frozen; he dared not move or say a word. Slowly the huge fish drifted towards the bait, the water parted noiselessly in front. It moved silently and effortlessly, like a monstrous error that had grown and multiplied for millions of years until it, and others like it, the alligators and snakes, and even the ridiculous little turtle in the boat at Foley's feet, were the only things that lived and never really died.

Escal was standing, clutching the pole, his right hand cupped on the blunt end, and his left grasping it midway from the point. Still the gar drifted towards the fish, and now even Foley could see it in detail – the long snout like a gator, and the eyes that peered out from small holes cut in the bony armour. It would pass behind the boat on the way to the bait; it had to be then, the down-plunge of the spear, and only once if his brother was to kill it.

Escal waited nervously for his only chance. It would come at any second. The gar showed no sign of avoiding the boat, though it could not help but see it. A little faster now, it was starting its run – the fins flipped in threshing circles and the water flashed white. Escal began the thrust of his spear and screamed 'Ai-yeh!' at the top of his lungs.

Foley could bear no more. He closed his eyes and held his head in his hands, between his legs. He felt the convulsion of the boat as the spear struck the plating of the gar, and he heard the sharp crack of the pole as it splintered. And the sound of Escal's feet slipping on the poling ledge –

he heard that just before the short muffled scream and smacking splash.

Foley straightened up and looked out on the water. Deep swirls at the back of the boat, and two pieces of the shattered pole; that's all he saw. The shiners still floated belly-up, now a little closer to the boat. He picked up the body of the turtle with both hands and slipped it into the water. His eyes were weak in the late afternoon sunlight, and began to water. They ached and wanted to close, but he forced himself to keep looking. The kingfisher was perched now, staring at him from the topmost spire of the cypress. Soon the boat would drift over to the shiners. He would pick them up and put them in the boat with him, and wait till somebody came along.

Giant Turtles, Gliding in the Dark

The buzzards, wheeling high over the chicken coop, reminded the boy of nuns; always in pairs, graceful and black. He remembered last summer, driving down the Tamiami Trail to West Palm, when his father had been forced to stop the car because a row of buzzards was stretched across the highway, picking apart a gator carcass spattered in the middle. The birds wouldn't budge, even with all the backed-up cars honking, and finally his father drove straight through, and a single giant bird thumped against the window. Seeing them up close wasn't at all like watching them in the air – or like seeing nuns, he thought, unless under their bonnets they're red and bald too.

The grey sky seemed as close as his mother's sheets hanging dead on the line, and its bright greyness hurt his eyes. The pillow, cloud-grey, prickled his sweating neck. The worst kind of Florida day. In the kitchen, his mother had turned on the *Game of the Day* on the Orlando station, and the announcer, a Yankee, said it was nippy in Philly. How cold is nippy? he wondered. Will it snow in Philly?

He'd seen snow once. It was dirty, not white like the schoolbook pictures, but dirty like clouds. Two Easters before, the three of them had gone up to Virginia for a vacation – that was when they were living in Jacksonville – and on the same day they had gone down in the Caverns, he had seen snow. It looked like Kleenex blown against the trees, but his mother – who was a Yankee anyway – had said to his father, 'Oh, look, Gene, there's a little snow left,' and they had stopped so he could make a snowball. It had only made his hands cold and wet, and came apart when he threw it. Mother only said, 'Of course, silly,' when he cried. He would never see it again, he knew.

In the kitchen his mother sneezed. She always sneezed as though someone had hit her suddenly on her back, and half hurt, half frightened her. It never built up or even ah-chooed, but was more like a squeak through her nose. Then the trailer creaked as she started walking to the porch.

Her handkerchief was wadded, and he could see she had been using it for her eyes too.

'Your hay fever bad today?' he asked.

'Yes, dear.' Her eyes were puffy, and made his own feel sorer. 'I guess something's blooming.'

'Something's always blooming,' he answered. She sat down on his cot, and took off her glasses to wipe them. Without her glasses her eyes were sunk deep in her head and even though her hair was dark, she looked too old to be his mother.

'Dear?'

'What?'

'After you fell asleep last night, Daddy came home with some very bad news –'

'He was very quiet,' he said. They had been whispering, so he couldn't hear.

'I can't tell you anything yet because I don't know everything myself.' She put her glasses back on, and the glasses made her look younger. 'Dearest, will you promise me something?'

'What?'

'That when Daddy comes home for lunch – if he comes home – as soon as you see him, you'll run around back and wait for him to leave. And if you're asleep out here when he comes, just lie quietly as though you didn't wake up, okay?'

'Can I take the radio out back?'

'Of course, Frankie. I'll take the radio out back now. You keep it on low, and I'll bring you some iced tea.'

'Mommy? What was the news?'

'Something about the factory. We won't know until he sees some men in town that are trying to take it away.'

'Will we move again?'

'Dearest, not now ...' She stood, and dabbed her nose again. 'I'll put the chaise lounge in the shade for you,' she said, then left for the kitchen.

'What men, mommy?' he called, but she didn't answer.

He had been thinking of snow, and like a favourite dream, he wished it back. He thought of the third-grade reader, something he'd read last year. Frontier kids played in snow all winter, snuggling under buffalo robes in the horse-drawn sleighs, boys and girls together, and after the rides there were quilting bees and husking bees, and spelling bees, with maple syrup poured on snow tasting better than ice cream. How he had cried last year when he learned how the other kids lived. When Miss Hewitt had asked if anyone had seen snow, he'd said he had, and that it wasn't half as good as sand to play in. 'Don't believe Yankee books,' was what he said, and Miss Hewitt said she'd get some Southern books for next year. But he knew then that he had been lying, just because no one else could argue. He hadn't seen *real* snow and probably he never would.

He got up reluctantly and walked to the kitchen. His mother was sitting at the table, wiping her eyes with wet tissue paper.

'Something must be mildewed,' she said.

Mil-dew: another of her Yankee words. Quick – get outside, catch the door before it slams, and just listen to the radio, drink the tea, and dream ... he dragged the chaise into the trailer's shade, settled in, and turned the radio higher.

... leading off for the Phillies will be Richie Ashburn. Batting second is Granny Hammer ...

Granny? Yankee names were funny. He looked again into the sky. The buzzards had disappeared.

... Mike Goliat bats eighth, and plays second base ...

One good thing about buzzards, he decided, was that you never saw *them* in the woods, which was about the only thing you didn't. But for the clearing, with the trailer and chicken coop, and the narrow trail connecting to the highway, the woods covered everything like a cave, filled with noises you couldn't see, and swarming with things you couldn't hear.

... Well, fans, Del Ennis gets the Phils off winging on a two-run blast, his seventeenth of the season ... Philadelphia made him think of Quaker Oats that he made doughballs from. It was nice just to ram your fist into a drum of Quaker Oats, because they were cool and moist, and when your hands were sweaty, they came out coated with oats. Del Ennis or Pudd'nhead Jones always hit a homer when the Phillies were on the radio. He wanted them to win, because of the very bad things people said about the Brooklyn Dodgers.

He had seen two ball games in his life, both in Scottsboro at the fairgrounds, and he'd like to see Pudd'nhead Jones even try to hit a homer out of there. Or Bob Lemon last an inning against Jacksonville. Both games had been on the evening of the Watermelon Festival, and since they had been living in Scottsboro then, last spring, he had gotten in free with a third-grader card. The Scottsboro Pirates were in last place – they were always in last place – and once last summer some men from the bleachers had challenged them and lost only 2-1. But that night they had played Jacksonville, and the visitors were like their city – big and ugly – and the way they hit and fielded before the game made all the Scottsboro kids groan. They looked like convicts, all in grey, and the Pirates looked like milkmen, in red and white.

Sherree Hotchkiss, boy howdy! Just before the game, he'd been allowed to sit on the infield to watch the beauty parade, along with the other school kids and country Cub Scouts. The beauty parade was held on a ramp by the first base coaching box. Every kid had been watching Sherree Hotchkiss, because she was a senior at Scottsboro High, and her father was Kingsley Hotchkiss, who owned the Palace movie theatre. She was also the prettiest, and on her way to be crowned they had watched her ankles wobble, and even seen the dimple where her titties parted. Everyone in the stands was whooping it up for Sherree Hotchkiss, especially the sailors in the first base boxes, and the kids on the grass. And when she was crowned Watermelon Queen, mayor Lindsey Williams had kissed her, and then again after she was led off the ramp. Frankie had groaned, because the mayor was an ugly little man, about three inches shorter than the queen.

The Pirates had lost both games of course, and their left fielder had gotten conked on the head with a fly ball and was carried out on a stretcher while everyone booed. Frankie had started home after the games, but outside the ball park the crowd was just waiting and smoking and laughing, as though Scottsboro had won both games. A couple of men were handing out cardboard rebel flags. Then the crowd started running up the street to the middle of town, and Frankie had run with them. On Main Street they were already standing in line waving their little flags, and above the shouting he heard the thump of drums. He had nudged his way between two high school kids for a better view. A white convertible was moving slowly down the middle of the street, filled with men in white, with their hoods pulled down, smiling and waving. The driver had his still up. He didn't know the men by name, but a few ran stores in town. Next came the county sheriff's car, with its red light turning slowly and the policemen inside waving out. Then came another convertible that everyone was whistling at, because Sherree Hotchkiss herself was sitting up on the top of the back seat with a cut open watermelon in her lap. She had changed from her bathing suit to a blue dress which was cut down just as far in front, and the skirt bounced high around the watermelon with every little bump in the road. Mayor Williams was sitting up next to her with a big rebel flag in one hand, and waving with the other, while in the front seat and down low in the back were four more girls who almost won but weren't nearly so pretty, all of them with rebel flags and waving too, and still in their bathing suits. Frankie had kept walking down the sidewalk to keep Sherree Hotchkiss in view, but two blocks later the parade split up, with the girls and the Scottsboro High School Band going straight, and the first two cars, along with some smaller pick-up trucks that had been following the girls, turning right.

'C'mon,' the two older kids had said, and he had followed them down the side street. It was unlighted, and he knew it led to where some niggers lived. The head car with all the men in white stopped in front of the first shanty and everybody started shouting so loud he hadn't been able to make out a single word. He didn't know what was going to happen, but there was a terrible feeling in the crowd, with men shouting dirty words, and the two high school kids that had been so friendly started punching him in the arm for no reason. The red light kept cutting across the shanty then the crowd, lighting everyone's faces as though they were at a bonfire. Shadows moved behind the curtains. Then the pick-up truck drove up and two fat men in T-shirts and dungarees took out some nailed-together boards and stuck them in the front yard. After some minutes of silence – even the kids had quit punching Frankie – one of the men in white from the front car touched the bottom of the cross with his cigar lighter and the whole thing whooshed into flames. Everyone had started shouting again, and he had been tripped by the bully and almost trampled by the crowd that started running after the lead car, deeper into Niggertown. He was crying when he got home, and his clothes his mother had cleaned specially for the festival night were torn and dirty, and when he had told her what he had seen, she started whipping him then screaming herself until his father had come over and slapped them both until they shut up.

It was a hazy afternoon, drifting to a long twilight and rain. Frankie dozed on the chaise he had pulled from the back of the trailer to the side, so he could watch the clearing instead of the black wall of forest. He had the radio on at his side, and from inside the trailer he heard the sudden spatter of hamburgers being dropped in hot grease. The Phillies were leading 4-2 and the announcer was saying: *'And that brings to the plate Mr Roberts himself, and for a pitcher, this boy's a pretty fair hitter . . .'* when suddenly, Frankie noticed a thick wave of dust, like smoke from wet leaves, blowing from the trail towards the clearing.

'Mom! Someone's coming!' he shouted, but she probably didn't hear, over the clatter of frying meat. As the dust reached the clearing it was already lifting, but it still caused him to sneeze. Then the red Dodge pick-up tore into the clearing, and came to a lurching stop. He made out the shape of his father, slumped against the steering wheel, beating the ledge of the dashboard with his fist. Frankie snapped off the radio, with the count on Robin Roberts at one and two . . .

Then came a blast on the horn, then another which didn't let up. In just a second or two his mother was out of the trailer, running to the truck, clawing at the front door handle, which didn't open. Frankie drew himself up into the smallest ball he could, making sure he couldn't be seen. Finally his father threw the door open and jumped down. His tanned face was brown with rage, and his waving hands were fists. He was screaming but his voice was so hoarse Frankie couldn't understand a word.

Then suddenly there was a roar from the kitchen, and through the screen Frankie caught the flash of yellow flames and heard the mad gurgle of boiling grease. In the kitchen, petals of flame danced in the skillet and the wall behind was charred inside a ring of sparks. Frankie nudged the skillet, pushing it off the burner, then tapped a log that had been wedged near the burner's lip, back into the belly of the stove. His hands were shaking with fear, and the heat had nearly overcome him. As he dragged himself to his mother's bed, then fell across it, it seemed as though his head would burst.

He opened his eyes at the sound of shattering glass. He could see out the old door through the porch to the clearing. His father was swinging a hammer at the truck door, bashing in the lettering that his mother had painted on carefully just a month before: Gene Thibidault – Orange Blossom Furniture. With each crunch, glass from the rolled-up window cracked and shattered, flying in all directions. Frankie raised himself just enough to see his mother on the ground, holding his father around the knees and reaching up for his arm before he swung again.

Then he threw the hammer through the broken window and grabbed her by the shoulders and rolled her over as though she were a bale of furniture stuffing. She lay on her side in the sand, holding her hands over her glasses, and Frankie wondered if the glass had cut her. His father was yelling, then he started kicking his feet in all directions and the dust fell all over her, falling on her like snow. Frankie watched until the snow drifted again into dust, and his father was back in the truck. Then he started the engine, rammed the truck in reverse and spun long sprays of sand as he tore out of the yard. The mangled door was half open, and flopped with every bump.

His mother started crawling to the trailer, without her glasses. Frankie, moving faster, dashed to the kitchen to push the cooling meat back over the fire before his mother reached the porch, and had already dragged the chaise to the back of the trailer where it looked as though he hadn't seen anything out front, by the time he heard the screen door slam. A few seconds later his mother fell on her bed with a moan and sniffle.

'*... Young Mr Roberts might be in with his first twenty-game season, with twelve in the hopper, and number thirteen nearly sewn up,*' the announcer was saying (too loudly) as the radio finally warmed up. Frankie picked it up and held it in his lap. It was old and had markings for exciting places like Capetown and Kobenhaven, which he listened for sometimes at night but never got, but all that came over when the batteries were low, outside of Scottsboro and Orlando, were about ten Cuban stations and something from Lakeland. Scottsboro came in between Montreal and Moscow, and he turned it there from Orlando to hear the local scores on the five o'clock sports show. Closing his eyes, and trying to imagine the towns and the various stadiums, he let the names and numbers wash over him like a giant black wave: the Crackers downed the Pels, Mobile took Nashville; in the Sally, Augusta split with

Jax and Brunswick walloped Savannah with the rest under the lights; while in the Georgia State it was Valdosta over Waycross; in the Florida-Alabama League ...

Out of eight towns in the league, he had lived in six.

'Shut that off!' his mother cried from the kitchen. He face was red and her eyes were swollen as she swooped down from the kitchen and snatched the radio from his lap, then ran back. In a few minutes he became sleepy and didn't care. When she called him to dinner he was dreaming and almost asleep; getting up again, to eat what he had saved from the fire, took away his appetite.

The hamburgers looked burnt – the tops were crispy black. For him there was a salad, and iced tea. He took a long gulp. She stood by the sink fixing herself an onion.

'Your hamburger will get cold, Mommy,' he said. His, in fact, was cold, and still a little pink in the middle.

Her back was to him; her breath shuddered as though she had been crying, but her shoulders didn't shake.

'You weren't in, so I had to put a fire out. You see that spot on that wall? The hamburgers caught on fire when I was out back and I got in just in time.' He took a bite of salad but it was oily and made his lips warm and greasy. 'I'll bet you're glad I saw it, aren't you, Mommy?'

'I hope you didn't hurt yourself,' she said. She sat down with her plate of onion.

'Daddy never lets you eat onions.'

'I'm allowing myself this little treat.' Her eyes were red again behind her glasses, and watching them made his own eyes water. 'Would you like some?'

'You know I don't like onions,' he said. 'Is your hay fever still bad?'

'It's that, and the onion.' She sniffled. There were black lines of dirt in the wrinkles around her neck, as though her skin had cracked, and grey smudges on her forehead that she hadn't wiped off.

'How come you changed clothes?'

'It gets too hot. Does that make you happy? Now please quit asking me so many questions. I'm getting a very bad headache.'

'You should put a wet towel on your forehead.'

'I don't need any towels.'

The onion plate clattered on the table, like a spinning coin coming to rest. She looked angry, then apologetic. 'We both need something more than towels,' she said. 'That's what I mean.'

'Would you turn on the radio, please, Mommy? I didn't hear who won the Game of the Day.'

'No, dear, we've had enough baseball. Not now.'

'Maybe Daddy heard,' he suggested. 'They listen to it at the factory all the time.'

'I'll ask him when he gets home.'

Frankie finished his tea then sucked the lemon. Usually she stopped him and said it was bad for his teeth. She ate her onion but didn't touch the meat. Then she poured herself some tea. Frankie got up, sank his dish and glass in the tub of water, took the radio, and shuffled towards the porch.

'I'm going for a nap,' he said, 'and listen to the radio.'

She said nothing, and didn't even turn. It looked to him that she might be crying, for her shoulders were shaking and she had taken her glasses off. He listened a second, but heard no sobbing; then he made his final turn to the porch. From under the cot he picked up his souvenir from the Caverns in Virginia – a shiny, cold, white rock, streaked with brown. He held it against his chest. It was cold as a stethoscope. Then up, so it caught the light and seemed to sparkle; then to his nose, and the still-cool, still-wet mustiness brought back all the memories of the cave, just as a seashell brings the ocean back.

It had been so cold underground that he had seen his breath, and when he asked the guide if it was cold enough to snow, the man had lied and said it wasn't. The guide was a terrifying old man, like the blind pirate in *Treasure Island.* The guide had taken a special interest in Frankie, calling him 'Skipper,' and taking him ahead alone. Sometimes he waited until the last moment before turning the lights on, and would stand behind Frankie, with his arms on Frankie's shoulders. Finally, in a high-ceilinged room called the 'Court Room' the guide had stood him in front of a shallow, waist-high basin.

'Everybody gotta wash his hands before he sees the judge,' the guide announced, then turned the spotlight on. It cut into the water, exposing the worst thing of all: pale, blind fish.

'Bigger and fight'ner than they got anywheres outside,' the old man said. Frankie hadn't been able to get over the idea of fish underground, let alone blind ones. Thinking back now, he could of course; in fact he sometimes wondered if the rain itself didn't carry fish eggs and tadpoles. He'd never seen the smallest puddle that didn't have something swimming around in it.

He had pressed closer to the rim of the basin, and suddenly his hands had been grabbed by the old man and thrust into the water. It stabbed like boiling water, and Frankie had been too stunned to cry out. A second later, he realized it was freezing, not boiling, and it was the first time he had felt something colder than ice. His hands were numb but for the still-dry portions under the old man's fingers. Than an instant later, he found his hand clamped around a trout that couldn't see it coming: the smoothiest, slimiest thing he had ever felt. It was frightening; he had panicked and felt sick. He knew why now – it had frightened him the same way worms did. What was bad about worms was their helplessness. They were meant to be hurt, and he was always hurting them. There wasn't anything that could happen to a worm besides getting stepped on in the rain or being squished on a hook and eaten by a fish. And worms were good, or most worms that stayed out of your feet were good; everything he'd heard about worms said they were good and hard-working. And to see something bigger and smarter than a worm that was still just as helpless, had been sickening. The old man had held his hard old hand tight on Frankie's, and Frankie's tight on the fish. It had felt to him that his own hand was drowning, and that he had to get it out or else he would drown too.

'See here, folks, how a little nipper can catch hisself a big ol' trout –' the old man was saying when Frankie let out the loudest scream he'd ever mustered.

'You shut up!' the old man sputtered, then spun him around with his hard hand against Frankie's teeth. Frankie started to cry, and the old man let go. Then his father stepped forward from the party, and the old man dropped his hand from Frankie's face and patted his shoulder once or twice. His father looked as though he were deciding which one to hit, but ended taking Frankie back with him.

'He could of ... that is, mister, screaming like that he could of knocked something a million years old down,' the old man had explained, and his father had said, 'I don't care for none of your million-year-old rocks,' then pushed Frankie back to his mother. Up in the office before they left, the man who sold them the tickets had given Frankie a hunk of white, shiny rock that had been selling for five dollars. It was that rock he held now on his chest, against his lips and nose.

Thinking of the cave, and cooled by the breeze, Frankie fell asleep.

He awoke in a howling cave of night. Strong winds roared in the treetops, frogs screeched like sirens. Twigs and waterbugs plunked steadily against the invisible screen, and the light spray, broken by the screen, was freezing cold. He reached under the cot for the cave-cold rock; smelling like the wet darkness itself. He held it like a crystal ball to his forehead, closed his eyes tightly, reliving the time in the cave, and another time almost like it.

A month before, they had driven to Ocala for factory parts, and then had gone over to Silver Springs, just like Yankee tourists. Something so exciting had happened that day that even now, just thinking about it, Frankie dug his head deep into the pillow, to drown out the wind. When everything was quiet as the Springs, he started remembering. They had gone out in a glass-bottomed boat with a hundred-year-old Seminole guide named Billy Trailways. The water was as cold and blue as Canada must be, and as the boat headed over deeper water, everything got blue and dark, almost like night. And way below, where water rushed out so hard from the black caves that it blew the ferns and sand aside, monster turtles and catfish swam. Yankees trailed their hands in the water, and sprinkled meal on the water for schools of bream to nibble. But he hadn't touched the water. Yankees laughed and pointed to the pretty girls in white bathing suits who were swimming in ugly patterns a few feet below and waving back. Frankie had looked beyond them, to the bright shoulder of the deepest ledge, where giant bubbles burst.

'This here's the main spring we're over now,' Billy Trailways had said, and Frankie expected the glass to break when the old Indian told how strong the force was. He threw his hands over his eyes and shivered until they glided over the spring and back to the dock. And when they got back, a white guide in state-trooper uniform gave them a lecture about the Springs, which had turned out to be more exciting than the trip itself. The officer took down a map and pointed to all the lakes and rivers in Central Florida, saying they were connected, *underground*, like rooms in a cave, to Silver Springs. Rivers underground, he said, that carried this water for miles, and no matter where you dug you were sure to come across it, if you dug deep enough. Frankie had been afraid to ask the guide at the time, and now he was afraid even to ask his father: what about those fish and turtles, he wanted to know – do they swim underground too, just coasting in the dark like gators in the swamp or buzzards in the air? For often, at night when his parents were asleep, he heard the grunts and hisses of turtles, nudging each other in the rivers just under his bed.

'Frankie,' his mother whispered, shaking his leg. 'Dearest?'

He ground his face into the pillow, nearly smothering in the mustiness, and knowing he'd have to wake up for her.

'There's something I have to tell you.'

He stretched his leg, pushing his toes against her.

'Mommy's been in the bedroom crying ...' she said, then shook his leg. 'Frankie, look at me and listen.'

He sat up. The yellow light from the kerosene lamp was reflected in her glasses, dull yellow in the dark. Frankie narrowed his eyes until his vision blurred, and his mother looked like an approaching car with old headlights. Her shadow was huge on the wall behind. She kept her hand over his foot. 'Daddy came home this afternoon. He had some very important news to tell us.'

'What?'

'You must be a little man, and listen to what I'm going to tell you, because I'll only say it once.' She cleared her throat, and Frankie tingled in the cold.

'Dearest ... we've lost the factory.'

He giggled. 'How did we lose the factory? It's awful big.' The factory was really little, just an abandoned terminal building on an abandoned airfield, but the runways went on for miles, dying out in the woods. Every Saturday he went out and made sofa buttons on the button punch, and his father gave him a penny for each one.

'Listen to me, dear. This is very, very serious. If there was some way I could keep you from knowing, I would, believe me. But you're going to find out soon enough, I'm afraid.'

'Knowing what? That you lost the factory?'

'Yes, that too ...'

'That we're moving again? I don't want to move again.' This was the first place they'd ever lived that he liked a little, and they had lived all over Florida and Georgia. In the cities, people wouldn't let him be.

'Tampa was worse 'n Jacksonville,' he said.

'Frankie ...' she cried, 'listen and be quiet. We should pray that we'll be *able* to move again. Tonight Daddy went into town to talk to the men that stole the factory.'

'Stolen? Somebody stole it?'

'Don't interrupt. Yes, some people stole it. Yesterday Mr Smailey, the lawyer from Scottsboro, and Lindsey Williams, and the sheriff came out to the factory with a paper said they had legally bought our factory and if Daddy wasn't off the property in twenty-four hours, they'd arrest him for trespassing.

'How much did we get?'

'Frankie!' Her voice was just a whisper, soft over the wind in the trees. Her voice didn't show it, but tears were running down her cheeks, and in the lantern light looked like rivers of gold. 'Oh, you're just a baby, a poor old baby, and I know you can't understand,' she moaned. 'You don't know what it is to lose everything.'

'I do so understand.'

She let go of his foot.

'Then if you do, you know our factory isn't for sale, not after all we own went into it. We started so we can begin living decently for once, instead of roaming like sharecroppers, and now that it's almost started to pay.... Don't tell me you understand,' she cried. 'You don't know the first thing, not the first thing. You didn't see Daddy today – he swore if they don't give it back to him, he'll take it back.'

'Mr Williams' brother is the sheriff,' Frankie said, remembering the parade. 'Daddy better not mess with him. He can't kick sand on them tonight.' He wished he could see the fight, because the sheriff was strong and fat, and looked like Johnny Mack Brown.

At last the rain started; single plunks on single leaves, then the hiss of a million drops all at once, soaking the ground. His mother stood and pressed her face against the screen. She stood that way a long time, outlined in yellow by the lamp, with patches of red from the copper screen surrounding her face. It would be a wonderful night to sleep. Finally he heard a long sigh that sounded like a shiver. He dug his face into the pillow so that the light and her breathing were smothered out and only the roar of a violent storm remained.

'Wake up, Frankie!' His mother rolled him over and whispered hoarsely. 'I want you to get into the kitchen and stay there until I tell you to come out. Now – here, I'll help, get up, come ...' Before he was fully awake, she was pulling him out of bed and into her bedroom, then into the kitchen. 'You stay here and don't move,' she said, as she eased him into the corner.

He rubbed his eyes and looked around the doorway, back to the porch. It was still raining, and she was on her knees, behind the door frame, looking into the black clearing. Then in the dark, he made out something faintly red, going on and off, moving slowly down the trail.

'*Get in,* I said!' she cried, and raised her hand as though to slap him if she could reach that far. Cautiously, he looked out again. The red light had grown stronger, then finally it drew even with the clearing and turned in. Two yellow lights cut into the yard, with the revolving red one in the middle. The police, he whispered. The car pulled nearer, and his mother dropped to all fours, out of sight. Frankie heard the clicking of the windshield wipers. The light kept turning, but nothing moved inside the car.

They honked, a loud high honk, just like the truck. A light went on, inside the car. There were two men in the front seat. The one on the left side was moving around, and Frankie saw he was putting on a raincoat. Frankie started crying, afraid they were coming in to beat him and his mother. If he opens the screen door, Frankie thought, he'll step on her. He was too afraid even to crawl from the kitchen, or crawl deeper into it and hide. He knew policemen could see everything.

Finally the one on the left got out. He didn't head to the cabin, but just opened the back door instead. The still-open front door blocked what he was doing. The he closed the back door and honked again. Frankie choked on his crying, and his mother made a terrible sound in her throat. The car started backing away slowly. The clicking of the wipers grew softer and softer. Then they turned on the spotlight.

Frankie followed the light, which cut through the steam-like rain to the chicken coop, then jumped to the trees, to the underside turned white by the wind. It hopped across the clumps of grass, over puddles, then stopped on his father, lying almost still and shiny black in a slicker. His arm reached slowly for the steps; but it looked as though he were too beaten to pull himself up. The engine roared, and the car – with the red light off – spun out of the clearing. On all fours, Frankie inched his way to his mother, who was huddled against the cot and hadn't seen what happened. He crawled to her and laid a hand on her leg, and broke the roaring silence with a whisper.

'That's how it feels, Mommy,' he said.

Broward Dowdy

We were living in the citrus town of Orlando in 1942, when my father was drafted. It was May, and shortly after his induction, my mother and I left the clapboard bungalow we had been renting that winter and took a short bus ride north to Hartley, an even smaller town where an old high school friend of hers owned a drugstore. She was hired to work in the store, and for a month we lived in their back bedroom while I completed the third grade. Then her friend was drafted, and the store passed on to his wife, a Wisconsin woman, who immediately fired everyone except the assistant pharmacist. Within a couple of days we heard of a trailer for rent, down the highway towards Leesburg. It had been used as a shelter for a watermelon farmer, who sold his fruit along the highway, but now he was moving North, he said, to work in a factory.

A Mrs Skofield was renting the trailer. She was a fat, one-eyed woman who gave me a bottle of Nehi grape without my asking, then led us down the highway from her tiny gas-station-general-store to the trailer. As we walked she explained that the trailer wasn't exactly hers, but she reckoned she was entitled to what she could get from it, since a no-count farmer had skipped off in the middle of the night, owing her money and leaving the trailer behind. My mother asked if it had water, or electricity, and Mrs Skofield snorted, 'What y'all expect, honey? Weren't no tourist livin' there.'

It was blisteringly hot inside. Even the swarm of fruit flies buzzing around the mounds of lavender-crusted oranges were anxious to escape. The furniture was minimal: two upturned crates, a card table, a coverless bed, a wood-burning stove, and an icebox. Behind the trailer, away from the highway and facing the forest of live oak and jack pine, someone had built a porch foundation of planks and cinder block.

'We'll take it if you finish that porch,' my mother said.

'Screens is hard to come by,' Mrs Skofield said, 'but we got heaps of gunnysack. I'll get my brother to put up some curtains you can roll up and down that'll be better than any screens ever was.'

'What about –' my mother started, then looked out the door.

'The brother'll dig y'all a squatty-hole. And you can have five gallon of water a day from the store. We'll sell y'all ice cheap.'

'What about people?' I asked. 'Is there any kids?'

'Ain't nobody now, hon, but just you wait you a couple weeks and you'll have all the company you want.'

'How come?'

'Fambly named Dowdy lives down that there trail,' she said, pointing to a narrow cleft in the trees. 'They ain't come down yet, but they'll be here. Come down from Georgia.'

'They white?' my mother asked.

Mrs Skofield snorted, then said, 'Y'all just spot you a nigger in them woods and my Seph'll fix it. A single white lady can't take no chances.'

'My Billy is fightin' Japs,' my mother said. 'Leastways he will be.'

Mrs Skofield went on to describe the lake that lay behind the trees, and how it was world famous for fishing. We moved in that day, and by evening I had already discovered a quiet inlet where I caught sunfish with just a blade of grass on my hook. And even before the Dowdys came, I knew the woods. My tender feet itched maddeningly with tiny thread-like worms my mother kept removing with carbolic acid, but at last my feet toughened and I was no longer bothered. By July, when our neighbours finally came, I was lean, brown, and lonely, and craving friendship that would free me from my mother's needs.

Then on a muggy day in July the Dowdys' rusting truck loaded with children, rattling pans, and piles of mattresses in striped ticking churned down the sandy ruts I had come to call my trail. I helped them spread their gear on the floors of a pair of tarpaper shanties, and watched their boy my age, Broward, pour new quicklime down last summer's squatty-hole. Within hours, he had shown me new fishing holes, and how to extract bait worms from lily stalks.

A few weeks later, Broward and I were fishing from a half-sunk rowboat in the inlet, merely dabbing the hook and doughball in the water to attract a swarm of fish, and snapping it out fast enough to avoid hooking another one. It was hot and lazy, and we didn't talk.

'Brow'd, Brow'd,' came a cry from the shanties. It was his mother, whom we could see, sitting on the floor of the kitchen where a door should have been.

'Your mother's calling you, Broward,' I said, attempting to head off a showdown.

'I'm fixin' to come,' he answered. 'She ain't gettin' supper less'n I'm there anyhow. She ain't fixin' to whale me before dinner.'

'Brow'd,' she shrieked, 'you git the hell over here 'fore I tear the skin off'n your back, you hear?' We saw her get off the floor and disappear inside.

'See, I tolt you so,' he said, flashing his nervous smile. 'Here, got another doughball so's I can bait up?' I took a slice of bread from the cellophane package – the one my mother had sent me up to Skofield's to get – moistened it in the warm muddy water and shaped it into a ball the size of a marble. Broward thanked me as he always did, then formed it around the tiny hook that dangled on the end of the string tied to the long cane-pole. The instant it touched the water, a school of bream rose to meet it; Broward snapped the bait and two tiny fish – one hooked and one caught by the gills – were sent flying to the bank. I jumped ashore and dropped the new acquisitions into the reeking flour sack that half floated by the boat, attached to a flaking oarlock. Then I stretched my legs their full length to get back into the boat, for Broward suspected that under the old deserted landing where I had been standing, swarms of water moccasins made their nest.

'You watch you don't never leave your catch in deep water,' he cautioned. 'Once I lost me a whole day's catch to turtles that was just snappin' off their heads soon's I throwed them in. I hate them critters,' he said, untying the sack. 'Ever time you catch you even a li'l one, don't forget to chop off his head.' He leaped ashore, and pulled the sack after. 'I gotta go now. She's sent my brother down to fetch me.'

One of Broward's younger brothers was scampering through the tall swamp grass towards us. It was Bruce, about three, blond and blue-eyed like all the others. And like the rest of the family, his stomach was bloated out like a floating fish's. Bruce wore only a filthy pair of underpants, with large holes cut around his rump and penis. As dirty as the cloth was, it was difficult to distinguish where it left off and Bruce began. Bruce, Broward explained to me, was 'shy – real shy. He don't take up with strangers much.' He threw his grimy little arms around

Broward's equally soiled knees, and whined, 'C'mon, Brow'd.' Broward set the sack down to disentangle his brother's buried head and hugging arms, then took it up again – the precious, unrationed fish that fed us all that summer – and taking Bruce's hand, trudged back through the grass and mud to their two shanties.

'Why don't y'all eat with us?' he asked. It was the first time, after a month's daily fishing, that he had invited me home even though I passed through the clearing in front of their shanties twice a day.

'I can't, Broward,' I replied. 'You got all those others to feed as it is. Anyhow my mother's expecting me.'

'Set real quiet and they won't even see you,' he said, and I laughed. 'You gotta do what she says, I guess,' came his stock reply, accompanied with a shrug of his bone-sharp shoulders. 'Nobody's gonna eat less'n I fix it. Sure like to have you over. I ain't never had a friend to dinner.' We took a few more steps toward the Dowdys' in silence.

'Okay,' I said.

There was a slight clearing in the sawgrass in front of their shanties. On either side of the trail there was marsh, and the shanties had been elevated on stilts, with ladders leading to the interiors and planks forming a network of safe paths. One shanty was for cooking and eating, and the other for sleeping. Usually there were equal numbers in each shanty, either sleeping, or playing by the boards in what passed for a yard. The interior of each shanty was dim. They depended on the light that filtered in through the numerous cracks in the tarpaper framework. One particularly large rip just over the stove served for both the overhead light and the escape hole for smoke and the fumes of cooking. The flour sack, the same as Broward's fish sack, slumped next to the stove like a dumpy old man. The humidity in the central Florida air caused the top half-inch of flour to cake over. The bulging bottom was gnawed open and here and there lay conical deposits, like anthills. Broward set the still-flopping sack on the floor by the stove. The flies that had followed us from the inlet and those that had been waiting, blackening the pools of watermelon juice on the table, now bombarded the sack. Broward's mother, who had been in the other shanty when we arrived, came back.

'You get them things the hell out of here, you hear?' she shouted from her slumped position at the head of the ladder. 'And you hand me my pack Luckies on the table.'

'Yes, ma'm,' Broward answered softly, and slid the cigarettes across the floor.

'When I say I want my cigarettes, I mean for you to *hand* them to me, if you ain't too stupid, that is. Ain't you worth nothin'?'

'Yes, ma'm,' he replied quietly as he ripped a brown paper bag open and spread it on the table. 'Hand me them fish,' he directed.

'On the table?' Flies settled in my eyes.

'Sure.' I laid it on the table.

'Now dump 'em,' he said. I opened the top and tilted the sack downward, and the fish came sliding and squirming out. A little turtle, clamped onto the largest fish, started to walk away, dragging his prize behind. 'Goddamn it,' Broward hissed, 'that right there's just exactly what I was sayin'.' He scooped it up and shook the fish from its beak. He slammed it furiously to the floor, as though it were a tiny coconut, then fired it against the wall until at last, mercifully, the bottom shell snapped off. I couldn't bear the sight; it looked, I imagined, like a frog turned belly-up, white and helpless; but then an almost nauseating vision of the secret nether-parts of the turtle, half frog, half snake, took hold and when he asked me to come over and look, I only waved my arms frantically around the fish and around my head, to clear my face of flies. He tossed the remains underhand into a clump of sawgrass.

'Here,' he said, handing me his pocket knife. 'While's I'm lightin' the fire y'all scrape the leeches off and start choppin' up the fish.'

'How?' I asked. My father had been an angler, with artificial lures and a casting rod. He loved to fish and my mother had always done the cleaning.

Broward laughed. 'Y'all just watch. First stick the knife under here, see,' indicating the area under the gills, 'and then just cut through. Then you slit his belly and dump out all this. Got it? Then make sure there ain't no leeches in the meat.'

'Y'all get a mudfish?' his mother asked.

'No, ma'm.'

'Then how the hell you expect to feed your fambly? How can anybody be so goddamn dumb is what I want to know.'

'Don't get mad. We couldn't help it. I ast everbody that come in from the lake if they got anythin' they was throwin' out, like a mudfish, and there weren't nobody even heard of one. They was all Yankees anyhow.'

'If you wanted to get one, you could have,' his mother retorted.

'Ma, I tried, honest. Now I got me a friend to dinner.'

'Ain't enough you don't bring home no food, but you gotta bring home another mouth to feed. Tell me this – you see him invitin' us up there? Not for nothin'.'

'They would. Maybe not all of us, but me anyhow, and you and Pa too.' He looked to me for support.

'Sure,' I said weakly. My mother would die, cooking for migrants.

'Anyhow we ain't losin' any food. Val said she's sick again and she don't want nothin'.'

'She ain't sick any more'n I am. She's fixin' to run off is all. I know what she's sick from,' she laughed. 'They gets to be her age and all of a sudden they's regular ladies they think and their fambly ain't good enough for them no more and this place just don't suit them – it ain't elegant like Waycross is. Or they starts thinkin' how grand they can live in Leesburg and go to pitcher shows ev'ry night. Well, that ain't the way you was raised, and it ain't the way anybody was intended to be raised, and they all gone to the devil, ever single one. There ain't no more my children goin' to school, you hear that, Mr Smarty? Any body thinks they're too good for this house is free to sashay out and all it means is they ain't any goddamn good theirselves.'

While she was speaking Broward had been stacking wood around the burning paper. Then he came back to the table and took the knife from me.

'I'll go, Broward. It's not fair.'

'Now you're stayin'. Now it's fer sure you ain't leavin'.'

After the fish had been cleaned, or at least cleaned to his standard, Broward took out a cleaver from inside the flour sack and began chopping the fish into half-inch squares. Then he dusted the diced fish with a handful of grey flour and dropped the pieces into the oiled skillet. They spattered and spewed and smoked and occasionally the flames from under the skillet curled around and ignited the oil. The flames shot roofward, nearly lapping the paper ceiling. He smothered them with the wet fish sack, and then the frying settled down to the noisy gurgle of flour in boiling oil.

The smell of frying fish never changes no matter how you cook it. You forget how you cleaned it, what kind of sorry fish you caught, and begin to look forward to eating it. Broward took the stack of dishes from the end of the bench by the table – plates with bright purple designs, the kind you get at service station openings – and placed them evenly, seven to a side.

Meanwhile, the odour of frying fish had attracted the other Dowdys to the kitchen entrance. They seemed not to notice me, as though I were one of them, and Bruce even waddled up and hugged me around the legs. By the time the fish was lifted and in its place at the centre of the table, the family had all assembled in an evidently prearranged pattern on the benches. Broward stood at the end nearest the stove, while Bruce and I occupied the last seats on either side.

They all sat quietly about the table. All eyes were on the tall, thin, and red-cheeked father. His face was lined from sleep and his weak blue eyes were bleary from the light. He rose, bowed his head, and folded his hands piously. The children remained seated, but also folded their hands and closed their eyes as hard as they could, so that each face was a mass of folds and wrinkles.

'Lord,' the father shouted as though He were sleeping in the next shanty, 'Thou hast been truly good to thine sheep. We thank Thee that we have this delicious food on our humble table, health in our fambly, and that Thee, that guards all our blessings, hast kept our name and blood untainted.' All the family followed with an 'amen'.

'Brow'd, you take care of Bruce's food, now, hear?' his mother ordered. 'You know he ain't fixin' to eat less you cut it up. I reckon your friend there can handle his own.'

'Yes, ma'm.' Bruce looked up at his brother and smiled his thanks.

'Here, y'all hold your fork like this and bring it up to your mouth.' As soon as Broward let Bruce's hand go, the fork clattered to the floor. 'Oh, it just ain't no use,' Broward said, looking at his mother. Bruce looked up smiling, with his mouth open.

'You feed that baby, you no good –'

'Wayc, you do it,' Broward pleaded. 'He don't remember from one meal to the next and anyhow I got me a friend to dinner.' Waycross Dowdy, who was fourteen and already taller than his father, and blubbery, scowled at Broward, then down at Bruce. Then he picked up the fish on Bruce's plate and stuffed it into his own mouth, and no one said a word.

On Wayc's other side sat Stuart. He never looked up from his plate, and was eating his fish with his fingers, cleaning them with a smack, then a swipe against his pants. Stuart often fished with Broward and me, and of the children, he bore the closest resemblance to Broward. Next to Stuart sat Starke, one half of a twin combination. Though much younger, he was built on the order of Wayc, with a low forehead and wide neck, and muscles already thick on his arms and shoulders, that jumped with the slightest movement of his hands. As I looked from the children to the parents, particularly to the mother, I noticed something of the final maturity of Waycross Dowdy in nearly all of them, made all the more terrible for its softened femininity. Starke's twin sister, Willamae, the only girl at the table except for a baby in her mother's arms, was a wisp of a girl whose eyes never focused on any object for more than a few seconds, and whose speech was so heavily 'cracker' that I couldn't understand it. She wore a pair of purple earrings which she kept swinging with a flick of her long red fingernails. Next to her was Henry, still wearing the cutout underwear of infancy. He was loud, a brat, and particularly antagonistic to his sister, whose earrings he kept trying to pull off.

'Wayc, you make Henry quit pickin' on Willamae,' Mrs Dowdy ordered. Wayc swung over the bench and lumbered up to his brother. Henry's fingers were on Willamae's earrings when he was sent headfirst into the edge of the table by a slap on the back of the head. He shrieked, Willamae's earring now lay in his hand, and Willamae, seeing it, shrieked with pain and delayed outrage. She dashed from the table, out of the kitchen, towards the other shanty, holding both hands over her ear. Henry's forehead, scraped a watermelon-red, was already purple in a long narrow band. Waycross went back to his seat, and Broward went over to Henry, whose face was red from crying. He looked down, then ran his finger across the cut. Then he took Willamae's plate and dumped her uneaten fish into his own.

'Take a little?' he asked Henry, who didn't reply.

Broward came back to his seat and offered some more to me, which I refused. Then he scraped half the remaining fish into the skillet and kept the rest for himself. After a few minutes Henry quit crying and shuffled over to his mother.

'Ma – Wayc, he hit me.'

His mother looked at the bruise. 'You know he didn't mean to go and do it,' she comforted. 'Y'all go back and eat up your dinner.'

As he walked back, he stopped for a moment behind Wayc, who didn't turn. I thought he was going to hit him back, and half hoped, half feared that he would. Henry waited for everyone to quit eating before he said, 'Anyhow, you didn't hurt me at all.'

Letters from my father came once a month, from Somewhere in the Pacific. During the sweltering nights of my ninth summer, my mother and I sat on the porch in the dark, with the burlap rolled up, listening to the Orlando station on the battery radio, to the network news.

Her face aged that summer, and her body grew thin on the fish I caught. She would read me parts of the letters and told me when to listen closely to the news, and very slowly I realized that the Pacific Theater was a battleground and not what it sounded like, and that men were dying all over, everywhere but home, and I would cry out to my mother, 'Why doesn't he come back to us?' and she would answer, 'Pray that he will.'

My memory of him blurred, although now we had a picture of him holding a coconut in his hand and grinning just like he did at home – looking happier in fact – surrounded by much younger men in shorts, wringing out their shirts. In his letters he called me 'little soldier' and always ended with an order for me to look out for my mother, and not to forget him, and he said that he missed us very much. Those orders I took seriously, and the fishing every day with Broward became in my imagination something of a tactical manoeuvre.

Broward knew nothing of the war, and asked me many times where my father was but never understood. He merely fished for food, but I reconstructed assaults and casualties. Turtles became tanks, and were thrown on tiny fires until – half cooked – the retracted parts surrendered; dragonflies were Zeros, and downed with a deluge of water; and the endless wriggling hordes of bream were Japs and their numbers hacked with glee. My father had been a driver for the citrus trucks going to port, and every so often he'd write that 'this island I can't name' would be a great place for growing oranges.

But the summer was an idyll. Whenever Broward and I roamed the woods we felt that unutterable sensation of being the first who had ever felt or heard the music of the place. For hours we would run along the beaches of the lake, prying our way through the twisted vines and stunted underbrush, skimming the ankle-deep run-offs, and building lookout blinds along the beach where we could watch the Yankees in their rowboats and hear their strange accents plainly over unruffled water. Alone, I would gaze over the water; the sun, piercing the calm surface of the lake, fluoroscoped the top two or three feet of lime-tinted water, often exposing a gator drifting like a log, or schools of bream dancing in the warm water like swarms of mayflies. I would think that there was just the lake, the beach, and me; then I would be startled by the splash of water from the swamp behind, and turning quickly, I'd often catch a glimpse of brown and know that I, or a prowling cat, had disturbed a deer and sent it in fearful bounds deeper into the forest. Then September arrived, and we received notice from the government that we were to be resettled in South Carolina in special quarters for servicemen's dependents. And with September came time for the Dowdys to leave the summer moss-picking grounds and head back up to the pecan-fields of Georgia.

'You know, this is the time of year I like best,' Broward confided the last time I ever saw him. 'When we get up north, we're right near a big city and all kinds of things happen that don't happen here. Last year they made Wayc and me go to school and I can almost read now. Pa says there ain't no reason to go to school, but I know there ain't nothin' you can't do if you can just read and write, ain't that so?'

Before the Dowdys could leave, they had to get their sole possession, the old Dodge truck, ready to roll. Over the humid summer months, rust had set in and a thorough oiling was needed. Naturally it was Broward who had been ordered under the truck to oil the bearings. The last I saw of Broward Dowdy were his legs, pale and brilliant against the sour muck, sliced cleanly by the shadow of the truck and the shanties beyond.

The Bridge

I

Studio One reached Fort Lauderdale from the Dumont station in Miami, and in the summer I was allowed up late enough to watch it. We had no set at home, having recently come down from Montreal. I watched it at Rifkin Brothers Furniture and Appliance Centre, where my father was the furniture buyer. The sets were round with magnifying lenses bracketed in front. The hostess of *Studio One* was Betty Furness, the Westinghouse lady.

An enormous sense of power, watching television behind locked doors while people press their faces to the windows – a seven-year-old responds to that. Behind me in the dark, mannequins in evening dresses stood by their washing machines, and upstairs my father worked on the books.

Around seven o'clock his secretary would come down from the office and sit with me in front of the television, and talk. She had a northern voice, and a harsh one, but no demands were in it. I knew (in the way of a boss's son) that she liked me. I knew, in fact, she thought I was amazing. She took me out to get the coffee and sandwiches, a high point of the evening. A child hungers for that. There's something illicit in going out with a pretty secretary for coffee and sandwiches.

Joan was her name. She'd been introduced to me as Joan and a boss's son has that privilege, even when he is fast becoming a *yes ma'am-no ma'am* Southern boy and is otherwise overly polite. I called her Joan because I never learned her last name. Born a Larivière up in New Hampshire (where they pronounced it 'Larry Veer'), she had been divorced from a Georgian named Holman after being widowed in the war by a man named Paulson. Widowed at eighteen and divorced on the rebound, and still only twenty-five. She was tiny but ample, and depending on the day and what she wore, became a trifle plump or unbearably voluptuous. The word, I know now, was *ripe*. Her arms were full and downy, her waistline faultless but a little too sudden, no room for a curving back and leisurely midriff, the gentle reach and suppression of breasts and hips, and I, at seven, responded to that. She was old enough to be my sister, but *just* to be my sister, and that accounted for the whistles she got on the way to the carryout counter at the big Walgreen's a block away.

With the television on and my father in the back behind the door, I would prowl the darkened store, trying chairs and sofas, and far from the windows where people could watch me, I dug my well-scrubbed hands into the mannequins' dresses, over their cold unnippled breast and up their fused and icy thighs. All of the mannequins immobile, unprotesting, Betty Furnesses. By the middle of the evening, I'd have all the girls unbuttoned, then by ten o'clock, have them proper once again.

II

We Thibidaults went to the beach one weekday, a day of perfect calm. My parents lay on a blanket sleeping and I ventured out. I couldn't swim. The Atlantic was glassy, even calmer than the Gulf but without the slime of jellyfish. Just the weeds with spotted crabs. I walked out in the perfect neutral warmth, in piss-warm water, not flinching with the darts of minnows against my legs, not worried about sand sharks and mantra rays, barracuda beyond the jetties. I'd read of the fishes, knew the dangers, but still I walked. No waves in sight, the convoy of giant tankers steamed across the horizon, and the illusion was firm that I could walk that day to Dakar or Lisbon. I bounced to shoulder-depth, knowing that if I stumbled or if something large should strike my legs, if a wave or undertow should suddenly arise, I would drown. At chin-depth I tried to turn and couldn't without taking another half-step forward to gain my balance. I opened my mouth to call, but only whimpered, and water entered. I thought I saw the dark funnelling shapes of my worst nightmares, and my throat closed with fear. I tried to walk backward and stumbled. My head went under, water invaded my ears, and then I was lifted, carried back a step or two, and set down in shoulder-depth water. My chest was still locked and my father struck me, hard, as he turned. I coughed as I ran behind him, afraid to look back. '*Dis rien à Maman*,' he said, and joined my mother who had not wakened. He never spoke of it to me, or to her.

III

Fort Lauderdale had a city pool, a Spanish-style fortress across from the beach. Swimming lessons were free in fresh, icy water under a murderous summer sun. We lived four miles from the ocean on a brackish, un-swimmable estuary called the Tarpon River. The river swarmed with eels, crabs, mullet, and catfish, and I had caught and studied them all, and lost yards of line and dozens of hooks to the garbage fish that gasped and bubbled under our dock. But such is access to the ocean; before you charter a boat you haul up eels; before skin-diving you learn to paddle. And you learn the ocean in the municipal pool.

I never learned. The water stunned me with its iciness. It was a July day in the upper nineties. The noontime sun was a lamp that bleached the skies and burned through the droplets of water on my back. I tried to float and felt torn by the scalding sun on my back and numbing cold that gripped my legs and belly. I wanted to sink into the dancing blueness, the cold Canadianness of the water. No one watched, and bronzed Florida kids played dangerous games in the deep end. I left.

I had biked out barefoot, towel around my shoulders, feeling very Floridian and almost at home. It was four miles from our house to the pool, down Las Olas Boulevard. A scorching day. Las Olas was intersected by an old swing bridge over the Inland Waterway which I, returning from the pool, towel on the handlebars drying, now approached. The bridge was out to let a string of yachts pass under. It wasn't returning in time to allow the backed-up cars to start and finally my bicycle began to wobble. I put my bare foot down to steady it and suddenly I screamed. The black-top was gummy from the sun, my foot already tar-stained and burning. The bicycle toppled, spilling the towel on the crushed limestone shoulder. The wooden bridge was now back in place and the guardrail was lifting, but I was crouched in the burning limestone. My bike and towel had rolled several feet behind me. The stones gave way to a sheer drop to the waterway about fifty feet below; my only hope was in dashing to the bridge, a splintery weathered thing, itself hot, but equipped with a rail that I could lean over until my feet quit burning. And then my bike was further away than ever and walking to it barefoot over the burning limestone or over the soggy black top seemed almost Fijian, something natives did in the *National Geographic*. My eyes watered in the blank sunlight. I looked at my arms and shoulders and they were as white as a slice of baker's bread.

Cars whizzed past, glittering in the sun, their windshield, hoods, and chromework so bright that I couldn't face them. Everywhere I looked there was a haze of pink. It was like coming out of a Saturday matinee after three hours in the dark and letting the white buildings blind you. No one was out walking, not at noontime over the unshaded bridge with just a bait and tackle shop at the far end. No one ever walked in the States, my mother had said.

The door of the bait shop opened. Way in the distance an old man started my way, drinking a bottle of orange and carrying a white carton of live bait-shrimp. He was still talking to the owner as he walked away, and finally he laughed loudly and waved. I could taste the orangeade prickling my mouth as the man shambled toward me. An old man, dressed warmly on a blistering day, took a final swig leaving an inch or so on the bottom, and flung the bottle over the railing and into the Waterway.

'Sir!' I called, long before the man could hear. My voice was weak against the traffic and seemed to be whining, like the voices of tourist kids in restaurants.

'Sir!'

The man drew near, holding the shrimp by a frail wire loop. The shrimp smelled, the water sloshed. I knew I could drink it.

'Sir – would you get my bike for me, please?'

The man walked past, smiling at his shrimp, a squinting against the oncoming cars. 'Sir – please, please. My feet are burnt and I can't walk –' but my voice was coming out a whimper and he didn't turn around. He just crunched on over the limestone in his thick oily boots and was past my bike without looking down. Then he faded and I had to blink to keep him in sight. He climbed down the bank and settled by the water to fish.

I lowered myself to the wooden planks. My shadow had made the wood bearable for my knees, then my legs, and finally I curled myself on the wood against the railings. There was a tiny knothole by my toes and I bent over, until my back seemed ready to split, like a roasted pig's I'd once seen in the *National Geographic.* The limestone looked like white-hot coals.

Through the knothole the water seemed even closer, like Coke at the bottom of a bottle. If I'd had a straw, I could suck it through, and I remembered the day I almost drowned, when ocean water hadn't tasted all that bad. Now, blue, running and deep, it seemed a cool blanket to wrap my shoulders in.

And when the water became olive-dark, strange shapes began to flutter; the channel seemed opaque, then shallow. I clung to the railing now, so large did the knothole seem; so close did the lapping of water against the pilings sound. The channel bottom was heaving and rolling; bubbles rose, currents dimpled, needlefish glided on the surface, mullet teemed around the pilings, snook leaped, a cabin cruiser that didn't need the bridge to turn, gurgled under me, shattering the water for several minutes, the old people on board drinking beer from ice chests, maybe trawling, and playing cards. I thought of taking down my swimsuit and pissing through the knothole on the next boat that passed. Maybe if I took off my pants and stood naked on the bridge someone would stop and give me water; but I was afraid of getting in trouble. I lifted my head a minute and stared at the highway, now vague and white. I had the impression that I was going to die and that dying on the bridge with hundreds of cars passing would be more pathetic than anything. People would know how I had felt. The old man fishing on the bank would be caught and thrown in jail. The bait man at the end of the bridge and the bridge man who must have been watching for the past two or three hours from his little perch at the far end, and the people on the boats who had passed underneath and all the cars that had hissed past on a film of melted asphalt; all guilty of letting me die. If I'd wanted to talk now I couldn't, my mouth was as dry as my back, and my tongue had grown to my palate. The water under the bridge was olive now and my gaze penetrated far below the surface. The wooden railing jiggled slightly. I held on, afraid that I might tip head-first through the peehole. I couldn't feel my body against the wood; it was as though I were asleep in bed with my head sinking into the cool pillow and my feet rising slowly. In the water, which now seemed shallow, something enormous, flat and brown tipped a wing and then settled back. The surface shuddered in response.

'I think –' A voice that seemed to be coming from the wood of the bridge, and I had to force myself to remember that I was just a foot or two from the highway, and in the middle of a sidewalk. I tried to look up to see who it was, for the voice was familiar, but, as in a dream, I couldn't. I felt now as though my feet were waving high and I was somehow balancing on the sharpened pupil of my eye. But when a hand came down on my back, I twitched, banging my nose.

'My God, the skin – look at his back! I told you that was his bike, didn't I? Go down to that bait shop and bring me some water. He's unconscious.'

My father.

I couldn't waken to speak. His hands were under me now, trying to lift me in my bent position, but any movement was like palming hot sand over broken blisters, and the moment I was lifted from the knothole, the instant water was removed and everything again turned white and wooden, I began to shiver, then to retch. I wanted only to be dropped in cool water and allowed to sleep. I opened one eye, just enough for light to enter, and saw the waterway, and on the surface, as though I had conjured them at last, a school of manta rays, skimming the surface and slapping their way out of sight. Then I slept, hearing voices and my father's response, 'I'm taking him home, yes, I'm his father, yes, I've been searching all over ...'

When I wakened it was shady, in a car, in the arms – I could tell even with my eyes closed – of a young woman who had recently showered. The doors of the car were open, I could feel a warm breeze, though I shivered, and the ashtrays had not been cleaned.

'It's frightening,' she said. 'How close –'

My back was cooler but the pain was deep, more like cuts than a burn. I would have vomited but felt too weak. 'I mean if we hadn't of ... You'd better take him now,' she said, 'he feels a little cooler.' The doors slammed and my father said, 'I'll let you off first,' I fluttered my eyes but couldn't keep them open. 'All right,' she said, and I could feel her looking down at me, stroking my hair, 'Such a little boy, really,' and then, 'It would be bad if he saw me here,' she said in that harsh Yankee voice. And before I slept she added in that soft Canadian French of her childhood, and mine, '*Mal s'il me voit.*'

A North American Education

Eleven years after the death of Napoleon, in the presidency of Andrew Jackson, my grandfather, Boniface Thibidault, was born. For most of his life he was a *journalier*, a day labourer, with a few years off for wars and buccaneering. Then, at the age of fifty, a father and widower, he left Paris and came alone to the New World and settled in Sorel, a few miles downriver from Montreal. He worked in the shipyards for a year or two then married his young housekeeper, an eighteen-year-old named Lise Beaudette. Lise, my grandmother, had the resigned look of a Quebec girl marked early for a nursing order if marriage couldn't catch her, by accident, first. In twenty years she bore fifteen children, eight of them boys, five of whom survived. The final child, a son, was named Jean-Louis and given at birth to the Church. As was the custom with the last boy, he was sent to the monastery as soon as he could walk, and remained with the brothers for a dozen years, taking his meals and instructions as an apprentice.

It would have been fitting if Boniface Thibidault, then nearly eighty, had earned a fortune in Sorel – but he didn't. Or if a son had survived to pass on his stories – but none were listening. Or if Boniface himself had written something – but he was illiterate. Boniface was cut out for something different. One spring morning in 1912, the man who had seen two child brides through menopause stood in the mud outside his cottage and defied Sorel's first horseless carriage to churn its way through the April muck to his door, and if by the Grace of God it did, to try going on while he, an old man, pushed it back downhill. Money was evenly divided on the man and the driver, whom Boniface also defamed for good measure. The driver was later acquitted of manslaughter in Sorel's first fatality and it was never ascertained whether Boniface died of the bumping, the strain, or perhaps the shock of meeting his match. Jean-Louis wasn't there. He left the church a year later by walking out and never looking back. He was my father.

The death of Boniface was in keeping with the life, yet I think of my grandfather as someone special, a character from a well-packed novel who enters once and is never fully forgotten. I think of Flaubert's *Sentimental Education* and the porters who littered the decks of the *Ville-de-Montereau* on the morning of September 15, 1840, when young Frédéric Moreau was about to sail. My grandfather was already eight in 1840, a good age for cabin boys. But while Frédéric was about to meet Arnoux and his grand passion, Boniface was content to pocket a tip and beat it, out of the novel and back into his demimonde.

I have seen one picture of my grandfather, taken on a ferry between Quebec and Levis in 1895. He looks strangely like Sigmund Freud: bearded, straw-hatted, buttoned against the river breezes. It must have been a cold day – the vapour from the nearby horses steams in the background. As a young man he must have been, briefly, extraordinary. I think of him as a face in a Gold Rush shot, the one face that seems both incidental and immortal guarding a claim or watering a horse, the face that seems lifted from the crowd, from history, the face that could be dynastic.

And my father, Jean-Louis Thibidault, who became Gene and T.B. Doe – he too stands out in pictures. A handsome man, a contemporary man (and yet not even a man of this century. His original half-brothers back in France would now be 120 years old; he would be, by now, just seventy); a salesman and businessman. I still have many pictures, those my mother gave me. The earliest is of a strong handsome man with very short legs. He is lounging on an old canvas chaise under a maple tree, long before aluminum furniture, long before I was born. A scene north of Montreal, just after they were married. It is an impressive picture, but for the legs, which barely reach the grass. Later he would grow into his shortness, would learn the vanities of the short and never again stretch out casually, like the tall. In another picture I am standing with him on a Florida beach. I am five, he is forty-two. I am already the man I was destined to be; he is still the youth he always was. My mother must have taken the shot – I can tell, for I occupy the centre – and it is one of those embarrassing shots parents often take. I am in my wet transparent underpants and I've just been swimming at Daytona Beach. It is 1946, our first morning in Florida. It isn't a vacation; we've arrived to start again, in the sun. The war is over, the border is open, the old black Packard is parked behind us. I had wanted to swim but had no trunks;

my father took me down in my underwear. But in the picture my face is worried, my cupped hands are reaching down to cover myself, but I was late or the picture early – it seems instead that I am pointing to it, a fleshy little spot on my transparent pants. On the back of the picture my father had written: 'Thibidault et fils Daytona – avr / 46'.

We'd left Montreal four days before, with snow still grey in the tenements' shadow, the trees black and budless over the dingy winter street. Our destination was a town named Hartley where my father had a friend from Montreal who'd started a lawn furniture factory. My father was to become a travelling salesman for Laverdure's Lawn Laddies, and I was to begin my life as a salesman's son. As reader of back issues, as a collector of cancelled stamps (the inkier the better), as student and teacher of languages.

Thibidault et fils: Thibidault and son. After a week in Hartley I developed worms. My feet bled from itching and scratching. The worms were visible; I could prick them with pins. My mother took me to a clinic where the doctor sprayed my foot with a liquid freeze. Going on, the ice was pleasant, for Florida feet are always hot. Out on the bench I scraped my initials in the frost of my foot. It seemed right to me (before the pain of the thaw began); I was from Up North, the freezing was a friendly gesture for a Florida doctor. My mother held my foot between her hands and told me stories of her childhood, ice-skating for miles on the Battleford River in Saskatchewan, then riding home under fur rugs in a horse-drawn sleigh. Though she was the same age as my father, she was the eldest of six – somewhere between them was a missing generation. The next morning the itching was worse and half a dozen new worms radiated from the ball of my foot. My mother then consulted her old *Canadian Doctor's Home Companion* – my grandfather Blankenship had been a doctor, active for years in curling circles, Anglican missions, and crackpot Toryism – and learned that footworms, etc., were unknown in Canada but sometimes afflicted Canadian travellers in Tropical Regions. Common to all hot climes, the book went on, due to poor sanitation and the unspeakable habits of the non-white peoples, even in the Gulf Coast and Indian Territories of our southern neighbour. No known cure, but lack of attention can be fatal.

My mother called in a neighbour, our first contact with the slovenly woman who lived downstairs. She came up with a bottle of carbolic acid and another of alcohol, and poured the acid over the worms and told me to yell when it got too hot. Then with alcohol she wiped it off. The next morning my foot had peeled and the worms were gone. And I thought, inspecting my peeled, brown foot, that in some small way I had become less northern, less hateful to the kids around me though I still sounded strange and they shouted after me, 'Yankee, Yankee!'

My father was browned and already spoke with a passable Southern accent. When he wasn't on the road with Lawn Laddies he walked around barefoot or in shower clogs. But he never got worms, and he was embarrassed that I had.

Thibidault and son. He was a fisherman and I always fished at his side. Fished for what? I wonder now – he was too short and vain a man to really be a fisherman. He dressed too well, couldn't swim, despised the taste of fish, shunned the cold, the heat, the bugs, the rain. And yet we fished every Sunday, wherever we lived. Canada, Florida, the Middle West, heedless as deer of crossing borders. The tackle box (oily childhood smell) creaked at our feet. The fir-lined shores and pink granite beaches of Ontario gleamed behind us. Every cast became a fresh hope, a trout or *doré* or even a muskie. But we never caught a muskie or a trout, just the snake-like fork-boned pike that we let go by cutting the line when the plug was swallowed deep. And in Florida, with my father in his Harry Truman shirts and sharkskin pants, the warm bait-well sloshing with half-dead shiners, we waited for bass and channel cat in Okeechobee, Kissimmee and a dozen other bug-beclouded lakes. Gar fish, those tropical pike, drifted by the boat. Gators churned in a narrow channel and dragonflies lit on my cane pole tip. And as I grew older and we came back North (but not all the way), I remember our Sundays in Cincinnati, standing shoulder to shoulder with a few hundred others around a clay-banked tub lit with arc lamps. Scummy pay-lakes with a hot dog stand behind, a vision of hell for a Canadian or a Floridian, but we paid and we fished and we never caught a thing. Ten hours every Sunday from Memorial Day to Labor Day, an unquestioning ritual that would see me dress in my fishing khakis, race out early and buy the Sunday paper before we left (so I could check the baseball averages – what a normal kid I might have been!), then pack the tackle box and portable radio (for the Cincinnati double-header) in the trunk. Then I would get my father up. He'd have his coffee and a few cigarettes then shout, 'Mildred, Frankie and I are going fishing!' She would be upstairs reading or sewing. We were still living in a duplex; a few months later my parents were to start their furniture store and we would never fish again. We walked out, my father and I, nodding to the neighbours (a few kids, younger than I, asked if they could go, a few young fathers would squint and ask, 'Not again, Gene?'); and silently we drove, and later, silently, we fished.

Then came a Sunday just before Labor Day when I was thirteen and we didn't go fishing. I was dressed for it and the car was packed as usual, but my father drove to the county fair instead. Not the Hamilton county fair in Cincinnati – we drove across the river into Boone County, Kentucky, where things were once again Southern and shoddy.

I had known from the books and articles my mother was leaving in the bathroom that I was supposed to be learning about sex. I'd read the books and figured out the anatomy for myself; I wondered only how to ask a girl for it and what to do once I got there. Sex was something like dancing, I supposed, too intricate and spontaneous for a boy like me. And so we toured the fairgrounds that morning, saying nothing, reviewing the prize sows and heifers, watching a stock-car race and miniature rodeo. I could tell from my father's breathing, his coughing, his attempt to put his arm around my shoulder, that this was the day he was going to talk to me about sex, the facts of life, and the thought embarrassed him as much as it did me. I wanted to tell him to never mind; I didn't need it, it was something that selfish people did to one another.

He led me to a remote tent far off the fairway. There was a long male line outside, men with a few boys my age, joking loudly and smelling bad. My father looked away, silent. So this is the place, I thought, where I'm going to see it, going to learn something good and dirty, something they couldn't put on those Britannica Films and show in school. The sign over the entrance said only: *Princess Hi-Yalla. Shows Continuously.*

There was a smell, over the heat, over the hundred men straining for a place, over the fumes of pigsties and stockyards. It was the smell of furtiveness, rural slaughter and unquenchable famine. The smell of boys' rooms in the high school. The smell of sex on the hoof. The 'Princess' on the runway wore not a stitch, and she was already lathered like a racehorse from her continuous dance. There was no avoiding the bright pink lower lips that she'd painted; no avoiding the shrinking, smiling, puckering, wrinkled labia. 'Kiss, baby?' she called out, and the men went wild. The lips smacked us softly. The Princess was more a dowager, and more black than brown or yellow. She bent forward to watch herself, like a ventriloquist with a dummy. I couldn't turn away as my father had; it seemed less offensive to watch her wide flat breast instead, and to think of her as another native from the *National Geographic.* She asked a guard for a slice of gum, then held it over the first row. 'Who gwina wet it up fo' baby?' And a farmer licked both sides while his friends made appreciative noises, then handed it back. The Princess inserted it slowly, as though it hurt, spreading her legs like the bow-legged rodeo clown I'd seen a few minutes earlier. Her lower mouth chewed, her abdomen heaved, and she doubled forward to watch the progress. 'Blow a bubble!' the farmer called, his friends screamed with laughter. But a row of boys in overalls, my age, stared at the woman and didn't smile. Nothing would amaze them – they were waiting for a bubble. The she cupped her hand underneath and gum came slithering out. 'Who wants this?' she called, holding it high, and men were whistling and throwing other things on the stage: key rings, handkerchiefs, cigarettes. She threw the gum toward us – I remember ducking as it came my way, but someone caught it. 'Now then,' she said, and her voice was as loud as a gospel singer's, 'baby's fixin' to have herself a cigarette.' She walked to the edge of the stage (I could see her moist footprints in the dust), her toes curled over the side. 'Which of you men out there is givin' baby a cig'rette?' Another farmer standing behind his fat adolescent son threw up two cigarettes. The boy, I remember, was in overalls and had the cretinous look of fat boys in overalls: big, sweating, red-cheeked, with eyes like calves' in a roping event. By the time I looked back on stage, the Princess had inserted the cigarette and had thrust baby out over the runway and was asking for matches. She held the match herself. And the cigarette glowed, smoke came out, an ash formed...

I heard moaning, long low moans, and I felt the eyes of a dozen farmers leap to the boy in overalls. He was jumping and whimpering and the men were laughing as he tried to dig into his sealed-up pants. Forgetting the buttons at his shoulders, he was holding his crotch as though it burned. He was running in place, moaning, then screaming, 'Daddy!' and I forgot about the Princess. Men cleared a circle around him and began clapping and chanting, 'Whip it out!' and the boy was crying, 'Daddy, I cain't hold it back no more!'

My father grabbed me then by the elbow, and said, 'Well, have you seen enough?' The farm boy had collapsed on the dirt floor, and was twitching on his back as though a live wire were passed through his body. A navy-blue stain that I thought was blood was spreading between his legs. I thought he'd managed to pull his penis off. My father led me out and he was mad at me for something – it was *me* who had brought him there, and his duties as my father – and just as we stepped from the tent I yelled, 'Wait – it's happening to me too.' I wanted to cry with embarrassment for I hadn't felt any urgency before entering the tent. It seemed like a sudden, irresistible need to urinate, something I couldn't hold back. But worse than water; something was ripping at my crotch. My light-coloured fishing khakis would turn brown in water, and the dark stain was already forming.

'Jesus Christ – are you *sick?* That was an old woman – how could *she* ... how could *you* ...' He jerked me forward by the elbow. 'Jesus God,' he muttered, pulling me along down the fairway, then letting me go and walking so fast I had to run, both hands trying to cup the mess I had made. Thousands of people passed me, smiling, laughing. 'I don't know about you,' my father said. '*I think there's something wrong with you,*' and it was the worst thing my father could say about me. We were in the car. I was crying in the back seat. 'Don't tell me someone didn't see you – didn't you think of that? Or what if a customer saw *me* – but you didn't think of that either, did you? Here I take you to something I thought you'd like, something any *normal* boy would like, and –'

I'd been afraid to talk. The wetness was drying, a stain remained. 'You know Murray Lieberman?' my father asked a few minutes later.

'The salesman?'

'He has a kid your age and so we were talking –'

'Never mind,' I said.

'Well, what in the name of God is wrong with two fathers getting together, eh? It was supposed to *show* you what it's like, about women, I mean. It's better than any drawing, isn't it? You want books all the time? You want to *read* about it, or do you want to see it? At least now you *know*, so go ahead and read. Tell your mother we were fishing today, OK? And *that* – that was a Coke you spilled, all right?'

And no other talk, man to man, or father to son, ever took place.

I think back to Boniface Thibidault – how would he, *how did* he, show his sons what to do and where to do it? He was a Frenchman, not a North American; he learned it in Paris, not in a monastery as my father had. And I am, partially at least, a Frenchman too. My father should have taken me to a *cocotte*, to his own mistress perhaps, for the initiation, *la déniaisement*. And I, in my own lovemaking, would have forever honoured him. But this is North America and my father, despite everything, was in his silence a Quebec Catholic of the nineteenth century. Sex, despite my dreams of something better, something nobler, still smells of the circus tent, of something raw and murderous. Other kinds of sex, the adjusted, contented, fulfilling sex of school and manual, seems insubstantial, wilfully ignorant of the depths.

At thirteen I was oldest of eighty kids on the block, a thankless distinction, and my parents at fifty had a good twenty years on the next oldest, who, it happened, shared our duplex.

There lived on that street, and I was beginning to notice in that summer before the sideshow at the county fair, several girl brides and one or two maturely youthful wives. The brides, under twenty and with their first or second youngsters, were a sloppy crew who patrolled the street in cut-away shorts and bra-less elasticized halters that had to be pulled up every few steps. They set their hair so tightly in pin curlers that the effect, at a distance, was of the mange. Barefoot they pushed their baby strollers, thighs sloshing as they walked, or sat on porch furniture reading movie magazines and holding tinted plastic baby bottles between their knees. Though they sat in the sun all day they never tanned. They were spreading week by week while their husbands, hard athletic gas-pumpers, played touch football on the street every Sunday.

But there were others; in particular the wife next door, our two floors being mirror images of the other, everything back-to-back but otherwise identical. What was their name? She was a fair woman, about thirty, with hair only lightly bleached and the kind of figure that one first judges slightly too plump until something voluptuous in her, or you, makes you look again and you see that she is merely extraordinary; a full woman who was once a lanky girl. She had three children, two of them girls who favoured the husband, but I can't quite place his name or face. Her name was Annette.

She was French. That had been a point of discussion once. Born in Maine, she would often chat with my father in what French she remembered while her husband played football or read inside. By that time I had forgotten most of my French. And now I remember the husband. His name was Lance – Lance! – and he was dark, square-shouldered, with a severe crewcut that sliced across an ample bald spot. He travelled a lot; I recall him sitting in a lawn chair on summer evenings, reading the paper and drinking a beer till the mosquitoes drove him in.

And that left Annette alone, and Annette had no friends on the block. She gave the impression, justified, of far outdistancing the neighbourhood girls. Perhaps she frightened them, being older and, by comparison, a goddess. She would sit on a lawn chair in the front yard, on those male-less afternoons of toddling children and cranky mothers and was so stunning in a modest sundress that I would stay inside and peek at her through a hole I had cut in the curtains. Delivery trucks, forced to creep through the litter of kids and abandoned toys, lingered longer than they had to, just to look. At thirteen I could stare for hours, unconscious of peeping, unaware, really, of what I wanted or expected to see. It was almost like fishing, with patience and anticipation keeping me rooted.

My parents were at the new property, cleaning it up for a grand opening. I was given three or four dollars a day for food and I'd spend fifty or sixty cents of it on meaty and starchy grease down at the shopping centre. I was getting fat. Every few days I carried a bulging pocketful of wadded bills down to the bank and cashed them for a ten or twenty. And the bills would accumulate in my wallet. I was too young to open an account without my parents' finding out; the question was how to spend it. After a couple of weeks I'd go downtown and spend astounding sums, for a child, on stamps.

While I was in the shopping centre. I began stealing magazines from the drugstore. The scandal mags, the Hollywood parties, the early *Playboy* and its imitators – I stole because I was too good to be seen buying them. I placed them between the pages of the *Sporting News*, which I also read cover to cover, then dropped a wadded five-dollar bill in the newspaper honour box, raced home, and feasted. Never one for risks, I burned the residue or threw them out in a neighbour's garbage can, my conscience clear for a month's more stealing and secret reading. There was never a time in my life when sex had been so palpable; when the very sight of any girl vaguely developed or any woman up to forty and still in trim could make my breath come short, make my crotch tingle under my baggy pants. In the supermarket, when young mothers dipped low to pick a carton of Cokes from the bottom shelf, I dipped with them. When the counter girl at the drugstore plunged her dipper in the ice cream tub, I hung over the counter to catch a glimpse of her lacy bra; when the neighbour women hung out their clothes, I would take the stairs two at a time to watch from above. When those young wives hooked their thumbs under the knitted elastic halters and gave an upward tug, I let out a little whimper. How close it was to madness; how many other fat thirteen- and fourteen-year-olds, with a drop more violence, provocation, self-pity or whatever, would plunge a knife sixty times into those bellies, just to run their fingers inside the shorts and peel the halter back, allowing the breasts to ooze aside? And especially living next to Annette whose figure made flimsy styles seem indecent and modest dresses maddening. Her body possessed the clothes too greedily, sucked the material to her flesh. She was the woman, I now realize, that Dostoyevsky and Kazantzakis and even Faulkner knew; a Grushenka or the young village widow, a dormant body that kindled violence.

The duplexes were mirror images with only the staircases and bathrooms adjoining. In the summer with Annette at home, her children out playing or taking a nap, her husband away, or just at work, she took many baths. From wherever I sat in our duplex watching television or reading my magazines, I could hear the drop of the drain plug in her bathroom, the splash of water rushing in, the quick expansion of the hot water pipes.

I could imagine the rest, exquisitely. First testing the water with her fingers, then drying the finger on her shorts and then letting them drop. Testing the water again before unhooking the bra in a careless sweep and with another swipe, peeling off her panties. The thought of Annette naked, a foot away, made the walls seem paper-thin, made the tiles grow warm. Ear against the tiles I could hear the waves she made as she settled back, the squeaking of her heels on the bottom of the tub as she straightened her legs, the wringing of a facecloth, plunk of soap as it dropped. The scene was as vivid, with my eyes closed and my hot ear on the warm tile, as murders on old radio shows. I thought of the childhood comic character who could shrink himself with magic sand; how for me that had always translated itself into watching the Hollywood starlets from their bathroom heating registers. But Annette was better or at least as good, and so available. If only there were a way, a shaft for midgets. It wasn't right to house strangers so intimately without providing a way to spy. I looked down to the tile floor – a crack? Something a bobby pin could be twisted in, just a modest, modest opening? And I saw the pipes under the sink, two slim swan-necks, one for hot, one for cold, that cut jaggedly through the tile wall – they had to connect! Then on my hands and knees I scraped away the plaster that held the chromium collar around the pipe. As I had hoped, the hole was a good quarter-inch wider than the pipes and all that blocked a straight-on view of the other bathroom was the collars on Annette's pipes. It would be nothing to punch my way through, slide the rings down, and lie on the tile floor in the comfort of my own bathroom and watch it all; Annette bathing! Ring level was below the tub, but given the distance the angle might correct itself. But detection would be unbearable; if caught I'd commit suicide. She was already out of the bath (but there'll be other days, I thought). She took ten-minute baths (how much more could a man bear?), the water was draining and now she was running the lavatory faucet which seemed just over my head. How long before she took another bath? It would seem, now that I had a plan, as long as the wait between issues of my favourite magazines.

I rested on the floor under the sink until Annette left her bathroom. Then I walked down to the shopping centre and had a Coke to steady myself. I bought a nail file. When I got back Annette was sitting in her yard, wearing a striped housedress and looking, as usual, fresh from a bath. I said hello and she smiled very kindly. Then I turned my door handle and cried, 'Oh, no!'

'What is it, Frankie?' she asked, getting up from her chair.

'I left my key inside.'

'Shall I call your father?'

'No,' I said, 'I think I can get in through the window. But could I use your bathroom first?'

'Of course.'

I checked upstairs for kids. Then I locked myself inside and with the new file, scraped away the plaster and pulled one collar down. Careful as always, aware that I would make a good murderer or a good detective, I cleaned up the plaster crumbs. I'd forgotten to leave our own bathroom light on, but it seemed that I could see all the way through. Time would tell. *Take a bath*, I willed her, as I flushed the toilet. It reminded me of fishing as a child, trying to influence the fish to bite. It's very hot, sticky, just right for a nice cool bath ... My own flesh was stippled, I shivered as I stepped outside and saw her again. She'd soon be *mine* – something to do for the rest of the summer! My throat was so tense I couldn't even thank her. I climbed inside through the living-room window that I had left open.

I took the stairs two at a time, stretched myself out under the sink to admire the job. I'd forgotten to leave *her* light on, but I thought I could see the white of her tub in the darkened bathroom, and even an empty tub was enough to sustain me.

How obvious was the pipe and collar? It suddenly seemed blatant, that she would entre the bathroom, undress, sit in the tub, turn to the wall, and scream. Do a peeper's eyes shine too brightly? In school I'd often been able to stare a kid into turning around – it was now an unwanted gift.

You're getting warm again, Annette. Very very hot. You want another bath. You're getting up from the chair, coming inside, up the stairs ... I kept on for hours till it was dark. I heard the kids taking baths and saw nothing. The white of the bathtub was another skin of plaster, no telling how thick. I'd been cheated.

Another day. There had to be another link – I had faith that the builders of duplexes were men who provided, out of guilt, certain amenities. Fans were in the ceiling. Windows opened on the opposite sides, the heating ducts were useless without a metal drill. Only the medicine cabinets were left. They had to be back-to-back. I opened ours, found the four corner screws, undid them, took out the medicines quietly (even my old Florida carbolic acid), then eased the chest from its plaster nest. It worked. I was facing the metal backing of Annette's medicine chest. The fit was tight and I could never take a chance of tampering with hers – what if I gave it a nudge when Lance was shaving and the whole thing came crashing down, revealing me leaning over my sink in the hole where our medicine chest had been?

The used-razor slot. A little slot in the middle. I popped the paper coating with the nailfile. I darkened our own bathroom. If Annette opened her chest, I'd see her. But would she open it with her clothes off? Was she tall enough to make it count? How many hours would I have to stand there, stretched over the sink, waiting, and could I, every day, put the chest back up and take it down without some loud disaster? What if my father came home to shave, unexpectedly?

I waited all afternoon and all evening and when eight o'clock came I ended the vigil and put the chest back up. With a desire so urgent, there *had* to be a way of penetrating an inch and a half of tile and plaster. When she was in her bath I felt I could have devoured the walls between us. Anything *heard* so clearly had to yield to vision – that was another natural law – just as anything dreamt had to become real, eventually.

I became a baby-sitter; the oldest kid on the block, quiet and responsible. I watched television in nearly every duplex on the street, ignored the whimpers, filled bottles, and my pockets bulged with more unneeded cash. I poked around the young parents' bedrooms and medicine cabinets, only half repelled by the clutter and unfamiliar odours, the stickiness, the greyness of young married life in a Midwest suburb. I found boxes of prophylactics in top drawers and learned to put one on and to walk around with it on until the lubrication stuck to my underwear. Sex books and nudist magazines showing pubic hair were stuffed in nightstands, and in one or two homes I found piles of home-made snaps of the young wife when she'd been slim and high-school young, sitting naked in the sun, in a woods somewhere. She'd been posed in dozens of ways, legs wide apart, fingers on her pubic hair, tongue curled between her teeth. Others of her, and of a neighbour woman, on the same living-room sofa that I was sitting on: fatter now, her breasts resting on a roll of fat around her middle, her thighs shadowed where the skin had grown soft, *This is the girl I see every day*, pushing that carriage, looking like a fat girl at a high school hangout. Those bigger girls in my school, in bright blue sweaters, earrings, black curly hair, bad skin, black corduroy jackets, smoking. They become like this; they *are* like this.

These were the weeks in August, when my mother was leaving the articles around. Soon my father would take me to the county fair. There were no answers to the questions I asked, holding those snapshots, looking again (by daylight) at the wife (in ragged shorts and elastic halter) who had consented to the pictures. They were like murder victims, the photos were like police shots in the scandal magazines, the women looked like mistresses of bandits. There was no place in the world for the life I wanted, for the pure woman I would someday, somehow, marry.

I baby-sat for Annette and Lance, then for Annette alone, and I worked again on the lavatory scheme, the used-razor slot, and discovered the slight deficiencies in the architecture that had thrown my calculations off. I could see from their bathroom into ours much better than I could ever see into theirs. Annette kept a neat house and life with her, even I could appreciate, must have been a joy of lust and efficiency, in surroundings as clean and attractive as a *Playboy* studio.

One evening she came over when my parents were working, to ask me to baby-sit for a couple of hours. Lance wasn't in. Her children were never a problem and though it was a week night and school had begun, I agreed. She left me a slice of Lance's birthday cake, and begged me to go to sleep in case she was late.

An hour later, after some reading, I used her bathroom, innocently. If only I lived here, with Annette over there! I opened her medicine chest to learn some more about her: a few interesting pills 'for pain', Tampax Super (naturally, I thought), gauze and adhesive, something for piles (for him, I hoped). And then I heard a noise from our bathroom; I heard our light snap on. My parents must have come home early.

I knew from a cough that it wasn't my mother. The Thibidault medicine chest was opened. I peered through the razor slot and saw young fingers among our bottles, blond hair and a tanned forehead: Annette. She picked out a jar, then closed the door. I fell to the floor and put my eye against the pipes. Bare golden legs. Then our light went out.

I looked into our bathroom for the next few seconds then ran to Annette's front bedroom where the youngest girl slept, and pressed over her crib to look out the window. She was just stepping out and walking slowly to the station wagon of Thibidault Furniture, which had been parked. She got in the far side and the car immediately, silently, backed away, with just its parking lights on ...

And that was all. For some reason, perhaps the shame of my

complicity, I never asked my father why he had come home or why Annette had been in our bathroom. I didn't have to – I'd gotten a glimpse of Annette, which was all I could handle anyway. I didn't understand the rest. *Thibidault et fils*, fishing again.

Jean-Louis Thibidault, twice divorced, is dead; buried in Venice, Florida. Bridge of Sighs Cemetery. I even asked his widow if I could have him removed to Sorel, Quebec. She didn't mind, but the *prêtre-vicaire* of my father's old parish turned me down. When my father was born, Venice, Florida, was five miles offshore and fifty feet underwater. The thought of him buried there tortures my soul.

There was another Sunday in Florida. A hurricane was a hundred miles offshore and due to strike Fort Lauderdale within the next six hours. We drove from our house down Las Olas to the beach (Fort Lauderdale was still an inland city then), and parked half a mile away, safe from the paint-blasting sand. We could hear the breakers under the shriek of the wind, shaking the wooden bridge we walked on. Then we watched them crash, brown with weeds and suspended sand. And we could see them miles offshore, rolling in forty feet high and flashing their foam like icebergs. A few men in swimming suits and woollen sweaters were standing in the crater pools, pulling out the deep-sea fish that had been stunned by the trip and waves. Other fish littered the beach, their bellies blasted by the change in pressure. My mother's face was raw and her glasses webbed with salt. She went back to the car on her own. My father and I sat on the bench for another hour and I could see behind his crusty sunglasses. His eyes were moist and dancing, his hair stiff and matted. We sat on the bench until we were soaked and the municipal guards rounded us up. Then they barricaded the boulevards and we went back to the car, the best day of fishing we'd ever had, and we walked hand in hand for the last time, talking excitedly, dodging coconuts, power lines, and shattered glass, feeling brave and united in the face of the storm. My father and me. What a day it was, what a once-in-a-lifetime day it was.

The Salesman's Son Grows Older

Camphor berries popped underfoot on a night as hot and close as a faucet of sweat. My mother and I were walking from the movies. It was late for me but since my father was on the road selling furniture, she had taken me out. She watched the sidewalk for roaches darting to the gutters. They popped like the berries underfoot. I was sleepy and my mother restless, like women whose men are often gone. She hadn't eaten supper, hadn't read the paper, couldn't stand the radio, and finally she'd suggested the movies. Inside, she'd paced behind the glass while I watched a Margaret O'Brien movie. The theatre was air-cooled, which meant the hot air was kept circulating; even so the outdoors had been formidable under a moon that burned hotly. The apartment would be crushing. She'd been a week without a letter.

I think now of the privileges of the salesman's son, as much as the moving from town to town, the postcards and long-distance calls; staying up late, keeping my mother company, being her confidant, behaving even at eight a good ten years older. And always wondering with her where my father was. Somewhere in his territory, anywhere from Raleigh to Shreveport. Another privilege of the salesman's son was knowing the cities and the routes between them, knowing the miles and predicting how long any drive would take. As a child, I'd wanted to be a Greyhound driver.

The smell of a summer night in Florida is so strong that twenty years later on a snowy night in Canada I can still feel it. Lustrous tropical nights, full of roaches and rats and lizards, with lightning bugs and whippoorwills prickling the dark and silence. I wanted to walk past our apartment house to the crater of peat bogs just beyond, so that the sweat on my arms could at least evaporate.

'Maybe Daddy'll be home tonight,' I said, playing the game of the salesman's son. There was a cream-coloured sedan in our driveway, with a white top that made it look like my father's convertible. Then the light went on inside and the door opened and a drowsy young patrolman with his tie loosened and his Stetson and clipboard shuffled our way.

'Ma'am, are you the party in the upper apartment? I mean are you Mrs Thee ... is this here your name, ma'am?'

'Thibidault,' she said. '*T. B. Doe* if you wish.'

'I wonder then can we go inside a spell?'

'What is it?'

'Let's just go inside so's we can set a spell.'

A long climb up the back staircase, my mother breathing deeply, long *ah-h-h's* and I took the key from her to let us in. I threw open the windows and turned on the lights. The patrolman tried to have my mother sit. She knew what was coming, like a miner's wife at a sudden whistle. She went to the kitchen and opened a Coke for me and poured iced tea for the young patrolman, then came back and sat where he told her to.

'You're here to tell me my husband is dead. I've felt it all night.' Her head was nodding, a way of commanding agreement. 'I'll be all right.'

She wouldn't be, I knew. She'd need me.

'I didn't say that, ma'am,' and for the first time his eyes brightened. 'No, ma'am, he isn't dead. There was a pretty bad smash-up up in Georgia about three days ago and he was unconscious till this morning. The report we got is he was on the critical list but they done took him off. He's in serious condition.'

'How serious is serious?' I asked.

'What?'

She was still nodding. 'You needn't worry. You can go if you wish – you've been very considerate.'

'Can I fetch you something? Is there anybody you want me to call? Lots of times the effect of distressing news don't sink in till later and it's kindly useful having somebody around.'

'Where did you say he was?'

He rustled the papers on his clipboard, happy to oblige. 'Georgia, ma'am, Valdosta – that's about two hundred mile north. This here isn't the official report but it says the accident happened about midnight last Wednesday smack in the middle of Valdosta. Mr Thee ... Mr *Doe*, was alone in the car and they reckon he must have fell asleep. The car ... well, there ain't much left of the car.'

'Did he hurt anyone else?'

'No, ma'am. Least it don't say so here.' He grinned. 'Looks like it was just him.'

She was angry.

'Why wasn't I notified earlier?' she asked.

'That's kindly irregular, ma'am. I don't know why.'

She nodded. She hadn't stopped nodding.

'We can call up to Valdosta and get you a place to stay. And we'll keep an eye on this place while you're gone. *Anything you want*, Mrs Doe, that's what I'm aimin' to say.'

She was silent for a long time as though she were going to say, *Would you repeat it please, I don't think I heard it right:* and there was even a smile on her face, not a happy one, a smile that says *life is long and many things happen that we can't control and can't change and can't bring back.* 'You've been very helpful. Please go.'

If my father were dead it meant we would move. Back to Canada perhaps. Or west to the mountains, north to cities. And if my father lived, that too would change our lives, somehow. My mother stayed in the living room after the officer left and I watched her from the crack of my door, drinking hot coffee and smoking more than she ever had before. A few minutes later came a knock on the front door and she hurried to open up. Two neighbour women whose children I knew but rarely played with stepped inside and poured themselves iced tea, then waited to learn what had brought the police to the Yankee lady's door.

My mother said there'd been an accident.

'I knowed it was that,' said Mrs Wade, 'and him such a fine-looking gentleman, too. I seen the po-lice settin' in your drive all evenin'-long and I said to my Grady that poor woman and her li'l boy is in for bad news when they get back from the pitchershow – or wherever you was at – so I called Miz Davis here and told her what I seen and wouldn't you know she said we best fix up a li'l basket of fruit – that's kindly like a custom with us here, since I knowed you was from outastate. What I brung ain't much just some navels and tangerines but I reckon it's somethin' to suck on when the times is bad.'

'I reckon,' said Mrs Davis, 'your mister was hurt pretty bad.'

'Yes.'

'They told you where he's at, I reckon.'

'Yes, they did.'

'Miz Davis and me, we thought if you was going to see him you'd need somebody to look after your li'l boy. I don't want you to go on worryin' your head over that at all. Her and her Billy got all the room he's fixin' to need.'

'That's very kind.'

I was out of bed now and back at the crack of my opened door. I'd never seen my mother talk to any neighbour women. I'd never been more aware of how different she looked and sounded. And of all the exciting possibilities opened up by my father's accident and possible death, staying back in an unpainted shanty full of loud kids was the least attractive. I began wishing my father wasn't hurt. And then I realized that the neighbour women with their sympathy and fruit had broken my mother's resistance. She would cry as soon as they left and I would have to pretend to be asleep, or else go out and comfort her, bring her tea and listen to her: be a salesman's son.

Audrey Davis was plump and straight-haired; Billy was gaunt, red-cheeked, and almost handsome. The children came in a phalanx of older girls who'd already run off, then a second wave ranging from the nearly pubescent down to infancy. At eight, I fell in the middle of the second pack whose leader was a ten-year-old named Carrie, with earrings and painted nails.

They ate their meals fried or boiled. Twenty years later I can still taste their warm, sweet tea, the fat chunks of pork, the chickpeas and okra. I can still smell the outhouse and hear the hiss of a million maggots flashing silver down the hole. The Davis crap was the fairest yellow. The food? Disease?

But what I really remember, and remember with such vividness that even now I wince, is this: sleeping one night on the living-room rug – it was red and worn down to its backing – I developed a cough. After some rustling in the back Miz Davis appeared at the door, clad in a robe tied once at the waist. One white tubular breast had worked free. The nipple was poised like an ornament at its tip. It was the first time I'd ever seen a breast.

Even as I was watching it, she set to work with a mixture for the cough. By the time I noticed the liquid and the spoon, she was adding sugar. I opened wide, anxious to impress, and she thrust in the spoon, far enough to make me gag, and pulled my head back by the hair. She kept the spoon inside until I felt I was drowning in the gritty mixture of sugar and kerosene. I knew if I was dying there was one thing I wanted to do; I brought my open hand against the palm-numbing softness of her breast, then, for an instant ran my fingertips over the hard, dry nipple and shafts of prickly hair. She acted as though nothing had happened and I looked innocent as though nothing had been intended. Then she took out the spoon.

After Audrey Davis's breast and kerosene my excreta turned a runny yellow. The night after the breast I was hiding in the sawgrass, bitten by mosquitoes and betrayed by fireflies, playing kick-the-can. The bladder-burning tension was excruciating for a slow, chubby boy in a running game, scurrying under the Davis jeep, under the pilings of the house, into the edges of the peat. My breath, cupped in the palm of my sweating hand, echoed like a deep-sea diver's as Carrie Davis beat the brush looking for me. Chigger bites, mosquito welts, burned and itched. I wanted to scream, to lift the house on my shoulders, to send the can in a spiraling arch sixty yards downfield, splitting imaginary goal posts and freeing Carrie's prisoners, but I knew – knew – that even if I snuck away undetected, even with a ten-foot lead on Carrie or anyone else, I'd lose the dash to the can. Even if I got there first I'd kick too early and catch it with my glancing heel and the can would lean and roll and be replaced before I could hide again. I knew finally that it would be my fate, if caught, to be searching for kids in a twenty-foot circle for the rest of the night, or until the Davis kids got tired of running and kicking the can from under me. Better, then, to huddle deep in the pilings, deeper even than the hounds would venture till I could smell the muck, the seepage from the outhouse, the undried spillage from the kitchen slops. No one would find me. I wouldn't be caught nor would I ever kick the goddam can. Time after time, game after game, after the kids were caught they'd have to call, 'Frankie, Frankie, come in free,' and it would be exasperation, not admiration, that tinted Carrie's voice.

My mother came back four days later and set about selling all the clothes and furniture that anyone wanted. There were brief discussions with the neighbour women who shook their heads as she spoke. Finally I drew the conclusion that my father was dead, though I didn't ask. I tried out this new profound distinction on Carrie Davis and was treated for a day or two with a deference, a near sympathy ('Don't you do that, Billy Joe, can't you see his daddy's dead?') that I'd been seeking all along and probably ever since.

But how was it, in the week or so that it took her to pack and sell off everything that I never asked her what exactly had happened in Valdosta? Her mood had been grim and businesslike, the mood a salesman's son learns not to tamper with. I adjusted instead to the news that we were leaving Florida and would be returning to her family in Saskatchewan.

Saskatchewan! No neighbour had ever heard of it. 'Where in the world's that at?' my teacher asked when I requested the transfer slip. When I said Canada, she asked what state. The Davis kids had never heard of Canada.

One book that had always travelled with us was my mother's atlas. She had used it in school before the Great War – a phrase she still used – a comprehensive British edition that smeared the world in Imperial reds and pinks so that my vision of the earth had been distorted by Edwardian lenses. Safe pink swaths cut the rift of Africa, the belly of Asia, and lighted like a rash over Oceania and the Caribbean. And of course red dominated and overwhelmed poor North America. The raw, pink, bulging brow of the continent was Canada, the largest and reddest blob of Britishness in the flat projection of the world. Saskatchewan alone could hold half a dozen Texases and the undivided yellow of the desert southwest called the 'Indian Territories.'

It was the smell of the book that had attracted me and led me, even before I could read, to a tracing of the Ottoman Empire, Austro-Hungary, and a dozen princely states. That had been my mother's childhood world and it became mine too – cool, confident, and British – and now it seems to me, that all the disruptions in my life and in Mildred Blankenship's have merely been a settling of the old borders, an insurrection of the cool gazetteer with its sultanates, Boer lands, Pondichérys, and Port Arthurs. All in the frontispiece, with its two-tone map of the world in red and grey, emblazoned, WE HOLD A GREATER EMPIRE THAN HAS BEEN.

We rode for a week without a break. Too excited for sleep, I crouched against the railings behind the driver's seat with a road map in my hand, crossing off towns and county lines, then the borders of states. We'd left in April; we were closing in on winter again. The drivers urged me to talk, so they wouldn't fall asleep. 'Watch for a burnt-out gas station over the next rise,' they'd say, 'three men got killed there ... down there a new Stucky's is going up ... right at that guardrail is where eight people got killed in a head-on crash ...' And on and on, identifying every town before it came, pacing themselves like milers, 'Must be 3:15,' they'd say, passing an all-night diner and tooting a horn, knowing every night clerk in every small-town hotel where the bundles of morning papers were thrown off. It had seemed miraculous, then, to master a five-state route as though it were an elevator ride in a three-story department store. Chattanooga to Indianapolis, four times a week. And on we went: Chicago, Rock Island, Ottumwa, Des Moines, Omaha, Sioux Falls, Pierre, and Butte, where my uncle John Blankenship was on hand to take us into Canada.

I watched my uncle for signs of foreignness. His clothes were shaggy, the car was English, and there were British flags in the corners of the windshield. But he looked like a fleshed-out Billy Davis from Oshacola County, Florida, with the same scraped cheeks, high colouring and sky-blue eyes, the reddened hands with flaking knuckles, stubby fingers with stiff, black hair. John's accent was as strange as the Davises'. The voice was deep, the patterns rapid, and each word emerged as hard and clear as cubes from a freezer.

The border town had broad dirt streets. A few of the cars parked along the elevated sidewalks were high, boxy, pre-war models I couldn't identify. The cigarette signs, the first thing a boy notices, were foreign.

'How does it feel, Franklin? The air any different?'

'It might be, sir.'

'You don't have to say "sir" to me. Uncle John will do. You're in your own country now – just look at the land, will you? Look at the grain elevators – that's where our money is, in the land. Don't look for it in that chrome-plated junk. You can *see* the soil, can't you?'

The land was flat, about like Florida, the road straight and narrow and the next town's grain elevator already visible. It was late April and the snow had receded from the road-bed. Bald spots, black and glistening, were appearing in the fields under a cold bright sun. Three weeks ago, when my father was alive, the thermometer had hit ninety-five degrees.

'Of course you can. Grade A Saskatchewan hard, the finest in the world.'

The finest what? I wondered.

'Far as the eye can see. That's prosperity, Mildred. And we haven't touched anything yet – we're going to be a rich province, Mildred. We have the largest potash reserves in the world. You'll have no trouble getting work, believe me.'

'And how's Valerie?' my mother asked. 'And the children?'

Around such questions I slowly unwound. My uncle was no bus driver and Saskatchewan offered nothing for a map-primed child. I was a British subject with a Deep South accent, riding in a cold car with a strong new uncle. So many things to be ashamed of – my accent, my tan, my chubbiness. I spoke half as fast as my uncle and couldn't speed up.

'Ever been to a bonspiel, Franklin?'

'No, sir, I don't think so.'

'You'll come out tonight, then. Your Aunt Valerie is skip.'

I decided not to say another word. Not until I understood what the Canadians were talking about

Uncle John Blankenship, that tedious man, and his wife and three children made room for us in Saskatoon. A cold spring gave way, in May, to a dry, burning heat, the kind that blazed across my forehead and shrunk the skin under my eyes and over my nose. But I didn't sweat. It wasn't like Florida heat that reached up groggily from the ground as well as from above, steaming the trouser cuffs while threatening sunstroke. The Blankenships had a farm out of town and Jack, my oldest cousin, ran a trap line and kept a .22 rifle in the loft of the barn. During the summer I spent hot afternoons firing at gophers as they popped from their holes. Fat boy with a gun, squinting over the wheat through July and August, the combine harvesting the beaten rows, months after believing my father dead, and happy. As happy as I've ever been.

I looked for help from my cousins, for cousins are the unborn brothers and sisters of the only child. But they were slightly older, more capable, and spoke strangely. They were never alone, never drank Cokes which were bad for the teeth and stomach (demonstrated for me by leaving a piece of metal in a cup of Coke), never seemed to tire of work and fellowship. They were up at five, worked hard till seven, ate hot meaty-mushy breakfasts, then raced back to work and came to lunch red in the brow, basted in sweat, yet not smelling bad at all. They drank pasteurized milk with flecks of cream and even when they rested in the early afternoon they'd sit outside with a motor in their lap and a kerosene-soaked rag to clean it. I would join them, but with an ancient issue of *Collier's* or *National Geographic* taken from the pillars of bundled magazines in the attic, and all afternoon I'd sit in the shade with my busy cousins, reading about 'New Hope for Ancient Anatolia' or 'Brave Finland Carries On.' I was given an article from an old *Maclean's* about my grandfather, Morley Blankenship, a wheat pool president who had petitioned thirty thankless years for left-hand driving in Canada.

What about those cousins who'd never ceased working, who'd held night jobs through college, then married and gone to law school or whatever? *My* cousins, *my* unborn brothers with full Blankenship and McLeod blood and their medical or legal practices in Vancouver and Regina and their spiky, balding blond heads and their political organizing. Is that all their work and muscles and fresh air could bring them? Is that what I would have been if we'd stayed in Saskatoon, a bloody Blankenship with crinkles and crow's-feet at twenty-five?

And what if we'd stayed anywhere? If we'd never left Montreal, I'd have been educated in both my languages instead of Florida English. Or if we'd never left the South I've have emerged a man of breeding, liberal in the traditions of Duke University with tastes for Augustan authors and breeding falcons, for quoting Tocqueville and Henry James, a wearer of three-piece suits, a user of straight razors. What calamity made me a reader of back issues, defunct atlases, and foreign grammars? The loss, the loss! To leave Montreal for places like Georgia and Florida; to leave Florida for Saskatchewan; to leave the prairies for places like Cincinnati and Pittsburgh and, finally, to stumble back to Montreal a middle-class American from a broken home, after years of pointless suffering had promised so much.

My son sleeps so soundly. Over his bed, five licence plates are hung, the last four from Quebec, the first from Wisconsin. Five years ago, when he was six months old, we left to take a bad job in Montreal, where I was born but had never visited. My parents had brought me to the U.S. when I was six months old. Canada was at war, America was neutral. America meant opportunity, freedom; Montreal meant ghettos, and insults. And so, loving our children, we murder them. Following the sun, the dollars, the peace-of-mind, we blind ourselves. Better to be a professor's son than a salesman's son – better a thousand times, I think – better to ski than to feed the mordant hounds, better to swim at a summer cottage than debase yourself in the septic mud. But what do these licence plates mean? Endurance? Exile, cunning? Where will we all wind up, and how?

Because I couldn't master the five-cent nib that all the Saskatoon kids had to use in school, and because the teacher wouldn't accept my very neat Florida pencil writing, a compromise was reached that allowed me to write in ballpoint. I was now a third-grader.

The fanciest ballpoint pen on sale in Saskatoon featured the head and enormous black hat of Hopalong Cassidy. The face was baby-pink with blue spots for eyes and white ones for teeth and sideburns. It was, naturally, an unbalanced thing that haemorrhaged purplely on the page. The ink was viscous and slow-drying and tended to accumulate in the cross-roads of every loop. Nevertheless, it was a handsome pen and the envy of my classmates, all of whom scratched their way Scottishly across the page.

One day in early October I had been sucking lightly on Hoppy's hat as I thought of the sum I was trying to add. I didn't know, but my mouth was purpling with a stream of ink and the blue saliva was trickling on my shirt. My fingers had carried it to my cheeks and eyes, over my forehead and up my nostrils. I noticed nothing. But suddenly the teacher gasped and started running toward me, and two students leaped from their desk to grab me.

I was thrown to the floor and when I opened my mouth to shout, the surrounding girls screamed. Then the teacher was upon me, cramming her fingers down my throat, two fingers when the first didn't help, and she pumped my head from the back with her other hand. 'Stand back, give him air – can't you see he's choking? Somebody get the nurse!'

'Is he dying?'

'What's all that stuff?'

What was her name – that second woman who had crammed

something down my throat? I could see her perfectly. For fifty years she had been pale and prim and ever so respectable but I remember her as a hairy-nostrilled and badly dentured banshee with fingers poisoned by furtive tobacco. I remember reaching out to paw her face to make her stop this impulsive assault on an innocent American, when suddenly I saw it: the blue rubble on my shirt, the bright sticky gobs of blue on the backs of my hands, the blue tint my eyes picked up off my cheeks. *I've been shot*, I thought. Blood is blue when you're really hurt. Then one of the boys let go of my arm and I was dropped to one elbow. 'That's *ink*, Miss Carstairs. That's not blood or anything – that's *ink*. He was sucking his pen.'

She finally looked closely at me, her eyes narrowing with reproach and disappointment. Her fingers fluttered in my throat. *Canadians!* I'd wanted to scream, *what do you want?* You throw me on the floor because of my accent and you pump your fingers in my throat fit to choke me then worst of all you start laughing when you find I'm not dying. *But I am.* Stop it. You stupid Yank with your stupid pen and the stupid cowboy hat on top and you sucking it like a baby. I rolled to my knees and coughed and retched out the clots of ink, then bulled my way through the rows of curious girls in their flannel jumpers who were making 'ugh' sounds, and, head down because I didn't want anyone else to catch me and administer first aid, I dashed the two blocks to the Blankenship house in what, coatless, seemed like zero cold.

I let myself in the kitchen, quietly, to wash before I was seen. In the living room, a voice was straining, almost shouting. It wasn't my mother and I thought for an instant it might be Miss Carstairs who somehow had beaten me home. I moved closer.

'John says you're a bloody fool and I couldn't agree more!'

Aunt Valerie held a letter and she was snapping the envelope in my mother's face. 'A bloody little fool, and that's not all –'

'I see I shouldn't have shown it to you.'

'He's not worth it – here,' she threw the letter in my mother's lap, 'don't tell me that was the first time. *She was there* – doesn't that mean anything to you? *That woman* was there the whole time. How much do you think he cares for your feelings? Does he know how you felt when you got there –'

'No one will ever know.'

'Well, someone better make *you* know. I don't think you're competent. I think he's got a spell on you if you want my opinion. It's like a poison –'

'I'm not minimizing it,' my mother broke in, and though she was sitting and didn't seem angry, her voice had risen and without straining it was blotting out my aunt's. 'I'm not minimizing it. I know she wasn't the first and she might not be the last –'

'That's even more –'

'Will you let me finish? I didn't marry a Blankenship. You can tell my brother that I remember very well all the advice he gave me and my answer to all of you is that it's my life and I'm responsible and you can all ...'

'Go ... to ... hell – is that it?'

'In so many words. Exactly. You can all go to hell.'

Go to hell: I remember the way she said it, for she never said it again, not in my presence. More permission than a command: *yes, you may go to hell.* But it lifted Aunt Valerie out of her shoes.

'Now I *know*!' she cried. 'I *see* it.'

'See what?'

'What he's turned you into. One letter from him saying he wants you and you're running back – like a ... like an I-don't-know-what! Only some things a woman can guess even when she doesn't want to. I don't deny he's a handsome devil. They all are. But to *degrade* yourself, really –'

Then my mother stood and looked at the door, straight at me, whom she must have seen. Her face was a jumble of frowns and smiles. I moved back toward the kitchen. 'This will be our address,' I heard her say. 'Mrs Mildred Thibidault.'

She didn't come to the kitchen. She went upstairs, and Aunt Valerie stayed in the living room. I pictured her crying or cursing, throwing the porcelain off the mantel. I felt sorry for her; I understood her better than my mother. But minutes later she turned on the vacuum cleaner. And I returned quietly to the kitchen then slammed the outside door loudly and shouted, 'I'm home, Aunt Valerie!' And then, knowing the role if not the words, I went upstairs to find out when we were leaving and where we would be going.

* * *

This long afternoon and evening, I closed my eyes and heard sounds of my childhood: the skipping rope slaps a dusty street in a warm Southern twilight. The bats are out, the lightning bugs, the whippoorwills. I am the boy on yellow grass patting a hound, feeling him tremble under my touch. Slap, slap, a girl strains forward with her nose and shoulders, lets the rope slap, slap, slap, as she catches the rhythm before jumping in. The girls speed it up – *hot pepper* it's called – and they begin a song, something insulting about Negroes. The anonymous hound lays his head on my knee. Gnats encrust his eyes. *Poor dog*, I say. His breath is bad, his ears are frayed from fights, his eyes are moist and pink and tropical...

All day the slap, slap. The rope in a dusty yard, a little pit between the girls who turn it. As I walked today in another climate, now a man, I heard boots skipping on a wet city pavement, a girl running with her lover, a girl in a maxi-coat on a Montreal street. *Tschip-tschip*: I'd been listening for it, boots on sand over a layer of ice. A taxi waited at the corner, its wipers thrashing as the engine throbbed. And tonight, over the shallow breathing of my son, an aluminum shovel strikes the concrete, under new snow.

What can I make of this, I ask myself, staring now at the licence plates on the wall. Five years ago in Wisconsin on a snowy evening like this, with our boy just a bundle in the middle of his crib, I looked out our bedroom window. Snow had been falling all that day, all evening too, and had just begun letting up. We were renting a corner house that year; my first teaching job. I was twenty-four and feeling important. I was political that year of the teach-in. I'd spoken out the day before and been abused by name on a local TV channel. A known agitator. Six inches of new snow had fallen. An hour later a policeman came to our door and issued a summons and twenty-dollar fine for keeping an uncleared walk.

America, I'd thought then. A friend called; he'd gotten a ticket too. Harassment – did I want to fight it? I said I'd think about it, but I knew suddenly that I didn't care.

Watching the police car stop at the corner and one policeman get out, kick his feet on our steps then hold his finger on the bell a full thirty seconds, I'd thought of other places we could be, of taking the option my parents had accidentally left me. Nothing principled, nothing heroic, nothing even defiant. And so my son is skiing and learning French and someday he'll ask me why I made him do it, and he'll exercise the option we've accidentally left him ... *slap-slap*, the dusty rope. Patrolmen on our steps, the shovel scraping a snowy walk.

I'm still a young man, but many things have gone for good.

Relief

Those with radios were safe from hurricanes, in their snug bungalows on landscaped streets. They nailed their shutters down, parked their cars under protection, and threw a card party till the storm blew over. In the morning, bleary-eyed but fresh with adventure, they'd drive down the cluttered streets, detouring around power lines, trees, temporary floods, then go home to sleep. Schools closed, and the kids gathered behind the fallen trees, firing kumquats at the clean-up crews of Negroes. The next day, blue skies and an autumn coolness returned; the town appeared cleaner, almost freshly painted. Errant hurricanes did that when they chanced across the state – made the townsfolk feel akin for a day to the blizzard-struck residents of upper New York who had also licked the adversity with candles, fortitude, and a supply of good hard liquor.

But with us things were different. We had no radios back in the swamps by the lake. Even if we had, what could we have done? Warn the moss-pickers who were the nearest humans? Tell them – on a hot, still day – that a voice from Miami had warned that a hurricane was coming tomorrow? Impossible. And in those days, had we known in advance, it might have been crueller. Had we known a storm was coming, we might have sat, terrified, a longer time, tempted to flee the flimsy shelter we had.

On normal days Lake Oshacola was an inland sea – not like Okeechobee, that shallow infinite puddle further south. Oshacola seemed fresh, moving, and deep; we could see ten miles across to the hamlet of Oloka, but the transverse shore, nearly thirty miles away, was hidden in perpetual haze. It seemed that we commanded an arm of the ocean, and we believed the lake contained the sharks and monsters of the sea. Of gators there was no doubt; I'd seen them at a distance pulling themselves up the rise over the Florida Central tracks, from the sawgrass sloughs on either side where they nested. We lived among the gators; little kids had to be kept in sight, and tied-up hounds were lost if the water rose.

That was thirty-five years ago. Now those shanties have been ploughed over and the hollows are getting filled. Bounty hunters have driven the gators back to the swamps with the otters and moccasins. Sprayers have killed the mosquitoes and the townsfolk are building cabins where I was raised, and their children have safer, drier yards to kick the can in, free of reptiles and migrant workers spoiling their fun.

But just before the war, those tracts between the lake and the highways, the sandy enclaves rising slightly above the swamps were still untamed. We had pumas then, and wildcats that shredded your wash if you left it out overnight. We were isolated from the town and separated from nearly everyone by the impenetrable channels of the lake that made the land we lived on a peninsula. On the same neck of land with us, but over the tracks and virtually in the permanent swamps, lived the family of migrant moss-pickers in two shanties raised on stilts. And on the inlet, Leon Sellers at his boat landing, living alone. Maybe there were people on Sem'nole Island about two miles offshore, but they'd be coloured or Indian, so we didn't speculate. On school mornings, three days a week, I walked up to the highway with my father and waited with him for our separate buses. He worked for the packing plant, dyeing oranges for shipment north by the Chamber of Commerce. He caught the Orlando bus into Hartley; I took the school bus going the other way.

Our schoolroom was a grey shanty car that had been part of a hobo jungle – now joined to a few others, a convoy of tin chimneys. Inside, the migrant agency had nailed in some orange crates for the dozen of us from Buck's Cove. There was a teacher's desk that looked like a vanity dresser, and a blackboard so tiny she could only squeeze on a quarter of the alphabet at a time – even now the alphabet divides itself into fourths whenever I recite it. There were other cars near ours, to take care of the Negroes and Seminole kids who lived in the other direction, but whom we sensed behind us in the swamps and never saw. The accumulation of shanty cars, a gas station, and a store was called Camp Hollow, Florida.

Inside that car, winter or spring, it was a cauldron, because of the peat-burning stove which was never banked. Since I was the only non-migrant taking instruction, and since I was able to read, I was allowed to sit up front to aid Miss Hewitt, and I would notice the beads of sweat on the slope of her breasts, for she usually wore revealing sun dresses that made school in such weather a little more tolerable. She was young, and fresh from St. Petersburg.

One morning in October, when the heat of day was just beginning, she announced that maybe there'd be no school the day after tomorrow.

'How come?' asked one of the littler ones.

'They say there's a hurricane coming,' she explained. All of us stood up and peered out the high screened windows. The sky was blue, a little hazy.

'Ain't no storm comin', ma'm', I said.

'You just wait you, Lester,' she said. 'The radio said a hurricane is coming tomorrow plumb through here.' We still looked out the window, smiling as we shook our heads.

'Ain't no storm comin', ma'm.' My reading assignment that morning had concerned a frontier family cut off by a blizzard, and their near-starvation before relief had come. 'Like this here storm, Miss Hewitt?' I asked.

'Worsen that,' she said.

I told my mother about the storm that afternoon, when innocent clouds were overhead. 'What kinda stuff they teachin' you?' she demanded, as she set out her wash. The clothes hung dead and took the longest time to dry, even when the sun came out. When my father came home, as he washed his arms of dye, he told us it was fixing to storm bad, with all this moisture in the air.

There was no school the next day, so I woke up early, slipped into my jeans, and left the cabin while my parents were still asleep. The sun had risen but was invisible, just a smudge under steaming clouds. Though I wore no shirt, sweat collected in the hollow of my spine. I headed down to the lake, following the slimy boards strung over the slough, then over the Florida Central tracks, then over more boards that the migrants used. They lived behind some cypress, where the puddles never dried. Several of their kids were running from one shack to the other.

When I got to the landing, Leon Sellers was bailing out his boats. He was a thin, pale man who smoked all day in what he called his office and lived on occasional boat rentals. A coloured woman sometimes visited him, according to the migrants. Two Yankees were standing by Leon, waiting for a boat. They were fat, sunburned men with tackle boxes and felt hats festooned with flies and hooks. They rubbed their arms with mosquito oil. Leon bailed a long time.

The Yankees paid and stepped aboard. They paddled out the inlet and Leon headed back to his office. His workshirt was stuck all over. The inlet was calm; ripples from the boat froze into creases on the surface. But in the cypress tops, the wind rattled. I took a cane pole from the rental rack, then went around back to the tray of coffee grounds where Leon raised the worms. I unknotted a few, wrapped them in paper, then ran to his wooden dock where I baited up.

There were whitecaps on the open lake. I fished and paid no more mind.

Leon Sellers got no more customers, and in a while fried bacon smell lay heavy on the air. I could even smell his cigarette, as though he were beside me. There were bass in the inlet that I tried for but never got, and a few gar and moccasins that I'd tap with the pole-tip when they drifted by. The inlet, where it spread into the cypress groves, formed a shallow lake and while I fished alone I heard the splash of larger things – gators and otter – walking in the water, whacking their tails. I sat there many hours and caught a few dozen bream.

Some kids from the migrants' shacks came down to fish. They wore tattered shorts. 'Lake's drying' up,' one of them said. I noticed my string of fish, tied to the pilings, had lifted, and the top fish were out of water. The green, underwater part of the pilings was dry. I lowered my fish and several minutes later they had surfaced again. I quit fishing, walked off the dock, and peered into the swamp behind Leon's. There were puddles, but the drainage to the lake was pasty, cut by little run-offs.

'Shacks is all dry underneath,' said one of the moss-pickers. 'Fetch yourself some minnies. Jist pick 'em offn the ground.' He didn't seem excited – not the way I became when I heard. I looked out on the lake and thought of running to Oloka, knee-deep in dying fish.

'It can't dry up,' I said. Leon Sellers had told me once the lake had a little tide, so small we couldn't notice unless we were boatmen, since it was connected somehow to the ocean. That's why it had sharks, too, he said.

'It's a tide.'

'What's a tide?'

'Something that makes the lake go up and down, only you can't see it.'

They laughed. 'That's loony,' said one. I stood with them till the inlet muck emerged in glistening peaks, and the turtles, like stubby snakes, poked their heads out of their nests.

'There's a fierce wind, too,' the oldest kid said. 'She's kickin' up waves.' We looked out again, beyond the inlet which now was guarded by logs that had been submerged. On the open lake the wind blew whitecaps off the tops of swells. There were ripples now on the inlet. The stench of mud, as it dried, made even the migrants back off. The inlet – now shrunk to the outline of its deepest depressions – roughened, and the congregations of fish frothed to the surface, drinking in air with little gasps. We stood at the end of the dock and looked into the water. There were boats, far below, long sunk, housing bass and larger turtles. We hadn't known that the inlet was so deep.

Leon Sellers came out. His boats had dropped from view, I guess, when he had wakened after breakfast.

'Can the lake dry up, sir?' I asked.

'That teacher yourn,' he snapped. 'Ask her can the lake dry up.'

'She don't know.'

'I seen her oncet. Tell her from me I'll give her a boat all day free for nothin', hear?'

'She don't fish, I don't think.'

'You kids, help me with my boats,' he called to the moss-pickers. We all gathered on the bank, braving the odour. Leon Sellers in hip boots eased himself into the water.

'Them your boats, sir?' a migrant asked, pointing to the sunken ones still below the surface.

'Ain't mine. Them sunk a long time ago.'

'Won't see me in that water,' said the oldest migrant. He scratched his chigger bites all the time with one hand no matter what else he was doing, and he blinked a lot. 'Ain't no tellin' what's in that water now.'

'Nothin' that weren't there before,' said Leon Sellers. 'It's jist kindly squeezed together more.'

There were three of Leon's boats still in the water; we worked an hour securing them on land. We dragged them to the side of Leon's shanty where he kept a tarp. When it came time to speak, we had to shout.

'She ain't fallin' anymores,' he said, after checking the water level. 'If I was y'all' – he pointed to the migrants – 'I wouldn't stay back there today. She's fixin' to rise again. And you – ain't no need you hangin' round here neither. You go home.' He went back to the shanty, lowered the shutters from inside, and brought in his tray of worms.

The wind, as though reacting on signal, suddenly snapped the branches off the higher cypress, sending a shower of twigs and moss down on the inlet. The nest of a buzzard was blown apart and Oloka vanished in the rising of waves and the coming of rain.

The water was rising now, visibly, as it relinked the standing pools, then covered up the mud. Rain pelted the inlet. The migrants gathered their fish and raced back to their shanties, afraid as I was now of something more powerful than our curiosity. I followed them as soon as I had gathered my dead fish, and ran over the boards that were freshly slick. Back in the swamp, where our paths split and I was left alone, I saw the rest of the migrants running into the larger shack and rolling down the burlap for protection.

The sloughs on either side of the path were filling up. I kept to the centre of the path, in case anything hiding might try for the fish. I didn't look up until I came to the rise before the tracks. Then I froze. Churning the mud just a few feet in front of me were two gators. They couldn't see me, but I heard their snorting and was stung by the mud their tails threw up.

I dropped to my knees. The water was rising rapidly, inching up the sawgrass stalks. I kept turning, all directions, and I whimpered. The gators reached the tracks; if they turned, they would see me. I couldn't see them now. I waited as long as I dared, till snorts and hisses filled the slough, then traced their slimy ruts up to the tracks. Slowly I stood, and saw the path was clear to our cabin. I threw the fish behind me, and dashed numbly over the boards till I collapsed in the clearing, just outside our door.

My father came out and fetched me. He'd been sent home as soon as he arrived at the packing plant. 'It's a hurricane,' he said, as he carried me inside.

The eye of the storm was to pass near Hartley by early evening. It was well past noon now, and the sky was purple, screened by lower clouds that looked like smoke. I told my father that the lake had fallen and now was rising.

'It's like to keep right on. I seen it oncet down in Okeechobee. We lost everthin' then. But Oshacola ain't big enough to flood us here.'

'It's flooding the migrants.'

'Them's migrants.'

'Leon Sellers sent two Yankees out in a boat this morning.'

'I wouldn't take one of his boats acrost that li'l biddy inlet.'

The winds now cut across the clearing, causing the palmetto fronds to collide, or setting up little pockets of equipoise. The rain struck in gushes, letting up for several seconds as though suspended by the wind. Puddles formed in the sand, collared with yellow scum.

'This here's just the beginnin'. Just the beginnin',' said my father. Land tortoises scurried across the clearing, up from the tracks. Inside, the crevices of the cabin grew cold and moist. From the east, the clouds were black.

'I'm checkin' the water level,' my father decided. He threw on a slicker and took off his shoes. 'I'll be down by the tracks!' he yelled. We lost sight of him quickly, as the rain darkened him into a shadow. He came back several minutes later, with leaves plastered to his slicker and his face lashed red. 'She's still risin',' he said. 'Near up to the tracks on the far side. Them friends of yourn – they're gettin' wet.'

'Reckon she'll reach the clearin'?' my mother asked. I helped her arrange pans and glasses under the leaks.

'Can't say. High's a man's waist down at them moss-pickers'.'

'Let's get out,' I cried. 'Up to the highway while there's time.'

'Ain't no sense runnin'. Nobody's outn the highway anyhows.'

'I'm scared. I don't want to drown in *that*. I seen what's in that water.'

'Shut up. Ain't nobody drowndin' here.'

'Lookit!' my mother suddenly cried. 'Lookit out yonder!' Two gators hustled across the clearing, and battered into the underbrush, where they disappeared.

'I told you – it's them same two!'

'Probably ain't all,' my mother added. Then she turned to the puddle at the corner of the kitchen. 'I wonder can them cinder blocks melt?'

I kept silent. I had seen the new look in my father's eyes, after the gators crossed our yard.

We were stranded that night on a tiny skirt of threatened sand. All depressions were water-filled; the privy had blown away and the stench alternated with the wind. We had lanterns, and by sitting on the bed we could remain reasonably dry. The water inside was a few inches deep.

We dared not go out, with the moccasins stretched like nightcrawlers in the clearing. The only food was a few oranges my father had swiped when he learned of the hurricane.

At the far end of the clearing there were other lights, set on the ground in a half-circle. The migrants had strayed up to the dry land, set their lanterns down, then huddled around them to keep the flames going. They didn't bother us. The wind had slackened, but that allowed the rain to drive down cleanly. Hours later, the lanterns hadn't moved, so we figured the lake had stopped rising, despite the rain. I fell asleep.

Around midnight we were awakened by a kicking at our screen door. It was the father of the migrants, holding a lantern near his face so we could see he was white.

'Can we borry some kerosene? Our lamps done give out,' he asked when my father and I came to the door.

'Ain't got none to spare,' my father said.

'I reckon could the missus and me get warm by your stove then? She ain't got a wrap and she's suckin' a baby.'

'Just her then.'

'I gotta come too. Can't her go off alone.'

'Just her,' my father said. 'It's you come by my door at midnight.'

'There's niggers out there. I heard them. What are we gonna do if they come on us in the dark? We ain't got no knives even. There was niggers on Sem'nole Island.'

'I didn't make it flood.'

'Give us a little food.'

'What I got is two oranges. I got a wife and boy.'

'My boys, they know yourn. They gotta ride together on that there bus.'

My father motioned me back to the kitchen, but I turned away slowly. The migrant went on talking, in a new tone. 'That's three of mine to one of yourn.'

'Wait up,' said my father. He sloshed to the kitchen with a scowl, and poured half an inch of kerosene in a milk bottle. Then he took a pan of leakwater and leveled off the bottle with it. 'There any niggers on Sem'nole Island?' he whispered before handing back the oily water.

'I seen smoke oncet.'

The moss-picker took the bottle and hurried back over the puddles to the flickering lights at the far end of the clearing. A few minutes later, they flared, then went out. My father double-latched the door, and we lay awake for a long time.

We woke at daybreak. There was a thumping on the door, and my father took a butcher knife with him before opening up. Standing in a black slicker and rain hat was a woman, with several people behind her, each holding a lantern. Two trucks were parked in the clearing. It was raining softly.

'Miss Hewitt!' I cried. She introduced herself to my father, first as head of relief for Buck's Cove, then as my teacher. She brought us out to the clearing, to the rear of one truck which was loaded with sandbags and boxes of food. An old lady was serving coffee. The other truck was brimming with Negro kids that had been rescued from the flood. They weren't allowed down, and didn't try to get out. Several of the migrant kids got shirts to cover themselves, then took positions by the tailgate, where they could toss little pebbles into the truck. The coloured kids moved deeper inside. The oldest migrant boy was bruised all over his back, and his shoulder was cut and swollen. Two of the volunteers swabbed the cuts and helped him into the truck with all the food. They said his shoulder was broken.

'We picked up a dozen children during the night,' Miss Hewitt told my mother, and the migrants' father, as they blew on their coffee. 'We have just no way of knowing how many drowned. It was terrible further east, where the flooding was higher. I'm afraid dozens were lost.'

'Well –' said the moss-picker. My mother nodded, with a smile broadening around the lip of the cup. 'We could have used y'all last night,' he said. He pointed to the truckful of coloured kids. 'They found us last night, like I knowed they would. They fixed it so we couldn't see them comin'. But we still laid it on them heavy. Musta killed one them sons-a-bitches. I guarantee you won't find no more of *them* back here.'

'Who, sir?' Miss Hewitt asked. 'Who are you talking about? Because if you are referring to coloured, there is not a Negro within five miles of here.' Her voice was categorical. 'You must try living with the meaning of that.'

'Says you,' he chuckled, smiling at my mother. 'I know different.'

'There's the boatman,' said my mother. 'Down at the inlet.'

I followed them to the inlet. The trail stank now, but the water had receded, leaving everything coated with scum. The other side was still flooded out. The migrants' shacks were toppled, and their Dodge truck was windshield-deep in water, with little waves breaking against its doors. We could see clear through the swamp now to the open water.

'You said there was someone else over there?' Miss Hewitt asked me.

I tried to gauge where the inlet had been. Finally I spotted the bow of a boat pointing up, and the peak of a tin chimney.

'It's there, under the chimney.'

'God,' cried Miss Hewitt. 'Can't you people –'

'Ain't nothin' we can do here,' said one of the helpers. We walked back to the clearing. Miss Hewitt said I should have warned the boatman, at least. The sun was up now, looking raw and tired, just over our cabin. They piled sandbags around our door, to keep out snakes. 'Don't drink anything that isn't boiled first, *please*,' Miss Hewitt told my mother. 'And see that you get your outdoor commode repaired. We'll leave you some food now, enough till you get into town.'

The migrant family was led into the grocery truck. 'We'll take this boy to the clinic,' she said to the father. 'And there's shelter for you in town.'

'We're comin' back,' he promised.

My father carried the box of groceries in. The two trucks, filled with crying children, sputtered from the clearing.

A few days later Leon Sellers showed up. He had waited out the storm Seminole-fashion, fishing from a frogboat deep in the swamps, with his tray of worms for bait. The Yankees were never heard from. Our school cars were destroyed, and after a few weeks they found room for me in Hartley. The migrants did come back a few days later to work on the truck, which eventually started up. They loaded everything the water hadn't lost, and pulled out one night very late. Someone cut our screens that night, and since copper became scarce during the war, mosquitoes plagued our sleep for the next three years until we too moved to Hartley and gradually forgot those years on a promontory, threatened by swamps.

Notes Beyond a History

She lived on the same curve of the lake as we did, but in a stone cottage that was a good eighty years old and set far back, because Oshacola had not been tame in those days. She had not wanted to see the lake – what was it but an ocean of alligators, the breeder of chilling fevers? She didn't need the water. Her wealth, back then, had been a Valencia grove two miles square, planted in her youth. Yet all that remained, by the time we arrived, were the two hundred yards of twisted trees between her door and the matted beach. Cypress and live oak had replaced her untended citrus. From where she used to sit on her porch, I doubt that she had even seen the lake in thirty or forty years. Her name was Theodoura Rourke and she was ninety-two. The year was 1932.

We were the second year-round residents on the lake, having built a fine Spanish-style home of tawny stucco in 1928, set about fifty yards from the beach with a rich Bermuda lawn reaching to the water in front and to the hedge at the side that separated us from Theodoura Rourke. By '32 there were other residents, not yet neighbours, but none so well-established. It was still a risky five-mile drive into Hartley over sand trails given to flooding or sifting, and no one but my father trusted his car enough to drive in daily. When I say we were the second family most Hartleyans of today would be surprised; we've always been known as the leading family and one of the oldest. Theodoura Rourke, however, was the first by such a gulf that a comparison with anyone else is absurd. I should divide the history of Oshacola County into 'Modern Era' and 'All Time' so that both the Rourkes and the Sutherlands could enjoy their prominence, like Cy Young and Early Wynn, with no one confusing the equivalence of the records they set. We were the first family of Lake Oshacola, then; the Rourkes had come with the place.

She was Catholic. That was important, for we had no admitted Catholics in Hartley, and since she was the lone example of an absent conspiracy, we were taught that everything strange about her must be typical of the faith. My mother – poor tormented women – was a south

Georgia disciple of Tom Watson, and what she told my brother Tom and me about Catholics (especially the Black Sisters, which Theodoura must have been) was enough to keep us awake, sweating together under our sheets. Black Sisters walked in loose black robes, two at a time in the day, and then at night they shed their robes and took to flight on the black leathery wings their robes had hidden, invisible on moonless nights but for their white human faces and their cruel white teeth for sucking blood. My mother's full-time job, aside from raising Tom and me to love each other, Florida, FDR, and the Christ of her choice, was collecting the goods on Theodoura Rourke. Who delivered food to her and her daughter? What shape of clothes were drying from the trees, what black people visited and were taken inside, and what language did they speak?

My father was a Hartley man with education; being that, he had been mayor three times, schoolteacher, principal, state senator, and judge. Thirty years ago in Florida that was omnipotence. He was an old father to Tom and me (his first wife had died and he remarried at fifty), and his bent walk, white suits, stoutness, and eclectic learning have forever merged wisdom with self-righteousness, justice with legality, and history with just a little priggishness. He left us a great gift, however: an assurance that we need never answer for anything he did. It freed me for my manhood, this history, as it did for Tom, and his rockets.

I have never stopped wondering what it was that made my brother a builder of rockets – Apollo moon probes – and left me here in Hartley, a teacher.

My office is air-conditioned, wrapped in tinted glass, eight floors up on the main quadrangle overlooking the lake. Eight floors more than commands the lake. Oshacola is beautifully landscaped now – a pond on some giant's greens. The city of Hartley and its suburbs are gleaming white among the smoky citrus groves. More smoke rises from the processing plants – the stench of orange pulp – and the Interstate slices west from here in an unbroken line to the Gulf. That haze that never lifts, way way to the west, it could be Tampa; fifty miles isn't far and if eight floors of perspective can do *this* to Oshacola, why shouldn't Tampa be creeping slowly to my front lawn?

Oshacola was always this small, I'm forced to admit, but never this humanized. I was smaller then, of course, and places are always remembered as larger and more unruly – but *why* precisely? I've only grown six inches in the past thirty-five years; why then does my memory insist on an Oshacola too broad to be seen across, on whitecaps that would swamp a weekend cruiser, on softshell turtles Tom and I could only drag with ropes, on clusters of snakes thrashing mightily on Theodoura Rourke's warm sand beach? Not only has the lake been civilized, but so has my memory, leaving only a memory of my memory as it was then. I'm not a shrewd man (and more than a little bit my father's son), but I have a probing memory and what I see with my eyes closed, books shut, was also true, also happened, and Oshacola was once that inland sea and the things in it and around it would startle an expert today, men like my colleagues on the first seven floors.

Hartley had a population of forty-three hundred in 1932, approximately three thousand of whom were white. My father knew them all. Hartley had one main street, and cars were still so rare that even a lost Yankee could make a U-turn in broad daylight with the sheriff looking on and chances were he wouldn't be stopped. We had a movie house open on Wednesday for Negroes and on the weekends for us. The buildings were mostly dark brick – those were the days before we learned we were in the tropics and should show off everything in pink and white.

A few weeks ago I went roaming through the old Main Street section and couldn't find much I remembered. It's now on the fringes of a Cuban and Negro ghetto, and there are a few used-car lots, *casas del alimiento*, laundromats, and *tavernas*. The real centre now is east, creeping towards the complex at the Cape. A year or two from now the first Hartley outpost, a pizza stand most likely, may find itself on national television at blast-off time.

Hartley now is – I can't describe the difficulty of adding to that phrase – *bigger*. One hundred thousand white souls, ten thousand black, and seven thousand Cuban exiles. The power is still in local hands, the boys from my class at Hartley High, despite the eighty thousand Yankees now among us, and though they no longer wear white suits or practise oratory they've not improved on my father's generation. They're a measly, brainless lot, owned ear-high by the construction, citrus, and power companies. And not a one of these local boys has an accent or curries a drop of character. As the wisest of all wise men said, the more things change, the worse they remain. The reason of course is that *change* merely reflects the unacknowledged essence of things. That's what history is all about.

In 1932 I delivered a Jacksonville paper to the row of cabins that were strung along the beach road that ran past our back door. A bundle was delivered to the courthouse and my father would have a janitor take the pile to the drugstore, where I would pick it up after school. Then I'd ride home with my father, eat, and Tom and I would later carry them down the road by kerosene lamp. Sometimes, when it rained, we didn't deliver till the next morning.

Big Mama – Theodoura Rourke – was ninety-two; her daughter Lillian was in her middle seventies. It was the daughter who sent me a note one day (it took four days to reach us by customary post though she lived but sixty yards away): *please to have Boy commence the Paper for Big Mama and Me. L. Rourke (Miss).*

My father handed it to me discreetly; it would never do for my mother to know I was trafficking with witches, visiting at night, and taking part of their hoarded treasures. The fear of personal contact actually did delay my collecting until after Christmas. Their two months' bill had hit a dollar and there was always the chance of a tip.

One day I showed up at the foot of the steps to Big Mama's back porch. I wasn't going to climb up or go inside.

'Paper boy, ma'm,' I managed when the younger old woman answered the door. From the bottom of the stairs, she looked dark and immense.

'How much are it?' she asked.

'Ma'm?'

'Mind to me what I say.'

'A dollar and a dime,' I said, guessing what she wanted. She turned away, black behind the ancient screen, leaving me to wonder if I had asked for too much. Should she complain, I was willing to take a fifty-cent cut.

Then Big Mama appeared and shuffled to the door. Her daughter opened it and Big Mama started down towards me, her spotted brown hand trembling on the wooden railing. I took a step backwards, wanting somehow to accommodate her presence. She straightened up when she reached the bottom step and I noticed she didn't even challenge my chin. I was looking down on the oily, brownish-pink swath of her scalp, the clumps of cottony hair stuck amateurishly, it seemed, to its flesh. My mother had said the Black Sisters were bald as buzzards under their bonnets – she was right.

Then she looked at me. Her skin was tarnished and wrinkled on a thousand planes; her eyes simply colourless – not even the rheumy blue I had expected. Her nose seemed to have receded into her face and her jaw had almost melted away. It was a long time (it seems now an eternity that I looked into her face!) before I noticed she was holding her cold fist on my arm. I looked, and she opened it.

Her palm was pink, darkly lined. I'd never seen such coins as she held. Two round, golden ducats lay flat and heavy in her hand, like the hammered heads of copper spikes. She brought them closer and I took another step back; they were medals, I thought, charms to mesmerize me.

'You never seen these here things before, have you, boy?' she asked, looking behind me with those pale, opaque eyes.

'No, ma'm.'

'Take aholt of them.'

'No, ma'm.'

She dropped them on the sand at my feet and I jumped back, half expecting them to leap at me, like snakes from Aaron's rod. The daughter, watching from the porch, laughed. 'You skeered, boy?' she called down.

'You just owe me for the paper,' I said.

'Boy, I done paid you for the rest of your life. Now pick up what I throwed. Them is genuine ten-dollar gold pieces –' she finished in mid-sentence, as though she had decided I was not worth the rest, and when she ceased talking, she seemed to shrink.

The pieces were half buried in the sand. I picked them up; they were cool, half coated with sand where her moist palm had held them. But wasn't it magic, I wondered, that both the coins had dug edge-first into the sand instead of landing flat? I was still cautious.

'Would you be wanting a bit of cake?' the daughter suggested suddenly. She held the screen door open. 'You can have it on the porch.'

'No, ma'm.'

'Johnnycake?'

I climbed to the porch, then followed Big Mama inside, but not into the house. I could see into the parlour and it was filled unlike any room I have ever seen since, except perhaps an auction house. Paintings and photos lined the walls with a single desire to be displayed; the tables were piled with metal and porcelain objects that reflected the pale sunlight like the spires of a far-off, exotic city. How I wanted to step inside, and I might have, but for a gold cross centred above the sofa and its remarkable crucified Christ whose face was lifted in agony to the door where I was standing.

Around the Christ several paintings were hung and they now caught my eye, for even in the dullness they were vivid. Wildlife scenes, watercolours or India ink on white stock. The artist had wisely allowed the white itself to animate the studies of birds, fish, and smaller game of Florida ... not like the murky, quasi-fabulous things my father collected, the overworked paintings by those New England gentlemen in floppy straw hats who merely observed the shoreline from the deck chairs on St. Johns River steamers.... These fish and birds and otters' eyes seemed to stare into mine and follow as I glanced away. Their scales and pelts and feathers were eternally moist, eternally in the sun.

'I see you are coveting my daddy's paintings,' Miss Lillian noticed as she handed me the plate of cake.

'They're right nice,' I said. 'They are the nicest things I've ever seen.'

'He executed them in the winter of eighteen hundred and fifty-seven.'

I ate the cake silently. Christ's head, it seemed, had nodded.

'You live just over yonder, don't you, boy? I seen you.'

I picked up the last piece of cake and underneath it was a fine gold crucifix, the type a schoolgirl might wear on a light gold chain. I pressed the last crumbs into a wafer and let it drop back on the plate.

'Now you kiss the Lord, boy,' the daughter commanded. 'Put your lips on Him and tell Him you are sorry for all you done.'

'No,' I cried. 'I ain't going to!'

'You have got to, else He will follow you. You have accepted the gift of His immortal body and so now you must be forgiven.' She lifted the crucifix as though she might a dime, and thrust it in my face. I could see the faint outline of a Christ, head bowed, dripping blood, vague as an Indian head on a old penny. Had it been worn from so much kissing?

The daughter held it now to her thick, puckered lips. Her eyes were closed and her lips were quivering with prayer, forming sounds I couldn't understand. Magic! And that was my only chance to get away before she could drain my blood into a cup. I don't think she opened her eyes until I slammed the door, but as I threw myself into the brier hedge between our properties, I heard her crying out, 'Remember, He's a-going' to foller you....'

FACTS:

• Theodoura (?) parents unknown; birthplace (presumed), Oshacola County, Florida, 1840 (c.). d. 1937.

• Bernard Rourke, b. C. Galway, Ireland, 1822. Arrived New York, 1838. Buffalo, 1839–44. Mexico and California, 1845–52. New York, 1852–55. Sent to Florida on canal crew, 1856. Married Theodoura (?), 1858. Captain, CSA. State Senator, 1882–84. Judge, 1886–88. Died, Oshacola County, Florida, 1888.

• Children (records incomplete, but births recorded):
  Lucretia (d. Infancy, 1859).
  Lillian (1859–1946). Barren.
  Bernard, Jr. (1866–1902). Issue suspected; unknown.
  John Ryan (1870–1894). Issue suspected; unknown.

Theodoura Rourke, parents and birthplace unknown, according to the records I'm at the moment responsible for. But I know where she came from, though my *History of Hartley* will never record it, and therein lies the rest of my story.

Her birthplace is in Oshacola County, probably now within the city limits of Hartley. I've often looked for the exact spot, but the traces of the old canal have been filled in and chewed over for at least twenty years. Perhaps from a helicopter I could spot it: something subtle in the pattern of streets, a patch of parkland primordially rich, a shack or two that no one thought of removing. But from a car all Hartley is the same.

A word, historically, on the old canal scheme. Some states are driven by dreams – gold, oil, timber, ore – but Florida (long before the sun and oranges counted for much) was weaned on a dream of the Mighty Ditch. The maps show why: the St. Johns is wide and navigable from Jacksonville down; central Florida is blessed with a chain of deep, virtually continuous lakes, and there are dozen accommodating estuaries on the Gulf side, the best perhaps at Tampa. To the early speculators it looked as though nature herself had merely lacked the will or Irish muscles to finish what she had so obviously begun. Cuba was Spanish, and the Keys were often treacherous – and a canal through Florida offered no natural or diplomatic barriers. A guaranteed safe passage between New York and New Orleans. Nature had never smiled so sweetly on the schemes of capital. Not only that, certain local politicians reasoned, the canal would be a natural divider between the productive and enlightened north of Florida and the swampy, pestiferous south. We could sell the rest to Spain, give it to the freedmen, or make it a federal prison – 'What Siberia is to the Tsar of Imperial Russia,' a local editor once wrote. A dozen companies had been involved in a thirty-year period, to effect the cut from Atlantic to Gulf, and at least a couple had sent crews down to dynamite the forest and butcher the indigenous tribes – all before Bernard Rourke's arrival in 1856. Theodoura, we can assume, had been born some sixteen years earlier to an unmarried mother of unknown origins, and an Irish father similarly anonymous. By 1856 the heroic age of the canal was actually over; not many of the crew sent to Florida from New York ever saw the North again.

The summer of the year I had run from the Rourkes' stone cottage, I made a discovery that determined my life. My brother Tom, the builder of rockets, must have been affected too.

One morning in August we were fishing from the frogboat we had tied to our dock. A political fish-fry was coming up, so we were keeping everything edible: shellcrackers, warmouth, some channel cats, and dozens of bream. The boat was filling. We quit awhile and stuffed a burlap sack with fish, then tied it to the dock.

'Look!' Tom cried.

We saw a black, blunt tub rounding the arm of the cove, with a tall man in black robes poling furiously towards us. He was close to the shore, at poling depth, and we huddled behind the dock, afraid that he would see us. A man who would pole a frogboat like it was a canoe, in black robes, in August, from Lord knows where – terrifying! The visitor swung beyond us, not looking, and then put it on Rourke's scummy beach and made his way through the jungly orange grove to their cottage.

'The devil hisself,' Tom whispered.

And he looked it – a dark leathery face, sideburns, black cape and white collar, and a white sleeve with ruffles showing under his robes. He even carried a little black bag. It was a priest, I told Tom, a Catholic priest.

He was inside about an hour. We heard no noises from the stone cottage, no shrieks, no moans. When the priest emerged, we noticed that he had taken off his hat and robes, and he proceeded to pole out into the lake in his ruffled white shirt, without a look backwards or to us. We had a better look at him this time. Tom shook my arm, but I was already nodding. The priest had Negro blood; which meant, we knew in a flash, that Big Mama did too.

We had to follow – I wonder *why* we did; Tom would say, as he does of the moon, because it's there – but how did we ever find the nerve? He was already rounding the cove, poling rhythmically. We only wanted to keep him in sight.

About a mile from our place, Buck's Cove got sealed in with lily pads. Beyond the pads a stagnant creek emptied in. We'd never explored it – the pads repulsed a boat like rubber, and the mosquitoes hummed above the creek like a faraway power saw – but the priest was prying his way through the pads, into the mouth of the creek. We followed.

Cypress overhung the mossy water. In the shade, the water was brown, the colour and tepidness of tea. Mosquitoes hummed. The water was the calmest I had ever seen, rich with moss and minnows. The ripples died so quickly we barely left a wake. I could feel the bass and turtles knocking against my pole, but I couldn't see six inches underneath the surface. There was no real shoreline, just a thicker and thicker tangle of cypress and floating mangroves, and the heat was increasing as all the breeze died down. Our breath came hard, but when we tried to catch it, we sucked in gnats. The sweat rolled off my nose and chin, and my arms were spotted with flies, drinking in the salt. I looked up and the priest was out of sight.

I poled half an hour, never catching him. The creek curved and branched, trees thinned and thickened, birds hooted and then were gone. There were pockets of breeze, then deadness; places where the water dimpled around my pole and pushed with a sudden current, and places where I felt I was sliding on a thicker surface. Then a consistent current came up, and the mosquitoes died down. The water was deeper. I thought we were coming to another lake.

Up ahead I spotted a bright yellow cloth draped from a cypress whose roots overhung the water. To the right of the marked tree there was a broad, open ditch that emptied into the creek at right angles to where we were. The ditch, about thirty feet wide, was lined with a high dike of mud and crushed limestone and stretched before us straight as an avenue. We took it.

It was deep, very deep; we couldn't pole, so I paddled. I told Tom I could *feel* the fish knocking against my paddle and knocking on the bottom of the boat just like someone was hammering. Bass were jumping all around us, and a few gar were floating in the middle.

'Somebody made this,' said Tom.

But where did they come from, I was wondering. We shouldn't be here. I thought; my father told terrifying stories of Seminole bands, still wild on the hummocks, that had never signed a treaty. They stole white boys and fed them to their hunting gators.

'Reckon it's Indians made it?' he asked.

I kept paddling. Seminoles or something – I couldn't picture white men so deep in nature. *Maybe niggers*, I'd wanted to say to Tom, but my voice was gone.

'Look, smoke!' Tom cried. We smelled it as soon as we saw it, and it wasn't just a campfire; it was lumber mill smoke. *Jackpiners*, I thought with relief. The ditch was narrower, and beginning to curve.

There were voices, children's and women's, not far away. We couldn't make out anything, but we smiled.

'I'm getting me a Coke as soon as we get down,' said Tom.

'I'm getting me *two*,' I said.

The settlement was just ahead. *Work crew*, I thought as soon as I saw the grey shanty shapes behind the dike. Two boys, our age, were squatting in the water on either side of the dike, dragging a seine and netting our way. They were thin blondish boys and Tom laughed suddenly, for they weren't wearing a stitch of clothing. I waited for them to spot us but they didn't look up from the water. 'Hey, y'all,' I finally shouted, 'what you call this place?'

They stood up slowly, still holding the corners of the seine. They didn't move towards us. I looked down at Tom and I saw his smile begin to sag, and his eyes grow wide and frightened. He held that look for several seconds, and then he began to retch. Then he screamed.

'There's something wrong with them,' he cried, his voice high and quivering, 'there's something wrong with them – they ain't ... they ain't....' The boys dropped the tips of their net and pinned it in the mud with sticks. They were as light as we were but not the way we were, and their hair was light but it wasn't blond, it was just colourless. And then I seemed to be looking into the opaque, colourless eyes of Big Mama, and into the bleeding side of Jesus, and I could hear Miss Lillian commanding me to kiss Him, *kiss Him....* The boys' hair was fair and kinky, and we could see they weren't any whiter than the priest we'd been following. They were only lighter.

'Let's get out of here,' Tom wailed, his voice already breaking. I started paddling backwards as the boys climbed their respective sides of the dike and approached us slowly from above.

I looked up one last time and saw far behind them a gold cross on top of a pink stucco building, then it dropped from view.

'Say something to them,' Tom cried. He held the useless pole, ready to defend himself somehow. Then one of the boys let out a hoop. People came running.

We were reeling backwards now, as fast as I could paddle and Tom could slash. I tried to stay near the middle, but what good was it – ten feet on either side – when the rocks started flying?

'No!' Tom was screaming. 'I didn't do nothing – quit it!' He was ten years old; he didn't know it wasn't, finally, a game. I knew, but I couldn't believe it was happening. He curled himself under the poling ledge where I was sitting.

Each rock, as it struck me, took my breath away before it started burning. Tom was praying, *Dear God, get me home,* and I paddled with one arm and then with both, dodging what I could, trying to protect my head. They didn't have rocks, nothing big, just limestone gravel, but I remembered the story of David and the picture I loved of Goliath with blood between his eyes. Once more I looked up, hoping they'd see how young I was, how frightened, but all I could see were swarms of children, all the colour of dirty sand, and darker adults screaming down at me, '*Morte, morte!*' and others, 'Kill, kill!' They followed us to the end of the ditch, to the cypress hung with yellow, and then there was no place for them to stand as the dike and dry land petered out. We were suddenly back on the creek and I fell to the bottom of the boat, crying. We drifted awhile, until the current died, and then I poled and Tom paddled the rest of the way home.

The records show no settlement of mixed-blood Catholics in Oshacola County in 1932, or at any other time. The parish records, begun in 1941 by Father Enrique Fernandez, of Tampa, show no significant Spanish or Creole population this far east of Tampa. Theodoura Rourke and Lillian are both listed as 'white' on their death certificates, as was Bernard Jr (John Ryan Rourke, who died in 1894, was apparently buried privately without any records being kept), and since Big Mama's estate later endowed a public park and Bernard Rourke's paintings hang in the state galleries, there is no great enthusiasm in Hartley to investigate. Nor am I concerned about her genes in any quasi-legal sense – only historically. Theodoura Rourke and her line are dead, unless the suspected issue of her sons Bernard and John could ever be traced; but she is one of many who have left scars on my body and opened a path that time has all but swallowed up. If my instincts are correct, her race degenerated into whiteness and melted back to Hartley, or Tampa, or anywhere a lost people congregate. And the two children who discovered them a few years too early, before the transformation was complete, they too are only wanderers.

A passage I once marked from a story of Henry James reads '... the radiance of this broad fact had quenched the possible sidelights of reflection....' I too am a partisan of the broad sweep, of mystery that sweetens as its sources grow deep and dim. I live in the dark, Tom in the light; I wonder, to return to the original question, if my experience that afternoon thirty-five years ago did not compel me to become an historian – and prevent me from becoming a good one. And made Tom, eyes skyward in St. Louis, indifferent to it all – the broad facts and the sidelights – and everything else around us crumbling into foolishness.

How I Became a Jew

CINCINNATI, SEPTEMBER 1950: 'I don't suppose you've attended classes with the coloured before, have you, Gerald?' the principal inquired. He was a jockey-sized man whose dark face collapsed around a greying moustache. His name was DiCiccio.

'No, sir.'

'You'll find quite a number in your classes here –' he gestured to the kids on the playground, and the Negroes among them seemed to multiply before my eyes. 'My advice is not to expect any trouble and they won't give you any.'

'We don't expect none from them,' my mother said with great reserve, the emphasis falling slightly on the last word.

DiCiccio's eyes wandered over us, calculating but discreet. He was taking in my porkiness, my brushed blond hair, white shirt and new gabardines. And my Georgia accent.

'My boy is no troublemaker.'

'I can see that, Mrs Gordon.'

'But I'm here to tell you – just let me hear of any trouble and I'm going straight off to the po-lice.'

And now DiCiccio's smile assessed her, as though to say *Are you finished?* 'That wouldn't be in Gerald's best interest, Mrs Gordon. We have no serious discipline problems in the elementary school but even if we did, Mrs Gordon, outside authorities are never the answer. Your boy has to live with them. Police are never the solution.' He pronounced the word 'pleece' and I wanted to laugh. 'Even in the junior high,' he said, jerking his thumb towards the black, prison-like structure beyond the playground. 'There are problems.' His voice was still far-off and I was smiling.

DiCiccio's elementary school was new: bright, low and long, with greenboards and yellow chalk, aluminum frames and blond, unblemished desks. My old school in Georgia, near Moultrie, had had a room for each grade up through the sixth. Here in Cincinnati the sixth grade itself had ten sections.

'And Gerald, *please* don't call me "sir". Don't call anyone that,' the principal said with sudden urgency. 'That's just asking for it. The kids might think you're trying to flatter the teacher or something.'

'Well, I swan –' my mother began. 'He learned respect for his elders and nobody is taking that respect away. Never.'

'Look –' and now the principal leaned forward, growing smaller as he approached the desk. 'I know how Southern schools work. I know "sir" and "ma'm". I know they must have beaten it into you. But I'm trying to be honest, Mrs Gordon. Your son has a lot of things going against him and I'm trying to help. This intelligence of his can only hurt him unless he learns how to use it. He's white – enough said. And I assume Gordon isn't a Jewish name, is it? Which brings up another thing, Mrs Gordon. Take a look at those kids out there, the white ones. They look like little old men, don't they? Those are *Jews*, Gerald, and they're as different from the others as you are from the coloured. They were born in Europe and they're living here with their grandparents – don't ask me why, it's a long story. Let's just say they're a little hard to play with. A little hard to like, OK?' Then he settled back and caught his breath.

'They're the Israelites!' I whispered, as though the Bible had come to life. Then I was led to class.

But the sixth grade was not a home for long; not for the spelling champ and fastest reader in Colquitt County, Georgia. They gave me tests, sent me to a university psychologist who tested my memory and gave me some codes to crack. Then I was advanced.

Seventh grade was in the old building: Leonard Sachs Junior High. A greenish statue of Abraham Lincoln stood behind black iron bars, pointing a finger to the drugstore across the street. The outside steps were pitted and sagging. The hallways were tawny above the khaki lockers, and clusters of dull yellow globes were bracketed to the walls, like torches in the catacombs. By instinct I preferred the used to the new, sticky wood to cool steel, and I would have felt comfortable on that first walk down the hall to my new class, but for the stench of furtive, unventilated cigarette smoke. The secretary led me past rooms with open doors; all the teachers were men. Many were shouting while the classes turned to whistle at the ringing *tap-tap* of the secretary's heels. Then she stopped in front of a closed door and rapped. The noise inside partially abated and finally a tall bald man with furry ears opened the door.

'This is Gerald Gordon, Mr Terleski. He's a transfer from Georgia and they've skipped him up from sixth.'

'They have, eh?' A few students near the door laughed. They were already pointing at me. 'Georgia, you said?'

'Gerald Gordon *from* Georgia,' said the secretary.

'Georgia Gordon!' a Negro boy shouted. 'Georgia Gordon. Sweet Georgia Gordon.'

Terleski didn't turn. He took the folder from the girl and told me to find a seat. But the front boys in each row linked arms and wouldn't let me through. I walked to the window row and laid my books on the ledge. The door closed. Terleski sat at his desk and opened my file but didn't look up.

'Sweet Georgia,' crooned the smallish, fair-skinned Negro nearest me. He brushed my notebook to the floor. I bent over and got a judo chop on the inside on my knees.

'Sweet Georgia, you get off the floor, hear?' A very fat, coal-black girl in a pink sweater was helping herself to paper from my three-ring binder. 'Mr Tee, Sweet Georgia taking a nap,' she called.

He grumbled. I stood up. My white shirt and baggy gabardines were brown with dust.

'This boy is *not* named Sweet Georgia. He *is* named Gerald Gordon,' said Terleski with welcome authority. 'And I guess he's some kind of genius. They figured out he was too smart for the sixth grade. They gave him tests at the university and – listen to this – Gerald Gordon is a borderline genius.'

A few whistled. Terleski looked up. 'Isn't that *nice* for Gerald Gordon? What can we do to make you happy, Mr Gordon?'

'Nothing, sir,' I answered.

'Not a thing? Not an itsy-bitsy thing, sir?' I shook my head, lowered it.

'Might we expect you to at least look at the rest of us? We wouldn't want to presume, but –'

'Sweet Georgia crying, Mr Tee,' giggled Pink Sweater.

'And he all dirty,' added the frontseater. 'How come you all dirty, Sweet Georgia-man?' Pink Sweater was awarding my paper to all her friends.

'Come to the desk, Mr Gordon.'

I shuffled forward, holding my books over the dust smears.

'Face your classmates, sir. Look at them. Do you see any borderline types out there? Any friends?'

I sniffled loudly. My throat ached. There were some whites, half a dozen or so grinning in the middle of the room. I looked for girls and saw two white ones. Deep in the rear sat some enormous Negroes, their boots looming in the aisle. They looked at the ceiling and didn't even bother to whisper as they talked. They wore pastel T-shirts with cigarette packs twisted in the shoulder. And – God! – I thought, they had moustaches. Terleski repeated his question, and for the first time in my life I knew that whatever answer I gave would be wrong.

'*Mr Gordon's reading comprehension is equal to the average college freshman.* Oh, Mr Gordon, just *average?* Surely there must be some mistake.'

I started crying, tried to hold it back, couldn't, and bawled. I remembered the rows of gold stars beside my name back in Colquitt County, Georgia, and the times I had helped the teacher by grading my fellow students.

A few others picked up my crying: high-pitched blubbering from all corners. Terleski stood, scratched his ear, then screamed: 'Shut up!' A rumbling monotone persisted from the Negro rear. Terleski handed me his handkerchief and said, 'Wipe your face.' Then he said to the class: 'I'm going to let our borderline genius himself continue. Read this, sir, just like an average college freshman.' He passed me my file.

I put it down and knuckled my eyes violently. They watched me hungrily, laughing at everything. Terleski poked my ribs with the corner of the file. 'Read!'

I caught my breath with a long, loud shudder.

'*Gerald Gordon certainly possesses the necessary intellectual equipment to handle work on a seventh grade level, and long consultations with the boy indicate a commensurate emotional maturity. No problem anticipated in adjusting to a new environment.*'

'Beautiful,' Terleski announced. 'Beautiful. He's in the room five minutes and he's crying like a baby. Spends his first three minutes on the floor getting dirty, needs a hanky from the teacher to wipe his nose, and he has the whole class laughing at him and calling him names. Beautiful.

That's what I call real maturity. Is that all the report says, sir?'

'Yes, sir.'

'You're lying, Mr Gordon. That's not very mature. Tell the class what else it says.'

'I don't want to, sir.'

'You don't want to. *I* want you to. *Read!*'

'It says: "I doubt only the ability of the Cincinnati Public Schools to supply a worthy teacher."'

'*Well* – that's what we wanted to hear, Mr Gordon. Do you doubt it?'

'No, sir.'

'Am I worthy enough to teach you?'

'Yes, sir.'

'What do I teach?'

'I don't know, sir.'

'What have you learned already?'

'Nothing yet, sir.'

'What's the capital of the Virgin Islands?'

'Charlotte Amalie,' I said.

That surprised him, but he didn't show it for long. 'Then I can't teach you a thing, can I, Mr Gordon? You must know everything there is to know. You must have all your merit badges. So it looks like we're going to waste each other's time, doesn't it? Tell the class where Van Diemen's Land is.'

'That's the old name for Tasmania, sir. Australia, capital is Hobart.'

'If it's Australia that would make the capital Canberra, wouldn't it, Mr Gordon?'

'For the whole country, yes, sir.'

'So there's still something for you to learn, isn't there, Mr Gordon?'

The kids in the front started to boo. 'Make room for him back there,' the teacher said, pointing to the middle. 'And *now*, maybe the rest of you can tell me the states that border on Ohio. Does *anything* border on Ohio?'

No one answered while I waved my hand. I cared desperately that my classmates learn where Ohio was. And finally, ignoring me, Mr Terleski told them.

RECESS: on the sticky pavement in sight of Lincoln's statue. The windows of the first two floors were screened and softball was the sport. The white kids in the gym class wore institutional shorts; the other half – the Negroes – kept their jeans and T-shirts since they weren't allowed in the dressing room. I was still in my dusty new clothes. We all clustered around the gym teacher, who wore a Cincinnati Redlegs cap. He appointed two captains, both white. 'Keep track of the score, fellas. And tell me after how you do at the plate individually.' He blew his whistle and scampered off to supervise a basketball game around the corner.

The captains were Arno Kolko and Wilfrid Skurow, both fat and pale, with heavy eyebrows and thick hair climbing down their necks and up from their shirts. Hair like that – I couldn't believe it. I was twelve, and had been too ashamed to undress in the locker room. These must be Jews, I told myself. The other whites were shorter than the captains. They wore glasses and had bristly hair. Many of them shaved. Their arms were pale and veined. I moved towards them.

'Where *you* going, boy?' came a high-pitched but adult voice behind me. I turned and faced a six-foot Negro who was biting an unlit cigarette. He had a moustache and, up high on his yellow biceps, a flag tattoo. 'Ain't nobody picked you?'

'No,' I hesitated, not knowing whether I was agreeing or answering.

'Then stay where you're at. Hey – y'all want him?'

Skurow snickered. I had been accustomed to being a low-priority pick back in ball-playing Colquitt County, Georgia. I started to walk away.

'Come back here, boy. Squirrel picking you.'

'But you're not a captain.'

'Somebody *say* I ain't a captain?' The other Negroes had fanned out under small clouds of blue smoke and started basketball games on the painted courts. 'That leaves me and you,' said Squirrel. 'We standing them.'

'I want to be with them,' I protested.

'We don't want you,' said one of the Jews.

The kid who said it was holding the bat cross-handed as he took some practice swings. I had at least played a bit of softball back in Colquitt County, Georgia. The kids in my old neighbourhood had built a diamond near a housing development after a bulldozer operator had cleared the lot for us during his lunch hour. Some of the carpenters had given us timber scrap for a fence and *twice* – I remember the feeling precisely to this day – I had lofted fly balls tightly down the line and over the fence. No question, my superiority to the Arno Kolkos of this world.

'We get first ups,' said Squirrel. 'All *you* gotta do, boy, is get yourself on base and then move your ass fast enough to get home on anything I hit. And if I don't hit a home run, you gotta bring me home next.'

'Easy,' said I.

First three times up, it worked. I got on and Squirrel blasted on one hop to the farthest corner of the playground. But he ran the bases in a flash, five or six strides between the bases, and I was getting numb in the knees from staying ahead even with a two-base lead. Finally, I popped up for an out. Then Squirrel laid down a bunt and made it to third on some loose play. I popped out again and had to take his place on third, anticipating a stroll home on his next home run. But he bunted again, directly at Skurow the pitcher, who beat me home for a force-out to end the inning.

'Oh, you're a great one, Sweet Georgia,' Squirrel snarled from a position at deep short. He was still biting his unlit cigarette. 'You're a plenty heavy hitter, man. Where you learn to hit like that?'

'Georgia,' I said, slightly embarrassed for my state.

'Georgia? *Joe-ja?*' He lit his cigarette and tossed me the ball. 'Then I guess you're the worst baseball player in the whole state, Sweet Georgia. I *thought* you was different.'

'From what?'

'From them.' He pointed to our opponents. They were talking to themselves in a different language. I felt the power of a home-run swing lighten my arms, but it was too late.

'I play here,' said Squirrel. 'Pitch them slow then run to first. Ain't none of them can beat my peg or get it by me.'

A kid named Izzie, first up, bounced to me and I tagged him. Then a scrawny kid lifted a goodly fly to left – the kind I had hit for doubles – but Squirrel was waiting for it. Then Wilfred Skurow lumbered up: the most menacing kid I'd ever seen. Hair in swirls on his neck and throat, sprouting wildly from his chest and shoulders. Sideburns, but getting bald. Glasses so thick his eyeballs looked screwed in. But no form. He lunged a chopper to Squirrel, who scooped it and waited for me to cover first. Skurow was halfway down the line, then quit. Squirrel stood straight, tossed his cigarette away, reared back, and fired the ball with everything he had. I heard it leave his hand, then didn't move till it struck my hand and deflected to my skull, over the left eye. I was knocked backwards, and couldn't get up. Skurow circled the bases; Squirrel sat at third and laughed. Then the Jews walked off together and I could feel my forehead tightening into a lump. I tried to stand, but instead grew dizzy and suddenly remembered Colquitt County. I sat alone until the bells rang and the grounds were empty.

Every Saturday near Moultrie, I had gone to the movies. In the balcony they let the coloured kids in just for Saturday. Old ones came Wednesday night for Jim Crow melodramas with coloured actors. But we came especially equipped for those Saturday mornings when the coloured kids sat in the dark up in the balcony, making noise whenever we did. We waited for too much noise, or a popcorn box that might be dropped on us. Then we reached into our pockets and pulled out our broken yo-yos. We always kept our broken ones around. Half a yo-yo is great for sailing since it curves and doesn't lose speed. And it's very hard. So we stood, aimed for the projection beam, and fired the yo-yos upstairs. They loomed on the screen like bats, filled the air like bombs. Some hit metal, others the floor, but some struck home judging from the yelps of the coloured kids and their howling. Minutes later the lights went on upstairs and we heard the ushers ordering them out.

A second bell rang.

'That burr-head nigger son-of-a-bitch,' I cried. 'That goddamn nigger.' I picked myself up and ran inside.

I was late for geometry but my transfer card excused me. When I opened the door two Negro girls dashed out pursued by two boys about twice my size. One of the girls was Pink Sweater, who ducked inside a girls' room. The boys waited outside. The windows in the geometry room were open, and a few boys were sailing paper planes over the street and sidewalk. The teacher was addressing himself to a small group of students who sat in a semicircle around his desk. He was thin and red-cheeked with a stiff pelt of curly hair.

'I say, do come in, won't you? That's a nasty lump you've got there. Has it been seen to?'

'Sir?'

'Over your eye. Surely you're aware of it. It's really quite unsightly.'

'I'm supposed to give you this –' I presented the slip for his signing.

'Gerald Gordon, is it? Spiro here.'

'Where?'

'Here – I'm Spiro. Geoffrey Spiro, on exchange. And you?'

'Me what?'

'Where are you from?'

'Colquitt County, Georgia.'

He smiled as though he knew the place well and liked it. 'That's South, aye? Ex-cellent. Let us say for tomorrow you'll prepare a talk on Georgia – brief topical remarks, race, standard of living, labour unrest and whatnot. Hit the high points, won't you, old man? Now then, class' – he raised his voice only slightly, not enough to disturb the coloured boys making *ack-ack* sounds at pedestrians below – 'I should like to introduce to you Mr Gerald Gordon. You have your choice, sir, of joining these students in the front and earning an "A" grade, or going back there and getting a "B", provided of course you don't leave the room.'

'I guess I'll stay up here, sir,' I said.

'Ex-cellent. Your fellow students, then, from left to right are: Mr Lefkowitz, Miss Annaliese Graff, Miss Marlene Leopold, Mr Willie Goldberg, Mr Irwin Roth, and Mr Harry Frazier. In the back, Mr Morris Gordon (no relative, I trust), Miss Etta Bluestone, Mr Orville Goldberg (he's Willie's twin), and Mr Henry Moore. Please be seated.'

Henry Moore was coloured, as were the Goldberg twins, Orville and Wilbur. The girls, Annaliese, Marlene, and Etta, were pretty and astonishingly mature, as ripe in their way as Wilfrid Skurow in his. Harry Frazier was a straw-haired athletic sort, eating a sandwich. The lone chair was next to Henry Moore, who was fat and smiled and had no moustache or tattoo. I took the geometry book from my scuffed, zippered notebook.

'The truth is,' Mr Spiro began, 'that both Neville Chamberlain and Mr Roosevelt were fascist, and quite in sympathy with Hitler's anticommunist ends, if they quibbled on his means. His evil was mere overzealousness. Public opinion in the so-called democracies could never have mustered against *any* anticommunist, whatever his program – short of invasion, of course. *Klar?*' He stopped in order to fish out a book of matches for Annaliese, who was tapping a cigarette on her desk.

'*Stimmt?*' he asked, and the class nodded. Harry Frazier wadded his waxed paper and threw it back to one of his classmates by the window, shouting, 'Russian MIG!' I paged through the text, looking for diagrams. No one else had a book out and my activity seemed to annoy them.

'So in conclusion, Hitler was merely the tool of a larger fascist conspiracy, encouraged by England and the United States. What *is* it, Gerald?'

'Sir – what are we talking about?' I was getting a headache, and the egg on my brow seemed ready to burst. The inner semicircle stared back at me, except for Harry Frazier.

'Sh!' whispered Morris Gordon.

'At *shul* they don't teach it like that,' said Irwin Roth, who had a bald spot from where I sat. 'In *shul* they say it happened because God was punishing us for falling away. He was testing us. They don't say nothing from the English and the Americans. They don't even say nothing from the Germans.'

'Because we didn't learn our letters good,' said Morris Gordon. The matches were passed from the girls to all the boys who needed them.

'*What* happened?' I whispered to Henry Moore, who was smiling and nodding as though he knew.

'Them *Jews*, man. Ain't it great?'

'Then the rabbi is handing you the same bloody bullshit they've been handing out since I went to *shul* – ever since the bloody Diaspora,' Spiro said. 'God, how I detest it.'

'What's *shul*, Henry? What's the Diaspora?'

'Look,' Spiro continued, now a little more calmly, 'there's only one place in the world where they're building socialism, really honestly *building* it' – his hands formed a rigid rectangle over the desk – 'and that's Israel. I've seen children your age who've never handled money. I've played football on turf that was desert a year before. The desert blooms, and the children sing and dance and shoot – yes, shoot – superbly. They're all brothers and sisters, and they belong equally to every parent in the *kibbutz*. They'd die for one another. No fighting, no name calling, no sickness. They're big, straight and strong and tall, and handsome, like the Israelites. I've seen it for myself. Why any Jew would come to America is beyond me, unless he wants to be spat on and corrupted.'

'*Gott*, if the rabbi knew what goes on here,' said Roth, slapping his forehead.

'What's a rabbi, Henry? *Tell me what a rabbi is!*'

'What*ever* is your problem, Gerald?' Spiro cut in.

'Sir – I've lost the place. I just skipped the sixth grade and maybe that's where we learned it all. I don't understand what you-all are saying.'

'I must say I speak a rather good English,' said Spiro. The class laughed. 'Perhaps you'd be happier with the others by the window. All that *rat-tat-tat* seems like jolly good fun, quite a lift, I imagine. It's all perfectly straightforward here. It's *your* country we're talking about, after all. Not mine. Not theirs.'

'It's not the same thing up North,' I said.

'No, I daresay ... look, why don't you toddle down to the nurse's office and get something for your head? That's a good lad, and you show up tomorrow if you're feeling better and tell us all about Georgia. Then I'll explain the things you don't know. You just think over what I've said, OK?'

I was feeling dizzy – the bump, the smoke – my head throbbed, and my new school clothes were filthy. I brushed myself hard and went into the boys' room to comb my hair, but two large Negroes sitting on the window ledge, stripped to their shorts and smoking cigars, chased me out.

Downstairs, the nurse bawled me out for coming in dirty, then put an ice pack over my eye.

'Can I go home?' I asked.

The nurse was old and fat, and wore hexagonal Ben Franklin glasses. After half an hour she put an adhesive patch on and since only twenty minutes were left, she let me go.

I stopped for a Coke at the drugstore across from Lincoln's statue. Surprising, I thought, the number of school kids already out, smoking and having Cokes. I waited in the drugstore until the sidewalk was jammed with the legitimately dismissed, afraid that some truant officer might question my early release. I panicked as I passed the cigar counter on my way out, for Mr Terleski was buying cigarettes and a paper. I was embarrassed for him, catching him smoking, but he saw me, smiled, and walked over.

'Hello, son,' he said, 'what happened to the head?'

'Nothing,' I said, 'sir.'

'About this morning – I want you to know there was nothing personal in anything I said. Do you believe me?'

'Yes, sir.'

'If I didn't do it in *my* way first, they'd do it in their way and it wouldn't be pretty. And Gerald – don't raise your hand again, OK?'

'All right,' I said. 'Goodbye.'

'*Very* good,' said Mr Terleski. 'Nothing else? No *sir?*'

'I don't think so,' I said.

The street to our apartment was lined with shops: tailors with dirty windows, cigar stores piled with magazines, some reading rooms where bearded old men were talking, and a tiny branch of a supermarket chain. Everywhere there were school kids: Jews, I could tell from their heads. Two blocks away, just a few feet before our apartment block, about a dozen kids turned into the dingy yard of the synagogue. An old man shut the gates in a hurry just as I stopped to look in, and another old man opened the main door to let them inside. The tall spiked fence was painted a glossy black. I could see the kids grabbing black silk caps from a cardboard box, then going downstairs. The old gatekeeper, a man with bad breath and puffy skin, ordered me to go.

At home, my mother was preparing dinner for a guest and she was in no mood to question how I got the bump on the head. The guest was Grady, also from Moultrie, a whip-thin red-faced man in his forties who had been the first of my father's friends to go North. He had convinced my father. His wife and kids were back in Georgia selling their house, so he was eating Georgia food with us till she came back. Grady was the man we had to thank, my father always said. 'Me and the missus is moving again soon's she gets back,' he announced at dinner. 'Had enough of it here.'

'Back to Georgia?' my father asked.

'Naw, Billy, out of Cincinnati. Gonna find me a place somewheres in Kentucky. Come in to work every day and go back at night and live like a white man. A man can forget he's white in Cincinnati.'

'Ain't that the truth,' said my mother.

'How many niggers you got in your room at school, Jerry?' Grady asked me.

'That depends on the class,' I said. 'In geometry there aren't any hardly.'

'See?' said Grady. 'You know five years ago there wasn't hardly no more than ten per cent in that school? Now it's sixty and still going up. By the time your'n gets through he's gonna be the onliest white boy in the school.'

'He'll be gone before *that*,' my father promised. 'I been thinking of moving to Kentucky myself.'

'Really?' said my mother.

'I ain't even been to a baseball game since they got that nigger,' Grady boasted, 'and I ain't ever going. I used to love it.'

'You're telling me,' said my father.

'If they just paid me half in Georgia what they paid me here, I'd be on the first train back,' said Grady. 'Sometimes I reckon it's the devil himself just tempting me.'

'I heard of kids today that live real good and don't even see any money,' I said. 'Learned it in school.'

'That where you learned to stand in front of a softball bat?' my mother retorted, and my parents laughed. Grady coughed.

'And let me tell you,' he began, 'them kids that goes to them mixed schools gets plenty loony ideas. That thing he just said sounded comminist to me. Yes, sir, that was a Comminist Party member told him that. I don't think no kids of mine could get away with a lie like that in my house. No, sir, they got to learn the truth sometime, and after they do, the rest is lies.'

Then Father slapped the fork from my hands. 'Get back to your room,' he shouted. 'You don't get no more dinner till I see your homework done!' He stood behind me, with his hand digging into my shoulder. 'Now say good night to Grady.'

'Good night,' I mumbled.

'Good night *what?*' my mother demanded. 'Good night *what?*'

'Sir,' I cried, 'sir, sir, sir! Good night, sir!' the last word almost screamed from the hall in front of my bedroom. I slammed the door and fell on the bed in the darkened room. Outside, I could hear the threats and my mother's apologies. 'Don't hit him too hard, Billy, he done got that knot on the head already.' But no one came.

They started talking of Georgia, and they forgot the hours. I thought of my first school day up North – then planned the second, the third – and I thought of Leonard Sachs Junior High, Squirrel, and the Jews. The Moultrie my parents and Grady were talking about seemed less real, then finally, terrifying. I pictured myself in the darkened balcony under a rain of yo-yos, thrown by a crowd of Squirrels.

I concentrated on the place I wanted to live. There was an enormous baseball stadium where I could hit home runs down the line; Annaliese Graff was in the stands and Mr Terleski was a coach. We wore little black caps, even Squirrel, and there were black bars outside the park where old men were turning people away. Grady was refused, and Spiro and millions of others, even my parents – though I begged their admission. *No, stimmt?* We were building socialism and we had no parents and we did a lot of singing and dancing (even Henry Moore, even the chocolatey Goldberg twins, Orville and Wilbur) and Annaliese Graff without her cigarettes asked me the capitals of obscure countries. 'Israel,' I said aloud, letting it buzz; 'Israel,' and it replaced Mozambique as my favourite word; *Is-rael, Is-rael, Is-rael*, and the dread of the days to come lifted, the days I would learn once and for all if Israel could be really real.

South

It was the South. My father had been in an accident in Valdosta, and the word they used was *crushed*: his legs, his back, his ribs, his hip. His arms were merely broken. We had no insurance. Until the accident we had been surviving in town. I was in the second grade. My mother stayed in the three rooms that weren't quite an apartment but served the landlady as one. They were three equal-sized rooms, all of them with long, screened windows, all of them wallpapered and carpeted. In the corner of one room she'd installed a refrigerator and a two-burner electric range; in another there was a shower stall and a chemical toilet, and in the third there was a dresser and a bed. I slept on a pallet in the kitchen.

A few months after the accident, my father was allowed to go home. He was still in the body cast for the broken back. He lay in his BarcaLounger, nearly straight out. He'd been selling BarcaLoungers before the accident, and he always believed fervidly in the products he represented. Later on, when he went back to selling, he would treat the BarcaLounger mystically, saying, 'This li'l honey saved my life,' and he could make his voice quaver like a Southern politician on Confederate Memorial Day. He wasn't even American. What he meant to say was that even a man crippled by pain and rendered immobile could master his convalescence, could still feel he had something useful to do with himself by going up and down in his BarcaLounger. In 1946, it was a whirlpool bath and physiotherapist in one moulded slab of aluminum. He needed that little mechanism. He couldn't read, and this was before television, and the only radio station, from Ocala, was hard to get and even harder to understand. He and my mother I don't ever remember talking.

They had no money, of course. And then they exhausted the resources of eventual recovery – the donations of friends up north, my mother's relations in Canada, her bonds provided by a provident father.

So we left the three rooms. Things got sold that I'd never even seen unpacked. My mother's family was well-to-do, and my mother was a woman of taste. She'd been a decorator, and she'd accumulated things in Europe and in England and then in Montreal, where she'd met my father. Those things – Meissen things, Dresden things, Prague things, sketches she'd done in German and British museums, watercolour renderings she'd done for clients in Montreal, heavy silverware in a rich, burgundy-velvet-lined case, candlesticks, cut-glass bowls, little framed paintings and etchings and cameos done on porcelain or ivory – they meant nothing at all to me. She unwrapped them and cried; she tried to tell me the stories of their acquisition, the smuggling out. They meant nothing at all, to my shame. A BarcaLounger now – that was a valuable thing. When all my mother's boxes were empty, I carried them to the trash. All that I liked, and saved for a while, were the yellowed sheets of newspaper she'd packed them in, a dozen years before. I liked foreign-looking things. Some of the newspapers were in Gothic face. Some of them were in French.

So 'a coloured man' was paid a dollar or two to move us from the three rooms into something we could afford. For the move someone donated a wheelchair, and so we walked across town – my mother, the coloured man and me, each carrying suitcases and boxes – and my father trailed behind, pushed indifferently by another part of the coloured man's family, called a coloured boy. He nudged my father down the main street (there were no sidewalks) with bursts of energy the way a boy might kick a stone for a few blocks until it careens under a car or somewhere out or reach. The first time my father's chair began to tip, causing him to wrench his back in an insane balancing act, the boy was canned, and I was appointed to finish the task. He made room on his lap for a suitcase and a lamp. His legs were pink, withered and scaly and would remain that way for years, until the rest of him started to shrink.

The new place was actually larger than the three rooms. It might have been called a house – it was detached but set back from the street, as a garage or a laundry house might have been. It gave us an address with an 'A' at the end – something new in all our travels, 'a sign' my mother said. Its virtue was that it was very, very cheap. The figure of ten dollars a month sticks in my mind. The facilities were outdoors, in an overgrown garden heavy with many other scents. Florida to me is always a collection of odours; it's the only thing I miss, and it's the first thing I notice about any new place I'm set down in. The outdoor commode – as my mother termed it – hadn't been used in a very long time; it was, like our small house, tilting and in need of paint. The virtue of an unused toilet cannot be exaggerated. It was quiet, neutral, and hygienic as nature itself. We soon took care of that, but rankness and a need for lime didn't set in for a few weeks. I don't know how my father used it, or even if he did; I suspect now my mother had arranged something with boards and a bucket and newspaper-linings in the house that she slopped outside every morning.

School was going on. I hadn't missed a day. I had started kindergarten outside of Atlanta and had put in a chunk of first grade in Gadsden, Alabama, and we had come to Leesburg, Florida, at the end of the first grade, before my father's accident, so that I was remembered by a few kids when second grade started. I usually didn't have that advantage. Most of the moves in our life were timed for summer, so that each September I began a new school. In Leesburg, Florida, in 1946, I had a small history.

I was more sociable in the days before my father's accident and the move across town. I remember, in those warm twilight evenings under the bare bulb of street-lights, the endless circling of bicycles in the fine dust of our lane; the weekend work-up games of baseball. I remember the first time I caught a pass thrown by an older boy and the buoyant worn pigskin, the fine black bubble of inner tube bursting between the laces. I had a curious side-arm throwing motion with a baseball that older boys watched and tried to imitate, without my control. Let's just say it was a Southern town in post-war America, and so far as I knew anything about myself, I fitted in. I was accepted. Kick-the-can, fishing with doughballs, endless summers of bicycling, football and baseball; a subtropical life led out of doors, with rings of dust tamped down by sweat, scabs on the knees and elbows still forming or just falling off, a dingy, uneven tan, dingy, uneven blondness in all hair.

Things of course were working.

I was sociable. In the first grade, and in the summer, kids had come home with me; I went home with them. My mother baked, served, poured. Her exaggerated notion of Florida heat led her to elabourate formations of Jell-O and gallons of iced tea and lemonade and – universally rejected by everyone but me – buttermilk. She disapproved of

Coke, that Southern elixir, and wouldn't stock it. No one seemed to notice those three strange, papered rooms in the widow's house, or that my father was never home, or that my mother had an accent no one understood. She had no friends. My parents went nowhere, even on the five or six days a month when my father was home. He lived entirely for himself. My mother lived entirely for me. I found this a satisfactory arrangement. I lived entirely for the release from school.

After our move, Grady was my only friend. I remember walking over to his house after school. It was a small town in those days, and a child revealed everything about himself from the direction he nosed his bicycle in from the stands outside of school. Each cardinal compass point indicated who and what you were, what your father did and what your prospects in life were going to be. I was an exception because our little laundry shed of a house was the last white-occupied structure on that side of town. The county, I learned many years later, was 70 percent black. All street services – pavement, lights, water, sewage – ended half a block from our address, although houses like ours, unpainted and tilting on stilts, with old cars and refrigerators in the ungrassed yards, teeming with children and with sullen young men and women and old black women in straw hats with flowers on the brims, continued for many undemarcated blocks. My mother would embarrass me horribly by walking into Niggertown and running her hands over the heads of little girls and then standing in the yards calling up to women of her age, 'I'm your new neighbour. We live just on the other side of the streetlight there. I hope you'll come over for tea some afternoon.'

As I say, I was an exception, going east from school, down the Dixie Highway, and cutting through the alleys behind the stores where the Jim Crow serving windows were. Grady Stanridge went the other way, where the better families lived. They were the new people in town, people with businesses, people like us only younger and not from so far away. It's hard to understand, even now, that the parents were just starting out in life – they were in their twenties, the men navy and army veterans with tattoos and a hunger to repossess their lives; and that there were also a number of kids in my class who had never seen (and would never see) their fathers; and that the remarriage of young widows and subsequent moving to larger towns was a favourite topic in our first and second grades.

Grady and I strolled down the Dixie Highway. His father had the Western Auto store. Grady could take anything he wanted from the store – games, baseball gloves, fishing equipment. He was generous and I was greedy. I took a yo-yo – one of those deluxe Duncans at thirty-five cents – and a wooden vial of fish-hooks. Grady also took a yo-yo, and we were back on the shaded sidewalk, 'walkin' our babies' and 'loopin' the loop', when I saw my mother across the street, making her way from the cool, deep shade of the west side of town.

I prayed she wouldn't cross over. She had the Canadian custom of smothering me with 'dears' and 'darlings' and even 'preciouses' in every conversation, and she even extended the custom to my little friends, as she called them. The one acceptable term of endearment – honey – she never used.

She was carrying a small package from the butcher's, and from the colour of stain on the outside I knew it to be liver, her – and my – favourite. We got it for ten cents a pound, since it wasn't considered fit for white consumption. It was assumed, whenever I was sent out to buy it, that we were getting it for our cleaning lady. I tried to keep my mother from going for it, since I knew she wouldn't go along with my lie.

She didn't see me. By the time we got to Grady's house I had mastered 'cat in the cradle' and my middle finger was cold and white and nearly asphyxiated.

His house was Florida Moorish, with a tile roof, Mexican grille work and rows of tall, narrow windows, curved on top. The outside was stucco; the grounds were well-tended, with oranges in the back, hibiscus and bougainvillea along the trellises and a tightly tufted, low-pile lawn. The walkway was crushed limestone, rendered white in the Florida sun.

Mrs Stanridge was smoking in the living room, taking her afternoon break, it seemed, with a tall drink in a frosted, narrow glass. The house was very neat; even with all the windows – which were clean – the glass tables and the various ledges showed no dust. There was a large portrait hung over a small fireplace; the woman was stout and grey-haired. Her black dress and the rows of pearls and the wavy hair reminded me of a movie matron, the kind of stuffy lady Groucho Marx would spill something on.

Grady led me to the kitchen for iced tea, made in the Southern fashion with no lemon and lots of sugar. Our house always featured lemons, and raw, tart foods were prized over all others. I used to chew rhubarb like celery, pop cranberries like cherries, suck lemons and chew limes. I didn't mind the way Southerners cooked their food, with pots of vegetables boiling all day till they were soggy brown messes, but I realized my friends couldn't eat at my place at all because they found everything, from meat to vegetables to dessert, raw. Of course, with my father laid out in his BarcaLounger, and with my living on the edge of Niggertown, I understood I couldn't bring anyone home at all.

We heard Mrs Stanridge out in the living room suddenly cursing and then shouting, 'Grady, get in here!' She seemed to be frantic; all the order that had been apparent a few minutes earlier had been overturned. She'd opened the breakfront drawers and had silverware out on the dining table. She had stacks of newspapers scattered on the rug.

'Where is it?' she demanded. 'Have you hidden it?'

'Hidden what, ma'am?'

'Hidden my purple flower pot. I have people coming over, and I went out to cut some flowers, and now I don't have my flower pot to put them in!'

'I don't even remember no purple flower pot!'

'It was purple. It was antique. It was right on the ledge under Big Mama's picture.'

Grady looked at the ledge. Not even a dust ring; the ledge thinly underscored the painting, nothing else.

'It's the onliest thing I care about. I had that flower pot before I even met Mr Stanridge.' Mrs Stanridge was almost whining.

'Well, don't look at me – I just got here,' said Grady.

'I'm upset.'

'I'll look for it.'

'I think I know what happened.'

'Maybe you took it to the kitchen.'

'I should have put two and two together,' she said. 'It was the lady done it.'

'What lady?'

'The cleaning lady.'

'May-Lou?'

'You know May-Lou quit on me. The cleaning lady that answered the ad.'

'Why would she want an old flower pot?'

'I seen her lifting it, even.'

I could see a purple flower pot nestled nicely in the upper shelf of the breakfront. 'Excuse me, ma'am,' I said.

Grady was in the kitchen. He shouted out, 'It ain't back here.'

'She stole it, that's what. May-Lou might have broke it and not told me. But this one was too careful. She stole it.'

'Ma'am?' I asked again.

'And her acting so superior. Like she was too good to clean a white lady's house. I even let her eat on my good plates.'

'Is that it, there?' I pointed, and Grady's mother reluctantly followed its direction. She hugged the pot like a rescued child, then set it back on the ledge and stepped away from it, just to admire it all over again.

'Thank God,' she said. 'And I promise you,' she said, as though she were speaking directly to the pot or maybe someone's ashes inside it and not to Grady and me, who were walking our yo-yos just above carpet level, 'I promise I ain't never hiring a white woman to do coloured work again!'

How easy it is for a boy, and then a young man, to write praises to his father. He sat there through my childhood and through my high-school years, and then he left, married two more times, and died. Never did we talk, never did he explain to me the passions (here I am again, calling them *passions* when I know for sure they were nothing but blind lusts) that drove him. And I have so deliberately mythologized him, the manly force in my life, the dark, romantic, French, medieval, libidinous force in my life, the foreign element in my life, believing somehow that his eighteen siblings, his six wives, his boxing career, his violence and his drinking and his police record, his infidelities, in some way ennoble *me*, tell me I'm not just the timid academic son of my mother's rectitude.

And she, who cleaned other people's houses while I attended school and my father reclined on his BarcaLounger, and finally returned to schoolteaching herself in Winnipeg after she finally left him, and who now lives alone in an apartment in Winnipeg, forgetting if she's eaten, forgetting to cook the things she's bought and keeps shoving into the refrigerator (the final smell in my catalogue of odours is the aroma of age, the rotting in the cold of orange-juice cans and Chinese dinners) – how easy it is for a boy and for a young man and even for a man now embarked on middle age to see his mother as nothing exceptional in the universe, nothing at all, an embarrassment in fact, against the extravagance of his father.

Mother, why couldn't we love you enough?

The Fabulous Eddie Brewster

Etienne was my father's only brother, old enough to have enlisted in the Canadian army in 1915 when my father was only six. After the war, Etienne had stayed in France as an interpreter for the Americans. Finally he married, fathered an intemperate New World brood of children, and in the thirties dropped from family correspondence, after notifying my aunt Gervaise that he had been elected mayor of his village. During those same years, my father drifted off the Broussard family farm, near Sorel to a hardware store in Montreal. In 1938 he married my mother, *une Anglaise* from Regina. Eye trouble harboured him in Montreal when the new war broke out, and precipitated my arrival a few months after Dunkirk. When the war ended, my father took us into the States, where, he surmised, a fortune waited. He had relatives all over New England – Gervaise and Josephine were living with their husbands in Vermont – and none of them was breaking even, but my father easily explained their lack of success. 'They're afraid,' he said, 'afraid to leave Québec.' Just *habitants* by his standards, whose children would be raised on beans and black bread for Sunday breakfast. My father wasn't afraid; he'd learned good English and sensed the future flow of money was southward, far southward. And so we ended in Hartley, a north-central Florida town of five thousand crackers, where he started selling jalousie windows and doors. We waited several months for a break while my father bronzed in God's own sun, caught his fill of bass, and cultivated a drawl around his *canadien* twang. Then we heard from Etienne.

> Louis, mon cher, mon seul frère: Forgive me, my dear brother, for all these years of silence. All was well until the war took it away. Thinking of you all these years, believe me. I was the mayor and they put me in prison. My Verneuil-le-chétif is no more, just some buildings ... everything is taken from me. My boys, fine boys Louis, only two left and they fight in Indochine. My girls

> gone from me, two in the Church, God keep them. Louis, help me, whatever you can send – I will not beg but as your only brother, I ask for help. The food is not so good in this camp, but with money I can buy little things on black market. ... Louis, if I could only see you now, my boy, my dear, dear boy. Bless you, Louis, your own brother Etienne.

Immediately, my father cabled two hundred dollars. A few weeks later came a second letter blessing us, thanking us, and asking if it were possible for him to return to America and maybe find work in the States? Could we perhaps sponsor him until he could get a start? He included a snap taken next to a prison shed. He wore prison greys and stood Chaplin-fashion, with hands at his side, feet out, a look both forlorn and astonished in his eyes. The picture did it; thirty years of estrangement instantly healed. My father condemned his own good health, his youth, our relative comfort, then decided to bring his brother over.

'Not to live here,' said my mother. 'Not with Frankie needing his own room –'

'He needs rest, Mildred. After a while, he gets fattened up, rested, I'll find him work.'

'What could he do, Lou? We don't know a soul who would hire an old refugee – no matter what he's been. He just wouldn't be happy.'

But Etienne's letters came more frequently: twice a week. He was in a DP camp outside Paris. 'Everyone but French here,' he wrote, 'with every day the Russians and the Germans and the British identifying refugees and taking them back – if they want to go or not. Good food costs money like hell. For myself I buy nothing, but there are others here, from Verneuil. Chocolate for the old women, tobacco for the old men, shoes for the kids. I am still their mayor, *non?*'

Finally my mother relented and the government granted permission for my father to bring Etienne over. Etienne in the DP camp had collected nearly five hundred dollars in three months, wiping out our first year's savings in the States. 'Either forget him, Lou, or bring him over,' said my mother. 'God knows it's a rotten choice.'

'Maybe we could afford a hundred a month. I could write him.'

'Send him a hundred and he'll squawk. But I don't like getting drained long distance. If he's taking our money, I want him under my nose.'

'Mildred – he's suffered. We can't imagine how he's suffered. Those Germans – they're not human.'

'Well, maybe suffering's made him hard,' said my mother. 'And how do we know what they imprisoned him for, eh?' Suspicion was instinctive with my mother, but that suspicion extended finally to herself. 'Oh, Lou, don't just listen to me. He's your brother, if you think you should bring him over, then bring him. One look at this place and he'll head back to Paris anyway, if he has any sense.'

'And I don't know him at all,' my father muttered. 'That's what makes it bad. Why did he come to me?'

But it was decided. My father wrote his sisters in Vermont, and somehow they persuaded their husbands to share Etienne's passage three ways. They all met their brother in New York, in February 1947. Down in Hartley, my mother transformed my toy- and map-strewn room into a study, suitable for a refugee mayor who had suffered but was accustomed to finer things. I slept the next year on the living-room sofa.

Hartley in 1947 was yet undiscovered by the prophesied boom. Inland towns in the north of Florida had no special interest in the tourist trade, being citrus regions intent on keeping the land in local, unreconstructed hands. It was small-town America with a Southern warp: proper and churchly, superstitious and segregated. As the only outsider in the school, I was a vulnerable freak and not allowed to forget it; as the only Yankees in town (the term outraged my mother – she remembered overturning Yankee cars in 1914 when the States had ignored their higher duties), we were treated cordially by the weekly *Citrus-Advocate* and Welcome Wagon lady, but suspiciously by the neighbours and businessmen. Once the Klan warned us to move after an interview with my mother had been aired on the radio ('... well, I think certain social changes are desirable and inevitable, yes ...'). The night of the Watermelon Festival, the Klan had staged an unmasked parade down Dixie Highway with the unhooded mayor and sheriff leading the way.

Etienne was much heavier than the prison snap prepared us for. He had bought a sale-priced summer suit in New York, so all traces of his displacement had been left in port. He was silver-haired, very short, and classically fat, with the hard unencumbering fat of middle-aged Latins, even polar Canadian ones. Though he looked much older than my father, who was trim and dark-haired, the resemblance was arresting, and one was somehow certain they were brothers, not father and son.

'So – your lovely wife!' he cried, taking my mother in his bulging, tattooed arms. 'Louis tells me this was your idea, bringing an old man over. Bless you, bless you. You've saved my life!' He lifted her, pivoting her on his belly, then kissed her loudly as she settled down. She was three inches taller.

'This is Frankie,' said my father, urging me forward. I held out my hand.

'Kid,' he announced, taking my hand in both of his, 'it's good to see you. I'm your uncle Etienne and I've come around the world to see you.'

'You're home now, Etienne,' said my father.

'I feel it, Lou. I sure as hell feel it.' He carried in two belted suitcases – scuffed and greasy, plastered with stamps and permits – then showered while we met in the kitchen.

'Some DP!' said my mother. Her cheek was still red where Etienne had kissed her.

'He surprised me too, Mildred. But don't go by his English – he learned it all in the army, so it's pretty rough. But he's proud of it. He doesn't even want to speak French any more. Says he wants to be accepted by you and the town. He doesn't even want to hear it.'

'Why, for heaven's sake? He's the first Frenchman I've ever met ashamed of French.'

'Well, he's not a normal Frenchman.'

'I'm watching him,' said my mother. 'A special Frenchman doesn't have to be a typical American.'

'What do you want? He suffered *some*, but he wasn't tortured. I asked him that and he got offended. He asked me what kind of prisoner I thought he was. His family got scattered, but I don't think any got killed. His boys are fighting now in Indo-China. He was an important man and now he has nothing left.'

'And what about his wife? Or did he have one?'

'He didn't say anything. I guess she might have died, or maybe they're divorced.'

'Thank God for that,' said my mother. 'But what does he expect from us? He thinks it was me who brought him over. I'll tell him it was because we couldn't afford to keep him in France.'

My father traced a pattern on the oilcloth. 'That reminds me – he wants *you* to decide a proper allowance for him.'

'He what?'

'Mildred – he's a grown man. He doesn't want to beg, but he wants some freedom in town. Little things. He came over with nothing. He thinks I'm too generous, so you're supposed to decide.'

'Five dollars a week.'

'Don't be cheap, Mildred. Ten at least. Even so, he'll be running short. He needs shoes, shirts, a razor, a bathrobe – things to be respectable around the house.'

'You give him ten and all you're going to see for supper is this fatback and black-eyed peas, and that's a promise. Take your pick. Just settle it before you go back on the road again, because I want everything to go smoothly with Etienne. I don't want him begging.'

'It'll be settled,' my father promised.

Uncle Etienne at first spent his days inside in front of the fan, listening to the news reports and reading the morning paper from Tampa which he walked downtown to get. While my father was on the road selling the jalousie windows, Uncle Etienne would tell us tales of their childhood in Sorel: of inhuman poverty and his fatherliness towards Ti-Louis. God, he'd had some times, though, just after WWI, and it was clear to see why he had remained in Europe. His favourite story concerned the day the Americans, occupying a post next to the Canadians, had called for an interpreter. Young Broussard had scampered over, and for two weeks had been assigned to a young officer named Eisenhower. 'That s.o.b. couldn't make a move without me,' Etienne recalled. 'What a man he was! I could have sent him anywhere – imagine – me a twenty-year-old kid. And did we get along! We were buddies, Ike and me. He wanted me with him when we hit Paris, believe me, but we got separated. Remind me to show you some letters from Ike. I always *knew* he was headed for the top. Always knew it. And the crazy joker couldn't even crap without word from me, and that's the God's own truth....'

While my father was away, it had been customary for my mother and me to eat lightly: a salad and iced tea with a dish of ice cream after – all if the icebox were working. But with Etienne at the table, such informality was disallowed. First, there had to be bread, crisped in the oven, then meat, gradually potatoes, and – due to his stomach ailments – they had to be baked. He would help with the shopping too, picking up steaks and chicken after scrupulous comparing. The apartment grew hotter with the oven on (Hartley ovens went unlighted from April to October), and my mother's patience grew shorter. She refused to cook to his specifications any more, and he astonished her by not complaining.

'Right!' he said. 'One hundred per cent right. Why should you cook when you've got a genuine French chef in the house? I'll cook. That's a bargain, eh, a real French chef for nothing?'

Small towns in central Florida, however, supply few of the staples of *haute cuisine*. Lamb was unheard of; similarly, all the more delicate vegetables. Hardiness was all a Florida cook demanded of her greens, that like paper towels they not disintegrate from oversubmersion. The new meals concocted by Etienne were no better-tasting, but the failures were more interesting: okra *parmesan*, a bouillabaisse of large-mouth bass, turnip-heart salad. I retired to Cokes and grilled-cheese sandwiches, and my mother tried bits of the main course, but concentrated on the salads. Etienne kept cooking for himself, undaunted by our disinterest and proud of his indispensability. When my father was home for the weekends, he ate enthusiastically in the steaming spicy kitchen.

Aside from the dinner hour, Etienne was now rarely home. It was a custom, he quickly discovered, for the town's older citizens to leave their respective dwellings very early, before the sun sucked the town to dust, and seek the public benches by the courthouse or under the commercial awnings along the Dixie Highway. By eight o'clock he would finish his tea and corn flakes at home and step out in his beige Panama with the tricolour *boutonnière*. If I happened to pass him during the day as I bicycled to the Lake Oshacola Park in search of shade and a Coke, or to the air-conditioned drugstore to check the new comics, I'd wave, but he rarely waved back. His circle of cronies was wide, no matter where he sat: the retired locals at the courthouse, or the wretched Yankees on Dixie Highway who had shunned St. Petersburg and Winter Park, or heard tales of Miami Beach, and had finally selected – at not much saving and very little comfort – the grove of cabins on swampy Lake Oshacola. He'd then return late in the afternoon with his bundle of vegetables, baked goods, and meats, shopped for in the Parisian fashion at separate stores. He arrived in time for the news, the ugly news of

Communist riots, and he would curse in French. After iced tea, he'd calm down. The local news and Fred Peachum's hillbilly music came on, and we turned it off.

'How was your day, Etienne?' my mother would ask.

'Nice, nice day. Talked to friends. Nice town – you really should know more people, Mildred. I mean it. Very nice people.'

'Don't tell me about the people, Etienne. You had bad people in your village – we have them here. The majority.'

'Naw, Mildred. I mean it. You don't take an interest is your trouble. Louie's too. He won't get ahead working for other people.'

My mother agreed, but never said so. Though my father was making more selling the jalousie windows and doors in Florida than he had selling screws in Montreal, Florida had not been the gold mine he'd hoped for. I too missed the snow, hockey, French (which my mother barely spoke and Etienne refused to), and was uncomfortable in the heat. I'd forget to tap out my shoes for scorpions, I contracted foot worms, my allergies were stimulated, sand seeped in every place, and my mother's treasured Irish lace got mildewed. My father, however, was still hopeful. He greedily sought the sun, grew brown and striking, and felt at least that he had planted himself in fortune's path and had only to stay put and success would stumble across him.

But Etienne, we soon learned, had not been idle on those long afternoons. His cronies at the courthouse, or along the Dixie Highway, had a little power, a little influence, or at least helpful bits of information. One weekend, when my father had just returned from a lucrative venture into new territory – Mobile and New Orleans – Etienne mentioned that if *he'd* just made a thousand dollars, he'd know how to invest it.

'Property, Lou. Any town worth living in is worth buying up. Nobody advertises what's up for sale. If you got friends and if you're on the ball, you know what's up. Pay the taxes and it's yours. No one knows about it, so the mayor and his friends snap it right up. How you think he owns this town? Smart man, the mayor.'

'What could I buy with a thousand dollars, assuming I wanted to invest it?' asked my father.

'Ah – that's the hitch, Lou. You couldn't buy. They wouldn't let you. It's exclusive, who they let buy. They don't know you.'

'They know you, eh?' asked my mother.

'That's right. I'm not up there for nothing. If I hăd the money, I'd form a partnership with you. Land or business.'

'What's to stop me going down tomorrow and buying up one of those places?' my father persisted. He was smiling, but dead serious, a gambler.

'They'd dump something on you that was half in the lake, Lou. The deedskeeper is the mayor's son-in-law. Fine boy named Stanley.'

'Typically American,' snapped my mother.

'You got to keep in touch,' said Etienne. 'Small town, after all. Naturally I'm telling you first, Lou, but I know you're not a rich man. Some of these others – the retired ones out along Dixie Highway waiting to die – they're rich. And they're dying to make a little more. There's a lot of them in town.'

'Watch out for your visa, Etienne,' said my mother. 'There's nothing in it about investing while you're here.'

'Im not investing. I'm just advising. It's their money – or yours. I'd just have a job and maybe with a job they'd give me a visa. Maybe then old Ike would write them for me. I got to think of my future. My family – two boys getting shot at in Indo-China, that's no life for a boy, they get shot, crippled for life. Better I find them a place, maybe get them started. I got talents, Mildred, Lou, I may be bragging, but I got talents.' He took our plates to the sink, ran the water, and sprinkled some soap. 'Then my wife working like a slave in Paris,' he added.

'Your wife? What's this about a wife?' cried my mother.

'Sure I got a wife. Twenty-eight years married. What do you think? Her name's Arlette.'

Now my father joined in. 'How come you never told me about her?'

'Did you ever ask, Louie?'

'I thought maybe – the war.'

'Would I be here then?' he charged. 'Do I act like my wife is dead? She's working, that's all. A seamstress, like she was thirty years ago.'

'Well,' sighed my mother, 'you take the cake.'

'She was afraid you wouldn't bring us both over, or me alone if you knew I was leaving her back temporarily. She said, "Go get well with your little brother in America and, maybe if you can, send me a little something back." That's what I do with what you give me every week, send little things back she can't get in Paris. You think I spend it all on myself, maybe? I'm an old man, I don't need anything. Just a little safety, a little money so when I'm old they don't carry me off to the poorhouse. I've seen everything wiped out, Louie; I've got a few years left and I'm going to use them.'

'You still should have told us, Etienne,' said my father. 'We would have been happy to bring her over.'

'She's my responsibility,' Etienne insisted. 'Things will work out better this way. You think over what I said about your thousand dollars. In the morning, one way or another, I'm going into business.'

'Etienne – what an American you are,' my mother said.

My parents didn't invest with Etienne, and for several days the subject was dropped. The mention of Arlette had a softening effect on my mother, and the stories Etienne now told us of France included Arlette and were a little more suitable. Soon he received her letters at home instead of the post-office box he had been renting.

Then one night he asked, 'What do you think of my cooking?'

'It's fine,' said my mother. 'It reminds me of Montreal, when Lou and I used to eat out.'

This soured him; one thing he resented was those remote origins.

'Better than Montreal, Mildred. Etienne's really good,' said my father.

'What I meant was, would you pay for it?'

'We *are* paying for it,' my mother reminded.

'No – I mean at a restaurant, say. If I had all the right vegetables and the right meats, do you think people would pay for it?'

'I don't think so,' she said. 'There no money here, let alone taste. This is the worst food on the continent, why?'

'I know a man. Met him last week, comes from New Orleans, named Lamelin. Wife is dead and his boy died in the war –'

'How sad –'

'– and he had this restaurant in New Orleans, see, then he sold it when his boy was killed, and he came here when his wife up and died, so he's got money and he's itching to get back in the restaurant business. His wife was the cook, so he doesn't know much about that end. I do. He's the business type, see – has contacts all over, and lots of money.'

'What are you thinking about, Etienne?' asked my father.

'A French restaurant here,' he announced. 'Outside Hartley, a few miles, near the main highway. More like a night club, really, with drinks, good food, entertainment.'

'You're crazy,' my mother said. 'You know what they go for here? Hillbilly stuff.'

'I'll give them something better.'

'They don't want it. You could bring Chevalier and they wouldn't pay.'

'I'll educate them. We start with Cubans since they're cheap and maybe move up to French. Believe me, I know lots of kids would come over. That camp I was in – full of them. Singers, dancers, pretty girls, kids with talent – I saw them.'

'Lou – you tell him,' my mother pleaded. 'They don't *like* Cubans any better than they like Canadians. Look – all you can get on the radio is Havana; it even drowns out their hillbilly junk and they hate it. Etienne, as a businessman you'd fail utterly.'

'I'm not a businessman,' he reminded.

'But she's right, Etienne. You can't take any crazy chances here. Things are too expensive.'

Etienne slammed the table. 'So what do you know, eh? A window dresser? I don't see you making a big name for yourself. So, they want doors and windows and you supply them. Good, fine, the best of luck. But how bad does anyone want doors and windows? Not so bad they can't wait. Not so bad they got to have you and nobody else. But with me – I know what they need. Even if *they* don't know it yet, I know. French food, but not too French. Why waste it? Deluxe treatment. Beautiful girls – can you give them that? Maybe a chance to make a little money. I give them something just a little better than they got, but not so much better they feel bad they can't ever have it. And the entertainment – leave that to me. I'm not selling Havana music, I'm giving them Havana girls. So I'll ask you one more time – you want to back me up? Lou – what do you say?'

'Etienne, can't you see?' My father towered over him, speechless. 'Christ, it's just crazy.'

'I always thought the Germans were pigheaded, but you take the cake, Etienne, believe me,' added my mother.

'*Eh bien*,' he grumbled, 'no more – all right? No hard feelings, eh? You don't trust me with your money. That hurts me – once five hundred people trusted me with their lives – their lives, Louie – and I didn't let them down. No one was killed in my town. I can't wait now, Lou – I'm taking back everything I had and I'm taking it here. Let me stay here another month, that's all, and I'll move out. No more trouble from me.'

'Etienne, you stay with us. We insist,' said my father.

My uncle started to his room. 'No thanks, Lou – I wouldn't feel right any more. I'll be keeping late hours anyway. It's best like this.' He came out in a few minutes, dressed in the best he had.

'Just remember you had a chance,' he said. 'And now I'm off to the radio station. They're interviewing me, so you listen, eh?'

'Radio!' exclaimed my father.

'On the local news. The *Fred Peachum Show.* You be listening.'

Peachum was Hartley's own hillbilly, whose show cut into the network's *Swing Time from New York* each afternoon for two hours of jamboree music; the Clewiston Cowboys and some added talent from the pine flats of northern Florida. The local news was a reading of the police blotter including all traffic tickets, hospital records, court decisions, school awards, and crop reports, interspersed with tales, interviews, songs, weather, ads, and sports. We'd never listened to it in its entirety, except for the time my mother had irritated the Klan with her predictions. We waited that evening an agonizing hour for Etienne.

'Got a gentleman dropped in to say a few words here,' drawled Fred Peachum, 'and I reckon y'all gonna find him right interestin'. Come right in here and pull up a crate, Eddie. This here is ... ah ... Eddie Brewster I reckon is how you'd say it, and he come to Hartley out of Paris, France. Tell the folks listenin' in how long you been in town, Eddie.'

'Oh, jus' a mont',' said my uncle in a new accent, mellow as a *boulevardier.*

'Let's see here, accordin' to my information you got a brother in town permanent, don't you?'

'Yes, my brodder Louie. He sells door and window built special for Florida. He brought me over from France.'

'What's happenin' over there now, Eddie?'

'Ooh – terrible. So much is destroyed. Everything was beautiful before, now not so beautiful. I think sometimes there is nothing left. In my village, just the church.'

'Kindly like a miracle, ain't it?'

'Yes, many time I tell myself – a miracle.'

'That fake!' my mother cried. 'A miracle –'

'*Chut*,' hissed my father. 'He's a little nervous is all.'

'And how you makin' out in Hartley, Eddie? I reckon it's right peaceful, after the war and all....'

'Oh, this town is very nice. Very nice – nothing in the world I like more than to settle down right here. And this town is ready for big things, you believe me. There's gonna be smart people come down here, once everything gets back to normal. My brodder Louie – he's a smart boy – he come all the way down from Canada. There gonna be others, you see.'

'Like you say, Eddie, we got a nice li'l biddy town here. I'd kindly hate to see it change. But that's the reason you come by today, ain't it, Eddie, to tell the folks how you wanta change Hartley?'

'That is right. I want to give Hartley something for the way it has welcomed me. I think the best thing I can do is give the town something that is personal from me – a French restaurant, with entertainment. Everything cooked personal by me, and the entertainment is direct from Tampa, maybe even Cuba. My partner and me are looking for property now that is close to Hartley but near Gainesville too. It would be my little way of thanking Hartley and all the people.'

My mother was up now, and yelling above Fred Peachum's long reminiscence about Cajun soup in New Orleans. 'The humility of the man! Lou, he's crazy, he's out of his mind – he's going to show his undying gratitude by opening a restaurant, eh? He's already announced it. Do you realize we're responsible for him? What if he signs loans for ten thousand dollars? They can't touch him – they'll come to his sponsor, that's who. Lou – you've got to stop him. I thought he was sly, but I never realized he was incompetent. He's a sick old man, Lou, and we never realized it.' My father bowed his head, and nodded.

Etienne was talking again. 'We're just not free to give any more information now. My partner and me hope to announce everything next week. I appreciate letting me talk, Mr Peachum. You wait till you taste *my* turtle soup.'

'All right! Eddie Brewster, folks, come in to give you the dope on a gen-u-ine French restaurant right here in Hartley. You check your paper for the big news next week, hear?'

Our phone rang and rang in the hours we waited for his return. When he finally arrived, he brought with him Maurice Lamelin, lately of New Orleans, and a portfolio of documents. They had made a purchase and were business partners.

Lamelin looked as though he had suffered a double loss in the past year; he looked also, as Etienne had said, greedy to rebuild his fortune. He was a sallow little man, taller than Etienne, but in no way powerful. Technicalities were his specialty: he spoke with authority about vegetable distributorships, freezer consignments, licences, and fire laws. The building had been Etienne's contribution; through contacts at city hall, he had heard of the old Sportsman's Club – a stucco structure with a tile roof, plazas, and a courtyard – going for back taxes and an unspecified transfer fee. The building was a local landmark, hastily erected in the twenties for a boom that never came. It stood a few miles outside Hartley on the main road to Gainesville. Landing the Sportsman's Club, my father agreed, was a shrewd move; it was the only possible site for a night club in all north-central Florida.

'We've got a new name for it, the Rustique,' said Etienne. 'I figured anyone can translate that. Come on out, we'll show it to you tonight.'

We drove out in Lamelin's new convertible. Cadillacs, the Cajun apologized, were back-ordered for months, so he had settled for a Chrysler at the same price.

At night, by flashlight and matches, the old structure with its faded mosaics, cracked beams, and resident lizards scurrying ahead, seemed like a Hollywood imitation of everything it, in fact was: Fitzgerald and Gloria Swanson, darkies mixing drinks, mannered but desperate poker games in the smaller rooms. Upstairs were rooms suitable for overnight accommodations. Lamelin planned to renovate them as soon as the kitchen equipment was installed. Already, we learned, the freezers and special gas ovens were on their way. Local merchants were providing furniture, thanks to the mayor's endorsement of Etienne's credit.

'How deep is the mayor's interest, Etienne?' asked my mother.

'He's nothing. Like a stockholder you might say. He has no power in this operation.'

'I'm the proprietor,' said Maurice Lamelin, 'and Broussard's my chef.'

'And impresario,' added my uncle.

'We'll be set up in two months,' continued Lamelin. 'We're gonna be the biggest thing between Jacksonville and Tampa.'

'Well, you'd better put some screens up,' said my mother. 'These mosquitoes are murder.'

The next day we returned, at Etienne's bidding, 'for a better picture.' Things had improved indeed; trucks unloaded in the marshy lot, neon experts measured the gables, power saws whined, and new timber was stacked outside for panelling the guest rooms and subdividing the ballroom. Lamelin prodded the workers: a tiny man, expertly profane. Etienne took us inside, showed us the kitchen area, the private dining rooms, the main room and stage, and the smaller rooms – for gambling.

'But you can't have gambling here!' said my father.

'How do you expect a place like this to make money, then, eh? You said yourself these people won't pay for food alone. So, let them try to win some money – what's the harm?'

'*Mon Dieu* – it's against the law, that's what!'

'Louie, Louie, what's the matter, you a kid? It's all clear with the law. All you need is a special licence so the county can collect some money too.'

'You know it's under the table, Etienne,' my mother charged. 'Don't try telling me it's legal.'

'All I'm saying is in Oshacola County it's as legal as selling doors and windows. It's called a Special Revenue Permit and we bought it and it's good till December 31.'

'Etienne – you listen to me,' my mother cried, 'so far as I'm concerned, it's illegal and what you plan is wrong, all wrong. I don't want you around the apartment, understand? If you need money for a hotel room, I'll give it to you personally. But don't come around, because I don't want to expose Frankie to any more of your double dealings.'

Etienne stepped back and held out his hands, palms up. 'Louie, what is she talking about? Tell her I'm doing this to bring Arlette over. You think I like taking chances at my age? You think I like the Cajun even? Mildred – you're my family. I feel like a grandpa to Frankie. Would I do anything to – to corrupt a kid? Louie, Louie, tell her, you can't just throw me out on the street like a dog, not after what I've been through, Lou?'

My father grabbed my mother's arm and pulled her to him. 'Why did you have to say such a thing, eh? Can't I have some peace as few times as I'm home?' Mother looked straight on, silent, her lips Scottishly tight. My father turned to his brother. 'Look, why didn't you tell me about the gambling, eh? Hell, if I had known *that* ... how do I know I'm not responsible for any bills you run up, maybe any crimes too? I sponsored you, but I sure as hell didn't think you'd start up a casino, not here. I'm trying to build something too, ever think of that? I'm new here too, I got a lot to lose too, only what I might lose is all in the future. So –'

'Lou, look at it like this. Let me stay till the restaurant's going good. After that I'll be working so hard I'll just stay in one of the rooms upstairs. Arlette will come over anyway. I don't want to sponge off you. Hey – where's she going?'

My mother yanked me with her to the car. We watched them argue awhile, and saw the screening go up; and the first tubes of neon. My father handed Etienne some money, then came back to the car, and without a word we drove home. 'Don't you ever butt into my personal business again,' he threatened as he let her out. 'Now I'm taking him into Tampa. Just don't wait up for me.'

That night we had salad and iced tea again, then we saw a movie: Margaret O'Brien. 'Your uncle Etienne is a bad man, Frankie, understand? I want you to try to forget him.'

The grand opening of the Rustique was publicized in all the area papers, and from most rural telephone poles in Oshacola County. For entertainment, Etienne had hired a flamenco guitarist and his troupe he'd found rolling cigar leaf in Tampa. Though Etienne rarely showed up in our apartment, my father often went out in the evenings before the opening to deliver mail or have a drink. He'd watch the floor show rehearse, and come back with tales.

'I saw girls, Mildred, nigger girls that bend over backwards so far that they go under a pole just *that* high off the ground.' He held his hand at shin level. 'Etienne was driving down to Orlando and he saw these niggers out in the celery field doing this crazy dance, see –'

'Don't call them niggers, please, Lou.'

'So he watched awhile, then he went over and offered them fifteen dollars to do it at the Rustique. They almost fell over him, they were so glad, being Bahamian and all. So he figures he's got the best entertainment in Florida outside of Miami Beach, and it cost him about fifty dollars total. After that, he found some Greek girls in Ybor City that belly dance –'

'Good Lord, Lou, they'll close him down. He can't run a place like that in the middle of nowhere. What'll people say? The Klan – they won't stand for that.'

'What do you mean? They know all about it.'

We were presented tickets for the opening night; Etienne figured a thousand tickets offering concessions on food and drinks had been won in contests or given away all over north-central Florida. Hard-drinking veterans now dominated the fraternities at the university, and they flocked up from Gainesville for the opening to sample all the attractions, especially Etienne's 'Normandy Knockout,' a reported favourite of General Eisenhower's. Fred Peachum was the MC and many personalities (the mayor and Stanley the deedskeeper plus the sheriff) were interviewed by the table-hopping hillbilly. The whole operation was a huge success; even the guest rooms were rented by strung-out celebrators. My father came home high and happy but the next day cursed my mother for not letting him invest.

It wasn't long before the Rustique was returning an extravagant profit on weekends and breaking even most week nights. Etienne scoured the region for talent. The gambling – and even sportier – activities in the rented rooms were the proud secrets of the town. When the next winter came the tourists took an inland route, thanks to enticing posters as far north as Augusta and Macon. They stopped in Hartley nearly as often as Daytona. The whole town prospered, as the *Citrus-Advocate* pointed out, and new motels were frantically erected. There was talk of a northern citrus processor coming to Hartley with a new scheme for freezing orange juice. The representative came, and after several conferences which Etienne joined, the processor was politely refused and advised to go further south. Oshacola County, it was felt, could make its money from Yankees without the mixed blessing of their industries.

After the winter season, the business slowed down somewhat, enabling Etienne to return to France for a visit to bring back Arlette.

With Etienne gone, Lamelin closed the Rustique for two weeks to allow for some remodelling and general expansion. Already, rooms were being reserved for next winter by Yankees who would never get further south, and a golf course was contemplated, along with an improvement of the docks.

Etienne and Arlette had been back in Hartley a week before they visited us. Arlette was my mother's height and, like my mother, pale in her features. She was *alsacienne*, her hair blond-grey, and her eyes the palest blue. Had she been in Hartley, one felt, Etienne would never have started the Rustique. Her English, contrary to Etienne's report, was perfectly Gallic: proper in every respect, but barely understandable. In her presence Etienne sat quietly and humbly, while she answered my mother's questions. They were staying in the bridal suite at the club, but she would try to find a small home on the lake – maybe even on the ocean, thirty miles away.

'We cannot thank you enough, Etienne and I,' she said. 'Life was without hope for us in France. Etienne couldn't work, and I could only support myself –' she looked down at her fingers, those of an overworked, perhaps unpractised seamstress. 'It seems all that is behind us. Thank God.'

'Have you seen the town?' my mother asked.

'I have. It is very small, is it not? We lived in a village much smaller, of course, before the war, but very different, too. My husband was the mayor. But after the war things changed horribly. *They had no right*,' she cried suddenly, 'Etienne did nothing wrong. He saved many lives.'

'*Assez*,' he commanded. 'It's all forgotten.'

'How many would be killed? How many of our friends would they have killed if Etienne had not urged co-operation? One need not approve, in order to co-operate.'

'I saved many lives. I know it,' said Etienne. He stood, and placed his hands on Arlette's shoulders. She took his hands in hers, smiling, but not looking back. 'It's all in the past. I've proved I was right. One year in America and I'm one of the richest men in the county and they'll let me stay.' He looked over at us and said to my father, 'Who needs them, the little men who judge you after the danger's past? They're the bad ones – the little men who were not in sight but suddenly become the judges. France is full of them.'

Etienne and Arlette were silent, defensive, waiting for a response. Finally my mother said, 'I imagine you'll be very happy here, Madame. You'll find no one to judge you here.'

Ten years later, Etienne was elected mayor of Hartley. We were already North, predictably, a year before the authentic boom began. We sat out Etienne's salad days from dingy suburbs of Cleveland, Toronto, and Buffalo. We never heard from Etienne directly, but were sent clippings from the *Citrus-Advocate* (now a daily), third-hand from Gervaise. The winter my father introduced portable heaters for drive-in movies in Buffalo, his brother was able to bring over Gaspar and Gérard from Indo-China. A few months later, Gaspar married a local girl, a wealthy one, and at the moment he is sheriff of Oshacola County. Arlette, a woman I barely remember but for her fingers, died before their beach home was completed. Etienne has retired alone to a sumptuous home by the golf course on Lake Oshacola – a course he invited Ike himself to open. My father goes down each winter for fishing and golf with his brother; everything again is cordial.

After their divorce several years ago, my mother went back to Canada and now teaches history in Regina.

Snow People

A Novella

I

One moment there were girls jumping rope in the dust, his friends pounding their mitts and George Stewart waving his bat, and the next he was wandering out beyond second base with a ringing in his ears, his nose smelling bone and all his side-vision gone. George was the first to walk beside him, maybe because he was the oldest, too old to be playing hardball with nine- and ten-year-olds. Maybe also because George Stewart had saved his life the summer before when he'd paddled beyond the pier in Oshacola Lake on an old inner tube through which he had somehow slipped into a roar of bubbles. He had saved him then; now it was George, the boy felt, who had somehow killed him.

'Walk it off, you'll be OK.'

'Where'd it hit you at?'

He didn't know. He couldn't talk – in the throat perhaps? He was walking, pitched to one side and leaning hard on George Stewart. He walked across the red dirt road where the fine clay dust felt cool on his feet, up the driveway to the porch door, bursting camphor berries as he walked. The door off the porch was locked.

'Ain't they home?' George asked. The truck was gone. *I must have cut my mouth,* he thought, for his T-shirt was pink from drool. It was the first time he'd ever been badly hurt, but where was it coming from? His chest? His nose?

'Ain't you got a key even?'

He was a boy entrusted with keys, always had been. There was a key to the house since his parents had started a small furniture factory and were usually out working at it, and there were other keys kept on a ring around his belt-loop; some to the factory buildings and others to apartments and houses they'd rented and vacated over the years.

'I'll be OK,' he said, his first words, and a pink blood bubble built as he spoke. Inside, the house was stale and humid but a little cooler than it would have been with the windows open. He found himself in the bathroom still with George Stewart and maybe some others, sweating and shivering, bent over the toilet bowl while a pink film spread on the water. He vomited, but it came out his nose because his mouth wouldn't open. Only the smell and residue of talcum powder and the yellow carton of Serutan on the toilet ledge assured him that he was home, in a bathroom unlike anyone else's, especially in Florida.

The pain was locating itself: in the back of his neck, in his nose, in his jaw. He wondered how a baseball, like a bullet, could do all that at once.

'You can have my ups,' said George Stewart, who'd run the bases before helping him. 'You better wipe all that up with a towel.' He took the nearest at hand, a white one that his father used, but the boy rejected it. He used toilet paper instead. Blood, his mother always said, left a permanent stain.

In the mirror, after washing, he stared at an unknown face. Baked pink over his cheeks and nose – he'd been out too long in the late August sun – but then the dark, dried lips and lump in his cheek and jaw. Pink drool ran from the corner of his mouth.

'Going back?'

'I don't think I can.' Through clenched teeth his voice reminded him of the morons in his class, the fifteen-year-olds who once in a while attempted to answer a question. He wondered if the blow on the head had made him a moron. He wanted to sleep, but he thought of trappers caught in a blizzard; if he slept would he ever wake up?

Not that dying was such a bad thing. The summer before, he'd picked up a cube of rat poison from under the sink, dark and tempting as a chocolate caramel, unwrapped it and held it in his hand until it got soft. Then he licked his fingers and went to bed with a letter to his mother under the pillow saying that he'd done it out of curiosity and that he wasn't mad at her for anything (he knew she'd take it personally); she shouldn't feel that there was anything he'd wanted and couldn't have, or that there was anything she could have done to save him. He'd arranged his room neatly, dressed himself in school clothes, assigned his valuables to friends, then fallen asleep. When he awakened the next morning he'd felt grateful for the immortality he now indisputably possessed. By the time he remembered to retrieve the letter it had disappeared, though his mother never mentioned it.

So he shouldn't worry. He lay down on his cot in the back porch, under the screens where the bugs plopped at night. His head was pounding with each heartbeat, his vision throbbed, and his jaw ached. Then he slept, knowing he would wake, for he was immortal.

A week later he found himself in Orlando, three hours in a dentist's chair while his mouth was wired shut. Now he sounded like Zerlene the moron who lifted her skirts for the older boys. He had to eat by reaming crumbled food through the gap where his wisdom teeth would someday grow. He learned to manipulate a straw and to strain un-iced Cokes through his locked front teeth. He stood behind the teacher at recess, for to play anything was to risk an elbow, an errant bounce, or even the need for a sudden gulp of air. And so, standing behind the teacher as a junior referee, he found a niche that had been waiting for him though he hadn't known it; how much better it was, keeping track of his classmates' performances, carrying a rulebook and whistle, than trying himself against physical odds that were obvious if unadmitted. He was a reader and speller and if it had not been a Southern school where science and arithmetic lagged behind, he'd have been a wizard there too. His place slightly behind second base or at the top of the concrete keyhole, at the teacher's side with whistle and rulebook, was proper, though he didn't know it yet.

For perhaps a month it worked. The kids accepted him as an incompetent who had tried, who was slow and ball-shy and easy to fake but didn't mind getting chosen last. But after a month of hot September games (he had two more weeks before the wires were due to come off), they began to associate him with the gradebook he carried and the imperious whistle he'd learned to blow with limited wind while pointing his finger at a foul, an out, or a questionable tag. He'd become a freak, and it was an isolated school in the dusty pine flats of northern Florida and a few of the kids remembered that he hadn't been born among them and no one knew of a church he attended, if any, and there was talk that his parents sounded *really* funny and ran a factory out at the old airport so he must be rich too, and no one appreciated his reading or the dates he knew in history and the way he won the spelling bee against sixth graders and the capitals he knew of all the states and that he wore shoes in the classroom instead of leaving them on the steps outside. Their judgement was swift. If they could, they would have killed him. But being boys of nine and ten, they knew they couldn't really kill. They could only hurt. The boy was like someone in a wheelchair or on crutches – just asking for it.

It started one day at the bicycle racks. It was three o'clock, the temperature up around ninety degrees, the bicycles scalding to the touch. They drew their bikes in a circle under a tree to let them cool. When he came out they didn't let him join their circle; he stood in the sun balancing the bike by a sticky rubber handgrip, putting his books on the seat. He wasn't that good on a bike, they knew that, and they suddenly hated him more for that than anything. They knew his route home, the dusty road where the ball field stood, even his house just across. A few boys started off in his general direction, taking the back streets to come out on the cement part of the Dixie Highway at South Street, before the clay stretch where he lived. It was a thrill, organizing an ambush with maps drawn in the sand, like a well-executed passing play – 'run out for one, you go deep and you go short and I'll throw it here, at the X' – and the 'X' would be where South Street cut off from the Dixie Highway in front of Chambers's general store. In fact, they planned to have themselves a couple of Cokes inside as soon as it was over.

The boy knew it too. He knew they were after him and that the plan was complicated and somehow exciting, and he was excited too, being the victim. He simply didn't know how to avoid it. His parents were working at the factory and he was the boy entrusted with keys, nine years old and jingling like a janitor on his bike. He knew something was headed his way, like a football thrown right at him. He put on his pants-clip and pedalled off, the hot seat burning, his books bouncing, and the keys jiggling from his belt loop, down the Dixie Highway past the lake and high school and the fairgrounds and baseball stadium, turning at Chambers's store where the Greyhounds stopped and picked up the insolent young men with baseball gloves and cleated shoes who had failed to make the team. He started to breathe easier when he saw the dust ahead, and the red tire tracks in the hissing blacktop that was about to end.

They strung it just a little low for what they'd intended; they'd meant to catch him around the mouth or neck with the cat-gut line. As it was, with him not going fast and the line tangling first in the bike's basket, then popping up to catch him flush in the chest before snapping, two of the boys sliced their hands enough to yell from the bushes. But for the others it was beautiful, a little reminiscent of the Cisco Kid knocking a posse off their horses. The bike reared up like a stallion and the kid slipped off backward so fast they thought someone else had hooked him from the rear instead of sweeping him off his seat, and he was down on the pavement with the bike skittering for a second or two on just its back wheel before crashing down right on top of him. It didn't look like he was ever going to get up or even begin to cry, which wasn't too loud anyway in that closed-mouthed way of his, and there seemed to be a lot of blood, which frightened them enough to tell Mrs Chambers about a kid who had fallen off his bike in the middle of the road. And then they lit out, back down the Dixie Highway past the high school and the fairgrounds to their own parts of town, which were older and cooler and better shaded.

Most of the cuts were superficial, the usual scrapes on the elbow, banged knees. The knees of his pants were both ripped out and there would be bruises where the basket and handlebars had come dropping down. The bad cuts were in the mouth, where for the second time in a month the boy tasted blood and smelled the bone and gristle, but now it was worse, for the wires were sprung and came bristling through his lips and tongue and this time the blood was bright as it dripped off the ends of the wire onto the pavement. Mrs Chambers helped him inside. She didn't know what had happened. First she guessed he'd eaten something that had exploded, or that someone had stuffed a pin cushion in his mouth – both perhaps serving him right for some thoughtless prank – and the boy couldn't talk because the wires would cut him up worse if he tried. It was a general store and well-equipped with the semi-rural exigencies of farmers and fishermen, and Henry Chambers went to the back and found some small wire-cutters and commenced to pruning the boy's mouth and lips, working the lips out over the ends he'd cut, then keeping them lifted while he worked inside, twisting and clipping while the boy screamed and kicked the counters fit to break the glass on top.

'What I can't understand is how he picked up all that wire in the first place,' said Henry Chambers, a speculative man in a simple trade, and it was he who finally suggested calling a doctor. By that time the front of the boy's shirt looked like he'd spilled a Cherry Smash, or been shot, but the doctor, when he came, congratulated Henry for keeping cool in an emergency. As he cleaned the wounds, he told them all a story about coming across a nigger farmer who'd had his stomach slashed open by a harrow up in Georgia. The man was lying in his field with about twenty feet of intestine in his lap spilling out into the dirt. 'All you can do is work with what you got,' said the doctor, who had cleaned off what he could with some Coke and then commenced to stuffing the guts back in, cramming them in elbow deep while the nigger sat there calmly enough, everything considered, smoking some of the doctor's Lucky Strikes. And he lived – couldn't no mule, couldn't no dog hit out on a highway live with half his guts sticking out, the doctor said – but that man hitched his overalls up and got into the doctor's car and was dropped at the closest nigger hospital and they sewed him up and he was back in his fields inside a month. But the doctor, who told the story while cleaning out the boy's mouth with antiseptic, was a careful man, not the kind to belittle an honest injury, and the boy felt his was respectable enough to rank (being white and only a boy) with that of the farmer in the field but not, perhaps, of the same magnitude. The doctor asked him about the broken jaw he'd obviously suffered, and how long the wires had been on. 'You're going to have to start from scratch,' he said, and then he took him back to his clinic for more cleaning and clipping and since now at least the boy could speak, however weakly, he had him call his parents to explain what he thought had happened.

A week later, freshly wired in Orlando, and lectured to by the unforgiving orthodontist about playing dangerous games with a wire-shut jaw, the boy was back in school. He later tried to guess exactly what they had done that day when the bike suddenly bucked and he found himself bleeding on the pavement. He checked the spot, so indelibly marked with his blood – but found not a blemish on the surface. Perhaps it was something in the spokes, or in the chain. Whatever it was, it took on the aspect of a general principle with the boy, that whatever the comforting vision before him – that of the girls skipping rope and his team shouting encouragement behind him, or having finished a day in school without a headache and being only a minute from curling up on the sofa with *The Game of the Day* and a cold Coke, something dreadful could suddenly cut him down without warning. Or not quite without warning: without defence.

So life was unsafe even if he was the most careful boy in the school, who calculated risks before jumping in, whose older parents were more careful than those of the other kids, or so it seemed to him. He'd never seen his father drunk and his parents were too busy with the factory to have any friends in town. There was always something unsafe about other people's lives, their accidents and needless gashes, the way small kids ran around with knives and scissors, and broken bottles glittered in their yards. Their outhouses were never limed out, the stench mingling with unventilated cooking gas and boiled collard greens. He'd always pitied the kids who had little chance of growing up without scars or missing fingers, like the men who worked at his father's factory, all of whom were missing something. Yet it seemed, for all his caution, that he was the one who carried the scars.

He gave up officiating. He had permission to walk around the building during recess, or to stay in the room and wash the boards if he wished, and he did. He was a third grader, an almost perfect reader who had polished off the year's book on the first night of classes, and had been attending to other things after school – the various magazines that came to the house: *Time, National Geographic, Maclean's* and the *Reader's Digest* that went directly to the bathroom to accumulate the talcum, spent hairs and grains of Serutan. On his wall he'd hung the maps of the Geographic Society, and on the dining-room table after school he would copy out the Walter Weber wildlife paintings, committing them all to memory. He knew the capitals, all the capitals and he knew the birds and fish of Florida. He was as good at copying as he was on statistics. On dozens of sheets of the factory's letterhead he copied bloody scenes from the Everglades, or cavemen stoning a mammoth, accompanied till dinnertime by the baseball broadcasts from chilly Fenway. At night, after his mother had come home to cook him his supper and then gone back to the factory, he'd take out his baseball bat and stand in the living room, swishing with each reported pitch to their local, last-place hitters in a Class D entry.

One day in class after the jaw had healed but before he'd rejoined his classmates in games, or the teacher at the periphery, a strange thing happened. Normally when they studied geography, he and the teacher would carry on a dialogue about whatever state or country was being studied, its rivers, mountains, cities and products. In his private travels he had gone to whatever country was being discussed, had placed himself on the pre-war streets from the pictures in their old geography text, creating the world afresh with his own pronunciations of impossible names: Traffel-gar and Gibb-ral-tar. Veena and Pra-goo.

The teacher was talking that day of the great rivers of North America and the subject was the St. Lawrence which, she said, she'd once seen for herself in Cuebeck, Canada. She passed some photos around the class. The boy was about to raise his hand, but she went on about the trip she'd taken through Cuebeck, out on the Gasp Peninsula, and the boy found himself standing up – the teacher noticed, but she went on talking about the mountains in Gasp – and she asked if anyone could find them on the map. The boy was now walking slowly to the front of the class, and the teacher watched him from the corner of her eye, thinking that he should have asked permission to be excused, but it would be all right, this once.

'And they have a big rock at the end of Gasp called Purse Rock because it looks like a giant handbag stuck out in the ocean –' and then the boy picked up a piece of chalk and tapped the board for attention. '*C'n'est pas vrai,*' he cried, writing quickly, '*Percé = Per-say*' and '*Gaspé = Gas-pay.*' He tapped the first word. '*Ça veut dire un p'tit trou. Comme les Nez Percés, les Indiens. Ils ont un p'tit trou dans le nez . . .*' and he was smiling now, pointing to the side of his nose, looking around for other kids to laugh with him. 'Don't you know the Indian tribes? Crows, Blackfeet, Shoshone? Nez Percé? *Percé, ça signifie comme ça –*' and he began to draw an Indian in full headdress on a white pony, one of his best copies from Holling C. Holling's *Book of the Indians,* when he turned with the first laughs from his classmates. '*Un instant –*' he started to say, thinking himself at home, drawing something for his father to see, playing the geography games they sometimes played, when the teacher stepped between him and the class and with the thick paddle he'd often seen her use on the morons, brought it down first on his arm, scattering the chalk, then on his flank, spinning him around so she could catch him by the collar, which ripped, and with one hand, bent him just enough to administer five of the hardest she'd ever delivered, on any boy for whatever reason, even to the boy who'd once stolen her cigarettes from her purse years before, at another school, at recess time.

The boy didn't know that he spoke a foreign language, didn't even know the name of the words he'd always spoken with his father; not until he looked back in his book and associated *purse* and *gasp* with the map he knew so well did he suspect that he knew things other people, grown people, didn't. The knowledge had made him confident, suddenly an adult with an adult's right to correct an erring teacher, and when the paddle started to fall it was the humiliation, not the pain, that hurt him most of all.

To understand such a boy is to begin with the father. He was in his middle forties: a short, trim, muscular man with wavy black hair greying in a bar at the temples, once a hockey player in another country. To equals and superiors he was charming and co-operative, liking nothing better than drinks and a night on the town in Jacksonville or Tampa. The boy knew his father's friends, younger men from New Hampshire or Maine, French boys with the names that were all vaguely familiar. The boy was already looking for similar names in the textbooks and box scores, on main streets and Dixie highways of all the towns they travelled through.

They had come to Florida four years earlier, settling first in Hartley and then moving to Fort Lauderdale. Each stay lasted a year while his father perfected his contacts, his English, and learned that he was temperamentally unsuited to working for other people. He'd been a furniture buyer in both towns, and once took the family with him to the summer showings in Chicago and North Carolina (the boy remembered Chicago for its hotels, the long nights in a murky room on the crisp hotel sheets while his parents were out at salesmen's parties, and his midnight walks down the corridors with day clothes over pyjamas, sitting on the benches outside the elevators in order to greet his parents when they finally came up). Finally his father quit, and started a wholesaler's showroom in Fort Lauderdale. But after one successful winter, Gene Thibidault was suddenly frozen out. His neon sign was smashed, his windows doused with paint, and his bank credit shortened. He was learning about the lines of force in Broward County. He sold again, at a loss, and went on the road for a year to build up his savings and moved the family back to the north Florida town of Hartley where the living was cheap. The boy had all but started school in Hartley, missing only the first grade – an almost fatal lateness, as it turned out.

For a winter they lived like widow and son, with T.B. Doe spending only five days a month with them, off the road. It wasn't the life his father preferred, though he was good at it, even at milking the poorest third of the nation – North Carolina to Louisiana – for a living wage. His mother took up substitute teaching, though the students complained they couldn't understand her. She'd come from Saskatchewan a long time ago, married in Montreal, then gone to Florida. It was his father who was keeping them South, while he and his mother dreamed of the North and of snow.

How his father had heard of the old airport, or when he first got the idea for starting a factory, the family never learned. Perhaps while he recuperated after a serious accident, when the boy and his mother had gone back to Canada for the spring and summer. When they returned, his father had leased an airport and signed the papers for a furniture factory.

And so they had moved from the apartment near South Street in Hartley two years before the baseball game, deep into the country to be near their airport. Airfields like this, built during the war for undefined purposes, dotted the South: an octopus of concrete hacked through cypress and live oak in that Florida geography of sand and swamp, palmetto and cactus, behind a wall of palms.

The furniture equipment was housed in the lone standing hangar; the office and showroom in the old conning tower. The equipment – joiners, planers, saws, lathes, sewing machines and button presses – had been bought through the Citrus National Bank. The designs of Citrawood Furniture were his mother's, who'd been trained for that much at least, and the orders came from his father, still in casts and confined to a chair, who'd sold enough on approval to satisfy the bank.

For the boy there was the gift of concrete in the depths of the forest, a network of private highways leading nowhere. He was seven, he had a two-wheeler, and he explored.

They were not alone, back in the woods. During the war, there had been a barracks, a store, a gas station, a graded road leading in from the highway, even a cinema. Then the buildings had been ploughed aside, and even the bulldozer lay quiet in the woods next to the spilled ruins of windows, shingles, and walls – even soup cans and movie projectors – that had fallen under the dull blade of the giant machine, now furry with rust.

Not far from where they lived that year in the woods stood a cabin of a migrant-worker family, down over the Florida Central tracks, closer to the lake where the mud never dried for six months of the year. You could scoop up that foul mud, thinking it fertile beyond belief, and plant seeds in it the way his mother had done, but nothing would ever grow. The migrants picked moss, ten cents a hundredweight, and sold it to his father among others, who rubberized it for sofa stuffing. There were seven children all strong enough to handle the metal poles and hooks to pull moss down from the cypress. The boy was a little too young and weak to help, but he was attracted to the Dowdys' cabin on those steaming days when his parents were at the factory and he was bored, or frightened of being alone.

He never did understand how many children there still were. The younger ones all looked alike – straw-haired, naked, bloated, playing in the sour purple-black muck, even trapping minnows in the run-off waters in their front yard. The boy his age or a year older was named Broward as he'd been born in Broward County, out on a canal west of Fort Lauderdale. He was darker than the others, and thinner. He blinked and scratched, the film of dirt above his shorts was cut only where rain or sweat had washed across it. In return for the things he showed the boy – the nests of turtles and alligator eggs, the wild-cat beds, where to fish for something better than bream, what to rub on chigger bites, how to eat watermelon without a plate or a spoon and without stopping the motion or spilling juice – Frank tried to teach him about the rules of baseball, how to make figurines from plaster-of-paris and red rubber moulds, the rudiments of reading, and how to speak.

The boy had worked all summer on the plaster figures, glazing and painting them and then walking to the highway to sell them at a nickel apiece to tourists who'd been beaten off the coast road by curiosity or social conscience. The boy and the Dowdy children would sit in the dust near the turn-off to Schofield's general store and gas station, with a row of little Indian figures in Seminole dress set on an upturned orange crate.

It was April, well into summer in central Florida, when the watermelon were at their ripest, and cheapest. At the general store the melons were piled around the gas tank, the doors, under the windows, and along the highway like boulders. Even the Coke machine outside was crammed with melons, at ten cents a giant slice. After selling a few of his Seminole dolls, the boy would buy a slice, return to the roadside and begin eating it, just the way the Dowdys had taught him.

One day, Broward Dowdy and a few of his younger brothers came up from their shacks, each with a melon slice which they'd been eating along the way. Their bellies were glistening with juice, and flies had sprung where the liquid had dropped on their feet.

Just then a large dusty car with out-of-state licence plates slowed down and pulled into Schofield's drive. On the dashboard, the boy noticed, stood the plastic Jesus that also stood in the cars of his father's friends, and which the boy associated with furniture salesmen along with their open liquor bottles, their drinking as they drove, their turning to look at women on the sidewalks, and the dirty stories that anything in skirts seemed to start.

There were six people in this car: a couple in front with one small boy, an old lady and two kids in the rear. There were Kleenex boxes and sandwich wrappers along the back window ledge, and while the car was stopped the wife carried out a box full of litter. The little kids were pestering their father for slices of melon, and the man headed over to the boys, camera slung around his neck.

'Boys – this Route 401?'

'No, sir. Y'all lost 401 outside Leesburg.'

'We want to see the Silver Spring –'

'Ain't fixin to, not thisaway.'

The grandmother shuffled their way, followed by a girl younger than Frank.

'*Regarde-les, Henri!*' the old woman called to the man. '*Prends leur photo.*'

'*Papa – comment mangent-ils?*'

'It isn't hard to learn,' said the boy. 'Just got to keep your mouth full of seeds and find a way of spitting them out.'

'*Papa – âchètes-en pour moi.*'

'*Combien demandent-ils?*' the old lady asked her son.

'Ten cents a slice,' said the boy. 'It's cheaper for y'all if you buy a whole one.'

'*Henri – ce garçon-là me comprend.*'

'Sure I understand,' said the boy.

'*Ecoute, Henri – prends leur photo, vite.*'

'*Qu'ils sont tellement quioutes. Regarde la didinne – là.*'

'*Tais-toi, Lucille.*'

'*Mais y portent pas de caleçons, papa.*'

'They don't *own* any underpants,' Frank said to the little girl, Lucille, his age. 'Least, not in the summer.'

The man, Henri, was walking around the orange crates where the boy had grouped his figurines. The Dowdys were standing behind them eating their watermelon. The tourist children were laughing among themselves, still pointing to the nakedness of the younger Dowdy children who regarded the tourist family curiously, as half-tamed animals might, waiting for a lump of sugar. Henri's wife had been cleaning the faces of her younger children, and passing cold Cokes around. She came running, as though her husband had called her to see a snake, or something odd. The three adults, a man with a camera and two women, faced the children, and only Frank, hoping for a sale of his Seminole dolls, showed a ready smile.

'*Mance,*' said the husband to his wife, '*ce gamin-là me comprend. J'en suis sûr.*'

'*Toi,*' she said to the boy, '*avec les poupées-là. Que t'appelles-tu?*'

'Frankie,' he said.

'*Sacrement!*' whispered the old lady, crossing herself.

'*Vite, Henri, avant qu'ils disparaissent!*'

The man wound his camera hurriedly and pointed it at the boys, who all dug deeper into their watermelon.

'*Monsieur,*' said Frank, '*est-ce qu'on doit sourire ou plutôt manger comme ça?*'

The man was still looking into his camera, but his elbows dropped. The smaller Dowdys were backing away, afraid of the camera and the way the tourists spoke. 'Them's Yankees,' Broward tried to explain, 'and that's jist Yankee-talk. Ain't that the way they talk, Frankie?'

'I don't know. I reckon it is.'

'You a Yankee, ain't you?'

'I don't know. I don't reckon I am.'

'Then how come you know what they're saying?'

It was a question the boy couldn't answer, not then and not two years later when he rose to correct the teacher's pronunciation.

But the tourists – they were Quebeckers from a small town outside Montreal – were even more frightened. The grandmother entered the date and time, and, as nearly as she could determine, the place, of this Visitation. All necessary to the registering of a Miracle. They bought all of Frank's Seminole dolls, not asking the prices, just stuffing his hand with all the change they had. Working in English, they arranged the Dowdy children around Frank and behind the dolls, the smaller Dowdys looking down into their slices of watermelon. Poor white trash, Florida crackers, migrant workers, nothing in their faces to indicate otherwise. But for a family from St. Jérôme, driving down for their first Florida holiday after the war, a Miracle had taken place, a flesh and blood Miracle captured on film that would make all the apparitions of the Virgin Mary, all the shrines and grottoes of Quebec, Spain, and other pious backwaters, blush in embarrassment. The old woman walked to him slowly, both arms out to frame him, to carry him as though he were already a doll, a framed portrait in oils. '*Tu n'es pas réel, je sais bien. J'ai peur de Toi, mon Ange ...*' and she stopped short of touching him. '*Ni chair, ni sang,*' she said and bowed, making the sign of the cross, then planting a hesitant kiss on his dirty feet.

In days to come, the St. Jérôme paper would carry an account, and two Montreal papers, one English, would pick it up. The office of the Archbishop in Miami, to whom the entire incident was related two days later, took it under advisement, studied the photos, and put the whole story on the French-language bulletin supplied by the better hotels to their Quebec guests, under the heading, '*Miracle ... ou Mirage?*' At least one travelling salesman that day in Miami, staying in the Patrician and picking up the French news with his tomato juice on the patio by the pool, drying out from the night before, read the story and thought of Gene Thibidault who lived up near Hartley, and who had a boy of seven or eight. He folded it up and gave it to Gene the next time he saw him; and when his father read it to him the boy remembered it perfectly. It became the first evidence – and all the proof he would ever need – that nothing secret and remote was ever lost in the world, was ever perfectly private.

II

About the same time as the Miracle, the boy had been learning to bicycle on the deserted concrete strips of the airport while his parents, ten Hartley lumbermen and two black seamstresses worked inside the factory.

He discovered a stream beyond the last bank of rusted lights at the end of the longest runway. Probably it had been a ditch dug by a wartime bulldozer and then abandoned. Maybe they'd tried to drain the swamps, almost succeeded in the dry season, then become disheartened when the winter rains came. Out a few feet, the water rippled around something rusty, and turtles' heads often broke the surface. The banks were lily-clogged and the scum was a lush grass-green as far out as a small current in the middle. The surface was in nervous agitation; the lily stalks walked and jerked, mysterious bubbles squeezed through the slime and burst with loud popping noises in the thick water, and minute by minute the smaller fish flopped and larger ones fretted the scum with a sudden spurt. Never had the boy seen water so alive. Even the worms he cast were nibbled before they could sink through the algae.

He'd never caught so many fish ... bream, and the longer perch they called warmouth. He deepened his line and got nothing. Then he brought the bait closer to shore and didn't shorten it and in a few seconds the twig he'd tied as a bobber submerged and started limping away, slowly at first, then faster and more insistently. The fish was hooked; he merely had to pull it in. It was heavy, but not too lively. He hauled it up through the algae and watched closely as it squirmed on shore. The fish, if it was a fish, was a foot long, black and finless, though coated in scum, like an eel only thicker, with blunt reptilian head. He dragged it onto the concrete, then dropped his pole and jumped on his bike. He'd done something that his father would want to see.

T.B. Doe was sitting at a card table just inside the entrance. Paper plates and stained cups had been pushed to one side, the cigarette-roller stood in the middle resting on a stack of invoices. A thick-set man with a puffy face and blondish-grey crewcut hair was sitting with him. The boy's mother stood by the filing cabinet talking to a woman much shorter with very black hair and the shadow of fuzz on her upper lip. A younger, better-dressed man in a shiny olive suit and cream-coloured tie was in the wood room, walking down the aisles between the machines as though he were inspecting them. The boy caught his breath and walked to his mother's side.

'And this must be your li'l boy that you was tellin' me about,' said the dark-haired woman. Up close it wasn't fuzz, just very bad skin with a row of blackheads above the line of lipstick. 'Ain't he cute, though. What's his name?'

'Frankie.'

'Ain't that the cutest li'l name, though?'

'This is Mrs Lamb, dear,' said his mother. 'And Mr Lamb, from the bank.'

'My husband is givin' some money to your daddy,' said Mrs Lamb, 'and that gentleman back yonder is my brother, Mr Curry. Travis Curry, the lawyer?'

'Trav!' Mr Lamb called. The lawyer hurried back from the far end, and was given a stack of papers to read. He signed, then stamped them with a pocket seal. Hands were shaken all around.

'Daddy – come see what I caught.'

'What would you say to a drink?' his father asked, pulling out the bottom drawer. 'Bourbon? Scotch?'

The Lambs took bourbon, the lawyer and his father Scotch, his mother nothing.

'Daddy.'

'Now I want you to watch this,' said his father. 'Son – you heard what everyone wanted?'

'Yes, sir.'

'Then take the cups over to the cooler and mix the drinks.' He looked across to the lawyer and banker. 'Only seven years old and the best damn bartender in Oshacola County. Makes a damn good dry martini, Manhattans, name it – trained him myself.'

'Ain't that cute, though.'

'Daddy – I caught a fish –'

'– only wish you were asking for something *harder*. But we're out of gin –'

'– it's *big*, Daddy. It's the biggest fish I ever saw.'

'Find out how much water they want first, son –'

So the boy made the drinks, simple straight drinks with a dash of cold water from the cooler, all the while thinking of the fish that lay at the end of the runway and the other things that swam under the scum and caused the bottom to bubble, the lilies to walk. It was a new water cooler with a ten-gallon jug on top; three squirts on the button brought a single fluttering bubble to the surface. He leaned his face on the cool solid glass, pressed his eyelids on it, then drew back enough to look through the water back into the office. He could still make out the women and the lawyer, the water reducing them all to balls or sticks in appropriate clothing.

'We're waiting, son.'

The office seemed all the hotter, now, with his eyes still cool and rested, as though he'd just slept, as though the drinkers were in his dream.

'Can you see the fish now, Daddy?'

'What fish?'

'I've been *telling* you.'

'Oh, all right.'

The bike was just outside. When he stepped into the sun and began pedalling he realized how sweaty he'd gotten inside. Clouds boiled overhead, grey-on-grey flaring, like a pebble dropped into a muddy puddle, and thunder was rolling over the lake behind the trees.

He had dropped his pole and fish on the runway a few feet from the water's edge, but now he couldn't find it. Yet the concrete was wet, as though a truck had backed into the mud, and then gotten stuck, thrashed around, gotten out.

The pole was quickly found ... at least its handle. He pulled it toward him, wondering how the fish could have dragged it so far. But the line was light as he pulled. And when he'd tugged it out of the shrubs and back onto the concrete, he saw the strangest, most frightening thing he'd ever seen. On his line was the same scummy black head, the mouth open enough to expose a set of nearly human teeth; the gills still heaving, but nearly all the body was gone. There was a backbone and part of a fin, and under the bones, part of its black intestines. The meat had been shredded from the bones, even the hook gleamed cleanly between the ribs. The boy was aware of the wind roaring in the giant cypress, the slapping of water he couldn't see. He was seven years old; he didn't know yet who he was, nor had he yet suffered for what he would become.

But the fish at his feet, or whatever it had been, had seen the worst thing in the world, whatever that was. The boy knew now that both things existed, the unnameable fish and the thing that had eaten it, and knowing that, he felt he had seen the worst thing too.

Hartley was a southern town and the South was as foreign to him as the Canada and Europe he was always hearing about. He felt excluded by the holidays – Jeff Davis's birthday, Confederate Memorial Day, or the quiet explanation from a beloved teacher of why they couldn't celebrate Lincoln's birthday, though it appeared in red on most of the calendars – which added to the deep sense of deprivation that he felt in reading the northern school books. The smug references to playing in snow, the predicating of all nature experiments on the 40th degree of latitude. Yankee rituals like robins in spring, squirrels in autumn, the burning of leaves, ice skating and sledding. In their Yankee books, families went on picnics in the country. ('What's wrong with the beach?' he'd demanded, 'don't they have an ocean? Or is snow a compensation?') He thought of snow as a kind of sticky popcorn one played in warmly and drily, for whenever it froze in the town of Hartley and the smudge pots were set out under the orange trees and the kids pulled themselves to school with frozen fingers gripping their handlebars, the teachers would assure them it couldn't snow. It was too cold for snow.

And so the boy concluded that Florida was a special case that no one in those cavernous cities up north could even write about. None of the fishing books described the thing he'd caught that day at the airport; none of them dared to talk bout the giant fish and turtles he'd glimpsed through the glass-bottomed boat at Silver Springs; none of them mentioned the black-skinned people who filled the streets of Hartley and who howled from the balcony of the Palace Theater every Saturday morning.

It was autumn again, the boy's ninth autumn, and his last as a Southerner. He'd been sitting in the yard watching the boys play football across the street and their younger sisters skip rope in the fine clay dust of the road. The porch radio was turned on loud, the camphor tree gave shade, and an old dog had settled in the yard near his feet to chew on a bone. Suddenly over the noise of the kids and the hum of a hot Florida afternoon, he heard the high-pitched whine of their factory truck turning the corner off the highway (ambush corner, the boy called it), and ploughing its way faster than he'd ever seen it, only to lurch to a stop between the boy and the view of the game, partially on the grass and still in the road.

'Get inside, get, get!' his father cried, and now the boy heard a siren out on the highway, and he could tell it was turning too at ambush corner.

The boy flowed with the action, and soon it was furious; the older boys stopped in their tracks, the girls jumping rope hesitated, the hound lifted an ear and then settled back but the boy was already running up the stairs and onto the porch. The truck rammed farther onto the lawn, blocking the drive, and his parents jumped out. It was as though the dusty road were rising in a wave and the lawn had turned to water; a rebellion of nature that only the boy and his parents were fleeing. He flew into the house, into the living room, which was the most protected (he'd often told himself that in the event of a hurricane he'd be safest crouched under the dining table just where the living room pinched to an alcove); and he was under the table when the screen door slammed and the living-room door burst open.

This is my father, he told himself: my mother and father. But it was a dream to him, like a movie. His parents were acting; they had to be. 'Gene, Gene! Don't do it!' his mother was screaming, and she grabbed for his father's arms, but he wrenched free. She was blocking the door, trying to keep it open.

He saw his father framed in the doorway, against the broken light of the screen, and thought, I don't know that man. He had never seen his father pursued, never seen him clumsy, never seen him terrified and desperate, clawing at the furniture to barricade the door. From deep in the dining room under the table the boy wanted to cry out, 'Quick, call the police, Daddy!' but then he remembered the sirens. The police were already coming. So his father was blocking off the bad guys for a few minutes until the police could catch them in the front yard. But he'd left his wife unprotected on the porch. *Save her!* the boy again tried to scream, but he too was shaking in terror. Then from the outside he heard his mother's voice, piercing his whimper, his father's guttural straining, the frantic stacking of everything movable, 'Gene, Gene –

Frankie's in there. Think of Frankie. They're here. Gene, *listen,* they're here.'

His father couldn't hear, not the way he was dashing around the living room, not the way the air was popping from his lips, the sweat dripping off his nose and chin. *Never mind me,* the boy thought. The Cavalry is coming, I can hear the bugles. They've got us surrounded, but we're holding out – And then he turned, looking not to the front and his father, but to the side, and the kitchen. The dusty boots of two men stood at the doorway, and from the way their pants were stuffed inside their boot tops and the stripes ran up their side, he knew the police had gotten in the back door while his father was barring the front, and they were safe. 'Yippee!' the boy yelled, and almost embraced their legs, and while that small victory still burned in his throat, the policemen moved. One bent fast and jerked the boy out by his shoulder, and stood him up by grabbing his collar and holding him a few inches off the floor, his thick wrist hard against the boy's throat. The other levelled his rifle at the desperate man who now had turned.

'That's better,' he said. 'Hands against the wall.'

The room shuddered with the flashing red light coming in through all the windows, dull crimson, the heaving gills of a dying fish. Then the second policeman pointed his rifle at the china cabinet and flicked the row of Royal Doulton onto the floor. The china had always been packed in newspaper, first thing, each time they moved. 'Hey, stop that!' he cried. 'Gene! Frankie!' his mother screamed from the porch and his father sagged against the wall. 'You son of a bitch,' he said.

The first policeman still held the boy tight, but let him down.

'Reckon you'll come along now?'

From outside, over the throbbing of several engines, the bursts of a police radio through the dipping banks of red, his mother cried again. 'Gene, what are they doing? Gene, sign it, for God's sake. It's not worth it.' She pounded the living-room door, which didn't budge. The second cop looked once at the first and made a sign that the boy didn't understand. Then he walked toward the boy's father, rifle extended. The boy's eyes were covered by the policeman's hand, but he could feel the red lights.

'Gene, they're taking me away. Gene, do something!'

It sounded as though the furniture was being moved again. The trunk was slammed against the wall, chairs were being stacked, the dresser was rolled bit by bit away from the door. But the house was shaking on its pilings and there were other sounds that could only come from grown men trying to hurt. Then the racket died down; it was a regular noise, the expulsion of breath, like a cough, while another man chuckled.

'Leave off him, Billy Ray. Leave off him. He was in a cast.'

'What about –'

'Now take that child out to his momma. What kind of barbarians is he going to think we are?'

The boy was turned and marched through the kitchen to where the back door was sprung open and the screen punched in. The dark-haired lady with the row of blackheads stood with other men on the back porch. From the living room the boy could hear her husband, Mr Lamb from the bank, saying, 'Well, sir, it looks like a nigger Saturday night in here. You see the grief you've brought on yourself –' and as the boy was pushed out the back through the knot of people, Mrs Lamb was saying to her brother, the lawyer, '– and him such a fine looking gentleman, too. That's where I feel so bad about it all.'

The neighbour kids stood in the driveway, in and out of the row of police cars with their red lights turning, climbing up and jumping out of the cab of the Thibidault truck. His mother stood between two policemen with their hats in hand, and as the boy approached he could see that she was handcuffed to the bug-smeared grille of their big Dodge truck. She leaned against the hood, and the boy could tell she wasn't seeing him or anything, any more. Her face was grey from the dust, rubbed white where she'd brushed it, and everything about her seemed out of focus to the boy.

The crowd applauded as the deputy led him from the house. He was being dragged and rolled like the bales of moss at the factory. Why were they cheering? The boy tried to smile – heroic survivor – but the policeman treated him roughly, more arsonist than victim. 'How many more you got in there, Henry?' a deputy shouted from the street. Older people were lined up on the street, veiled by the dust from curious cars slowing down, and the lawn was filled with onlookers. The shaded part under the camphor trees where the boy had been sitting with the old hound dog was scattered with cars and the whole thing looked like a country auction, except for all the older men in shirtsleeves wearing deputy's badges. The officer, Henry, dropped him next to his mother in front of their truck. She reached out with her free hand and brushed his hair out of his eyes.

'Who in the name of Christ locked this woman up?' The same officer who had stopped Billy Ray in the living room had seen the woman handcuffed to the grille. All of the men milling on the lawn had handcuffs dangling from their belts, but only the uniformed men had guns. One of them quickly unlocked her, and apologized.

The other policemen were talking to the neighbours, answering their questions, good-naturedly and causing them to laugh. 'Naw, he didn't have no gun,' said one, 'leastways we bust in on him 'fore he could git it out.

'Yeah, so me and Billy Ray – that's Officer Moffitt, he's still inside with Mr Doe and Mr Lamb – I'm Henry Stokes, come in from Bushnell,' he was saying to an older man taking notes, 'bust in the back door and took him by surprise.... Naw, just him and the kid hiding under a table. I didn't see no guns, but that don't mean –

'Kid went peaceable. I expected some kind of fight out of him – the kid I mean – but he didn't give no trouble, you know? Like he figgered his old man was already guilty.

'Yeah –' he went on to someone else. 'It was Mr Lamb swore out the complaint. Assault with Intent, out at the old airport where he's got that factory. We follyed him here.

'– Right now it's Assault and Resisting Arrest and Trespassing. Trespassing at the airport –'

The policeman was going down the line of spectators, answering their questions, moving farther from the boy and his mother. Even through her skirts her legs seemed cold and dead, and her hand on his shoulder was heavy and still. He could hear a voice he knew, the lady-next-door's, snapping at the kids, 'Quit that, hear?' and seconds later he felt the little limestones striking his arms and raining from gentle arcs on his head and pinging lightly on the truck.

After a long time people moved away from the house and driveway and the kids started other games in the street. One deputy came to his mother and told her they were ready for her inside and that he'd look after the boy while she went. Without answering, she took the boy's hand and pulled him along with her, and no one objected. Mr Lamb and Travis Curry came out of the house and the people who still lined the yard cheered when they saw him. Mr Lamb was smiling as he walked toward their truck.

'We'll be needing your signature now, ma'am,' he said. 'Seems your husband was mistaken about the agreement we signed, and he's prepared to make a settlement. I can't tell y'all how sorry I am about his misunderstanding – I reckon it's a little bit my fault, not informing you earlier – and what with your husband taking it kindly bad –'

His mother was looking at the banker, in the same blank way she'd been looking earlier. 'Thief,' she said.

'Ma'am?'

'Scum. Trash.'

'Now, Mrs T.B. Doe. You are a refined lady. Don't oblige me to change my mind. It's like Mr Curry explained out at the airport, the bank was protecting the people's money by writing in an option clause to buy at the close of the second year.'

'To steal.'

'I'm pretending I didn't hear that. I'm pretending that a gypsy woman or a Jewess or whatever it is you are – hell, you ain't even Americans and you been leasing U. S. Government property – didn't call me what you done called me. A gypsy-Jewess that done took half the Oshacola County Police and two town marshals to restore order –

'Naw, I'll forget it. All I want is your signature and I'll forget all of it. I'm fixing to drop all charges of a personal nature. From the first day you signed that agreement you became the unpaid managers of Oshacola County Development Corporation. We let you draw your own salary without interference. You should have taken all you could get, 'cause that's the last penny you're fixing to see. Now we assert our rights of ownership.'

The sheriff interrupted. 'You don't have to go in if you don't want to, ma'am,' he said. 'Your husband done signed all the copies inside. Travis has them right here.'

'It's kindly hot and stuffy inside,' said Billy Ray Moffitt.

'He broke all your china,' said the boy. 'He put the barrel of his gun on the shelf and knocked everything off.'

'What did you do to my husband?'

'Convinced him to sign,' said the officer.

'They were fixing to kill him,' said the boy. 'That's why they covered my eyes and took me out.'

She looked at the banker and the lawyer, her eyes dry and hard. 'Well?' she demanded, and they held the papers out, smiling at her and the boy. 'I see,' she said. They gave her a pen. 'I see.' They brought his father out to the porch, handcuffed to one officer, leaning on another. 'I signed,' he said. 'What you wanted.' His face was dark, red under his tan, but he wasn't bleeding. *My father gets dark, my mother gets white,* thought the boy. *He gets small, she gets large.* 'They've taken it all,' and he coughed, bent double, coughed some more, and cried.

'I see, I see,' she kept repeating to no one especially, taking the pen and finally signing below the purple clot that even the boy could see was just a travesty of his father's legal signature.

Only his teacher seemed to care that they were leaving. His father had left that same night as soon as the driveway cleared and his mother had packed without talking to either of them. They threw out boxes of books and of broken china, tropical clothes and the little things that the police hadn't smashed but that wouldn't fit in their four mouldy suitcases. At school the next day the boy had been surrounded by his classmates who'd all by then heard of it – 'What'd your father do, Thibidault?' The sheriff was a hero of the boys in Hartley, a muscular man built on the order of Johnny Mack Brown. They'd heard that a man had been shot out at the airport and the sheriff had tracked the owner back to Hartley and singlehandedly captured him by rushing the back while Mr Doe was shooting it out in front. 'How many did he kill, Thibidault?' they demanded, and the boy was laughed at when he said there had been no guns except the deputy's and no one killed, but that the factory had been rushed by cops and taken over and his parents ordered off it, and the proof of that was that his father had been allowed to leave town after signing everything over and he was already on his way to North Carolina, and would send for them later. A week later a post card came from High Point and the next morning his mother went with the boy to school to collect the necessary transfer letter and report card. The teacher announced to the class that Frankie was moving and that everyone would miss him. Then she took down his drawings that lined the walls, and cut the top line with all the gold stars off the reading and spelling charts. Out in the hall she said that Frankie had made her teaching somehow worth it. She herself was thinking of quitting, she told his mother.

They'd been living out of boxes for a week; when they got back home his mother finished packing sheets, some clothes, a pan, the toaster, and they were finished with Florida. That afternoon they boarded the old Greyhound to Jacksonville and sometime around midnight, in that last of the Florida cities, after hours in the bus station drinking Cokes, they boarded the chrome-plated bullet-shaped New York local. The boy took the seat behind the driver and with a road map open to Route 1, traced the coming journey.

Wherever they went, bus drivers were friends and heroes, bringing news and carrying messages, making the waitresses put on lipstick and run a wet comb through their hair, making the old men tell what seemed to be dirty stories, and the boy realized that he was once again in his father's world, with the salesmen who travelled all night and depended on coffee and the jokes they could tell. It seemed to the boy that he'd learned more in two nights of staying awake with the drivers than he had from all his years in school and reading books.

They got off in High Point, North Carolina – the furniture city in the hills – and his father was there to meet them. It was Furniture Mart time and the town was jammed with buyers and salesmen from everywhere east of the Mississippi. The conventions in Chicago and High Point were cornerstones of the furniture life, the sort of thing the boy associated with the plastic statuary in the salesmen's Chryslers: all the young Tonys and Mikes who swapped stories about niggers and kikes and Miami Beach. And now, suddenly, the boy and his mother were at a convention and his father was there without a job or friends. He'd already bought a used Chevy and he'd found a place for them in a rooming house in Thomasville ten miles away. For T.B. Doe there would be the hotel in High Point where the men with jobs drank all night and a clever man could pick up leads. He was seeing men night and day about a job, not letting on that the factory was gone, and that the money he carried in his wallet was all he had. Meanwhile they were to sit tight in Thomasville and Frank was to stay inside during the day, since he wasn't dressed for the cold and the truant officers might pick him up for not being in school.

They'd had their dishes broken that day in Hartley and his mother hadn't cooked a kitchen meal in nearly a month. They'd been eating out and the boy had acquired the childhood taste for French fries, hamburgers, Cokes and pie, and with no place to play or run a bike, he'd immediately begun to put on weight. His mother had bought new pants and a shirt at a Montgomery Ward's in Georgia while the bus was stopped; three weeks later he'd outgrown them and he was beginning to look – even to himself – like the sons of some of the older salesmen who used to visit back in Florida, the ones with older mothers who would talk of glands while their pale, moist-skinned sons wearing their father's cast-off white shirts and their own shiny pants, with rolls of fat like cushions on their necks and stomachs, eyes pressed into slits over their mounting cheeks, had sat with a Coke. They'd all looked alike in those days, those clumsy boys with high whining voices and adult-styled shoes, whose pockets chimed with change as they waddled. Frank had always been embarrassed when the Jackies and Herbie Juniors, were brought over to visit – he'd gotten on his bike and sought out the neighbour kids. Now he could frighten a kid himself and his wrists were so pudgy he couldn't wear his watch and all the veins had disappeared off the tops of his hands.

And yet these idle days were among the best he'd known. He would waken to the sidewalks clogged with school kids, and he'd all but rap on the window with a kind of arrogant self-assertion. After breakfast his mother would go out and buy him drawing paper and new comics, and she'd pick up whatever local papers were available for herself. Sometimes his father would drive over from High Point to share a cup of coffee and let them in on job leads. They were looking for a buyer at Rosenbaum's in Pittsburgh; another in Buffalo; a man in New Jersey wanted someone to manage his furniture investments. Baumritter needed a man for Kentucky and Tennessee; Kroehler was looking for a Boston man. The boy thought he would like Boston, it was the farthest north. There was not a city in America the boy would not like to live in except perhaps Hartley, Jacksonville, and Tampa, and most certainly, High Point or Thomasville, North Carolina. Every name except the one they were living in filled him with wonder for the new things there were to learn. It was, as far as he could see, the main reason for living, with comics, drawing, and the nightly meal of hamburgers, French fries, Coke, and cherry pie coming in second.

Then just as suddenly as they'd arrived, they were gone. His father had wanted leads and now he had them, and he wasn't going to do any more rushing, he said. He'd learned with the factory. No more trust and no more lawyers, ever. And so it would be more motels, rooms where the boy drew dinosaurs from memory, or rooms in the worst parts of the cold black cities where flecks of snow (at last!) drifted against the black walls of tenements, like ashes from a distant fire. Richmond, Baltimore, Philadelphia. Always interviewing while his mother wrote letters to old friends in Canada and he traced the maps from his mother's old atlas they'd saved from Florida. On the walls of those overheated November rooms hung sentimental portraits of the Dionne quintuplets, and his mother told frightening tales of Catholicism and old Quebec.

Each week led them closer to New York. All those towns read New York papers, heard New York radio directly ('Temperature in midtown Manhattan now 38 degrees'), and now and then, with enormous antennas, pulled in New York television on their tiny sets. New York was the legendary place that his mother feared and had never seen, but his father knew well and felt would be lucky for him. But New York was too expensive for all of them. Better to store them in Newark or Elizabeth, while he scouted the city for a job.

The boy was sleeping later and later, not knowing the day of the week any more, or if his parents would be in when he woke up. A series of landladies would bring him breakfasts, pouring cornflakes into a bowl, toasting some bread and leaving out the softened butter, and he would stroke their cats and watch every minute of television from the time it came on. They moved every week or two. The winter deepened. It snowed and melted, grew black, lingered on the north side of things. He still wasn't allowed out in the daytime; embarrassing questions might be asked. When they stayed in hotels, there'd be a paper bag on the dresser when he woke up, left by his mother, filled with fresh pastries and a Dixie cup of milk with a lid.

In the early weeks of the trip, he had gloated as they passed the rows of yellow windows in the sooty school buildings, but after Christmas he longed to learn something, however stupid, again. He'd take his chances with the kids, be pleased to be put in a school if only for a week or two. He was tired of filling notebooks with designs of cars and airplanes, drawings of animals and portraits of imaginary bearded men. He wanted more gold stars and perfect papers. Only when he saw the schoolyard fights developing (and how often their tourist rooms stood opposite an old brick school), with three or four kids pushing around a fatter one, the circling and punching near the bicycle racks that he knew so well, was he glad there'd be no school, no fights, for him that day, or week; not in that city, or that state. He'd never learn New Jersey history or the counties of Pennsylvania, all the battles that had taken place in Maryland, or the constitution of Delaware. Not having to learn the names of the new teachers and thirty classmates, only to leave them again six weeks later. The millions of possibilities he'd never convert! He looked out the windows, fed landladies' parakeets; drew maps of imaginary countries, harbours, rivers, coastlines, and lost himself in highway nets, urban sprawl, then named his cities in invented languages, devised their flags, labelled the rivers and bays based on private words for water; watched them grow, and then with a cheap fountain pen dropped from a foot above, bombed them into rubble.

Then they were once again in another hotel, this time in Jersey City where the tips of Manhattan skyscrapers were faintly visible beyond the bluffs. It was the oldest hotel yet, with high-ceilinged rooms that were still overheated, cracked hexagonal tiles on the bathroom floor, spots of old tomato paste along the wall near the electric outlet. A single yellow bulb too high for changing, overhead. The smeared windows made his eyes water. It seemed to the boy that first night in Jersey City that they had come to the end of the world; the swamps and river separating them from Grand Central Station, museums, subways, the Empire State Building, the Stork Club, Central Park, Radio City, the Yankees and the Statue of Liberty was the same intractable, impassable barrier that had doomed him always. New York was *there,* five miles away! The same network radio voices that had thrilled him in Florida were at home in those towers! He pressed his face on the windows, steaming the glass with the whispered magical names: Times Square, Flatbush, the Bronx, Fifth Avenue, Macy's, Madison Square Garden, Coney Island, Brooklyn, Waldorf-Astoria. Those names were all he knew of *America;* the rest of the country was an endless roadside that hardly existed.

Instead of a ring of keys, he was left with a single room key attached to a bulbous rubber tail – too fat to stuff in a pocket and carry away but just right for lobbing in the air, and counting the revolutions it made before plunging down. He lay on the cot the next afternoon, studying the ceiling as though it were a floor, tossing the key upward as though it were diving. It snowed a little that day, enough to whiten the tops of cars. In the schoolyard below him, kids scraped together enough for a snow-ball fight before their recess ended. It had once been his dearest wish, in Florida, to play in snow. But now, the snow no longer excited him.

As he watched the melting snow outside, the idea struck him to build his own snowman. Indoors, with what he had. He'd always drawn things, never built. Afraid of cluttering things, of cutting himself. He bundled all the old papers into balls and began stuffing a shirt and pair of pants he could no longer wear. He stuffed them good and fat until the buttons were popping, then blew up a paper bag for the head and painted on the hair and features. He had no carrot for the nose, but he did have paste and more paper bags, and he blackened a gaping hole for a mouth crying out. He put mittens over the shirt cuffs and socks over the ends of the pants. It took him the better part of the day and it suddenly seemed vital to have it done before his mother got home.

He sat the model on a chair, then in bed. He thought of sitting him on the ledge outside their window to see if a crowd would gather, but the window was locked for the winter. Then, with his parents just minutes from coming, he took off his belt and looped it around the dummy's neck, and then found a place on a chandelier to hook the buckle. The dummy jerked and tightened and then swung back and forth, just so. The boy waited by the elevators, running back to the room each time the arrow started up from the lobby. He was waiting behind the door when the familiar crinkle of shopping bags and his parents' talking filled the hall. He gave the dummy one last turn as they rapped. They knocked louder and his father cursed as he put down the bags. 'He must be sleeping,' said his mother, and his father said, 'I sure as hell hope he hasn't gone out,' and his mother answered, 'No, he knows not to,' and his father replied: 'All he does is sleep.' The boy was almost hysterical with suppressed laughter and his bladder burned with sudden urgency.

The moment the door swung open, his mother screamed; sharp

inhuman screams with every breath she took, that brought an opening of doors and rushing of feet down the hallway, as she sank to the floor, and the groceries she'd dropped. Her screaming went on as his father, arms free, rushed in and pulled at the dummy's pants and they came off in a shower of paper balls, and the boy took his hands off his mouth so they could hear his hysterical giggle. 'Mildred, Mildred!' his father was shouting though no one heard, and looking straight over the boy to the woman slumped in the doorway, hands – arms up to the elbow – covering her head and chest, dry breathless sobs ripping from deep inside. No one heard his laughter. The hall was jammed two and three deep with women in housedresses and men in bathrobes, some smiling, others stunned and whispering. Even the boy himself had joined his mother at the door, shaking her, saying, 'Hey, it was just something I made, that's all. I thought you'd like it, I really did.' His mother looked out once from behind her arms, like a child lifting his head against a blow that he knows is coming, and his father jerked him up, lifted the full hundred and thirty pounds his son had become, and shook him, shook him as though he had indeed been paper and stuffing, then threw him in the direction of the bed. 'Get back, get out, get the jesushellout-ofhere all of you!' he screamed, kicking the rubbish, the bottles of milk, the slices of meat for the hot plate, the broken bottles of instant coffee into the hall, laying his hands on the shoulders of men to push them further and faster so the astonished women would follow. And while his father was in the hall the boy climbed on the bed. His mother ran to him and fell across him, and the deep jerking sobs began again.

His father, returning, must have looked once, then slammed a door they couldn't hear, for he didn't come back that night, nor for several days. A week later he told them only of a blizzard that had caught him outside of Rochester. Then he mentioned he'd found a room off Broadway on 92nd Street, and they'd be moving into the city that very night.

The Love God

He greases my griddle,
Chops my meat,
He wets my dreams
He keeps his horses in my stable.
('My Handy Man', Victoria Spivey)

My earthly father is listed as Lyle Coombs, a beans-and-cotton farmer from Pocahontas County, Arkansas. My mother, Elvina Tulleson Coombs, was a tenant farmer's daughter from outside Tupelo, Mississippi. They had been barren for twelve years of marriage prior to my arrival in 1940. Both were God-fearing Pentecostals and part of my childhood was spent under the eye-smarting swelter of canvas revivalism. I record these facts from my birth certificate in the interest of total candour.

I do not know where I come from. I do not know who I am. In these eerie byways of the self, I know I am the direct descendant of Michelangelo and Shah Jahan. Certainly I fought with Genghis Khan and Alexander the Great. Everyone recognizes me, but no one knows what I look like. Lyle Coombs thought I looked just like him – a scrawny little guy with chest, back and arms so woolly, and a head so bald, you thought he was the victim of some misdirected drug experiment. In the mirror, any given day, I see a fit young blond with a California tan, a swarthy Italianoid with gold chains and wiry hair, an uptown dude, a tweedy professor in Oxford cloth button-downs. I am not certain that I exist, despite the comforts I have taken in others' bodies.

Penny Path, my true, eternal father, was, when I got to know him, somewhat arthritic in the hindquarters from nearly twenty years of hauling and occasional plough-pulling through Lyle Coombs's dense, hill-country clay. Further to my commitment to total candour, I must acknowledge that I am not Penny Path's only child. By his reckoning, which was necessarily dimmed by time and circumstance, he had sired several thousand offspring, though I was the first to assume a general human form and demeanour. He thinks I look exactly like him, but if I did, I'd have four legs and whinny at the mares.

Do not be fooled by outer appearance.

I have the true story of my conception from my mother's telling, though even she is unaware of the full details. She remembers a pinkish cast to a cloudy, late-summer afternoon in 1939. She was on the porch shelling peas into a large wooden bowl. With Lyle away for three days, Penny Path had worked his way nearly to the fence near where the truck was usually parked.

It was a quiet, drowsy afternoon with war just breaking out in Europe, and cotton farmers like Lyle immediately speculating on a rise in cotton prices. He'd gone to the bank in Jonesboro to raise money for his first tractor. Failing that – he was a man accustomed to failure, and the New Deal hadn't transformed much of that west-central corridor of Arkansas into a solid money economy – he was also to see a vet about the care and feeding and cost advantage of breeding mules for labour and either selling or even destroying old Penny Path. To breed a mule, of course, you needed donkey sperm and a scrub mare to receive it. While it was true that Penny Path didn't show much inclination to slow down as the best local stud, and that his bloodlines, though lost on paper stood out handsomely enough in his progeny, it's not as though he was worth all that much, either. He was getting on, and he'd become a mite touchy.

She remembers the heat of that night, alone in bed. The moon burned like an auxiliary sun, worn and scarred and nearly orange till it climbed. Lyle had installed a generator to keep a light on in the shed where he raised a few hogs and chickens, and the house lights were tied to it, along with a radio. She was lying in that moon-bright dark listening to ballroom music from radio station WWL in New Orleans and thinking how much she'd like to have a baby to look after on nights like this, and how much she hated having to go out in the bug-crawly night and unscrew the housefeed from the generator when the moonlight suddenly cut out, as though a giant cloudbank had moved over it.

Then she saw why. She saw the form of a stranger just standing at the bedroom window. His head and shoulders and half his body filled the window and the moonlight outlined his deep, broad shoulders, sculpted and smoothed the bulges of an enormously strong but totally unscarred body. She said it reminded her of white marble, like pictures she'd seen from Greece and Italy. He looked serene, not frightening to her at all. He'd entered her life the way images enter in a dream, without warning, without even the noise of his breathing.

Now, the house in which I was born was a simple, pre-Depression catalogue item, commonly used to shelter a farm's tenant family. While it was all on ground level, the bedroom window was still a considerable distance to the ground. The house was set high on a stone foundation, so that Lyle Coombs, for example, a man of normal height, could not be seen from the bed when he walked past the window. She had a good view of the windmill and the fence posts and the roof slope of the outbuildings, but the idea that a human being could even be seen, unless he was standing on a ladder, and that he could fill the entire double-hung window frame was unthinkable.

He didn't speak. He held out his arms – there were no screens – and my mother went to him. He simply lifted her through the window, holding her out flat in his arms like an offering, and she felt a cool breeze against her cheek and shoulders as a wind came up. She knew she was being borne away at great speed in the arms of a god-like giant, but she could only hear hoofbeats below her, and at a distance. She kept her eyes closed and when he set her down in the highest field under a line of cottonwoods, she surrendered to him with such shuddering totality that she knew her barrenness had ended for all time, like a queen bee after the first and final penetration.

One may wonder how a son learns such facts from his mother, and I can only say I am uniquely blessed in eliciting the most intimate sexual details from everyone I meet. In me they see their fantasies, a man who understands, who has experienced everything and passed beyond all curiosity, all need, all prurient interest. The blankness of my response often leads to deeper engagement and more self-exposure than ever intended.

My mother remembers the aching of her full breasts and my refusal to take them, my preference to hold them in my hand and dangle the nipples over my eyes, to lick and not to suck. I could lie in her lap for hours gurgling to her unbuttoned fullness, tracing each pulsing vein, twanging a few stiffened hairs at the edge of her aureole. She remembers visitors pulling down the ruff of my loosened diaper and seeing an organ there that belonged on a man of heroic proportions, though she, of course, saw only a baby. She remembers the embarrassment of taking me into Jonesboro to the park around the Confederate Memorial, and as she wheeled me in, dogs would begin their humping, tulip trees and magnolias would shower petals on the benches. I remember fishing in the ponds near home, the squirming black balls of catfish larva bobbing around my cork, the copulating dragonflies resting on my line, the canopy of bugs and birds over my head, the clotted flies tumbling from the air.

I remember the night of my conception, and I have it not only from my mother, but from my father himself. My mother knew her experience had not been of this world – she only wondered if she'd been dreaming it. When she dared to open her eyes, she saw only old Penny Path standing under a cottonwood and pulling up clumps of grass. He was an ornery beast and no one had ever tried to ride him. She'd never exactly ridden a horse, having been raised around mules on a Mississippi tenant farm, but she found herself approaching the unsaddled animal in her flimsy night wrap and pulling herself on him, practically lying on her belly over his back and holding tight to his neck as he slowly bore her home. He stopped at the bedroom window without an order being given and she was able to slide off and stagger back to bed.

It is fortunate, in those times and in that Pentecostal home, Lyle Coombs arrived a day early and that my mother, with unaccustomed vigour, was able to lure him to bed and even to engage him in formats that she said she'd dreamed would lead to a pregnancy. Lyle had given up all hope, but still surrendered – he held a nearly Catholic view that the end of sex was procreation, and their sustained barrenness, rather than challenging him to greater effort and frequency, had discouraged him from participating in the whole humiliating activity.

Of course we communicated, my father and I. His true name was Panipat, named for the battleground where Emperor Babar brought the lone true faith to pagan India. His ancestors had boiled from the sands of Arabia, carried emperors east and west, had borne the most regal and powerful men of their times into battle and ceremonies. He had been the private mount of Emperor Shah Jahan; he had watched the building of the Taj Mahal, and his throat had been slashed, along with the throats of eighty camels and two royal elephants to be buried in the tomb at the moment of its completion. He grew to full amorousness as the lead stallion in Emperor Ranjit Singh's Imperial Cavalry, and bore His Majesty himself, a man of three hundred pounds and two hundred concubines. He had borne the British to India and Afghanistan and the Crimea, pulled cannon on the continent, and was auctioned off by Scotsmen and sent to Canada and the United States, and sold down river into the beans-and-cotton lands to be used like mules and donkeys.

My father hated mankind. He harboured the hatred of a slave who remembered his kingdom.

In the war years, Lyle Coombs prospered. The old steam tractors of an earlier era rusted near the windmill. 'First came steam, then draft horses, then mules,' said my earthly father, pitchforking a bale of hay at my eternal father, 'now it's diesel tractors, soon's this war's over. This ole son's days are numbered. A stud stallion these days is worth his weight in catfood. Got a pet-food processor been sniffing around. Big ole boy like you'd go for forty dollars, easy.' It was Lyle Coombs's little joke that Penny Path could understand his insults.

Little did Lyle Coombs know the ways of the world.

Like a boa constrictor swallowing a cow, my real father once told me, the days of men are numbered. For the first few months the cow will still be standing, chewing her cud. All she knows (he had a low opinion of cattle) is her tail's too heavy to twitch at flies. A few months later, her hind legs have nowhere to go. A year later, she'll be half digested and still be mooing.

He could not forgive the farmers of Pocahontas County, especially Lyle Coombs. Watching the mares he'd consorted with – just about every available mare in Pocahontas County and some from eastern Oklahoma had been backed into his special stall, for his pleasure. The rough equation of pleasure: a woman weighs a hundred pounds; a mare weighs ten times that. A man's apparatus is what – six inches, he snorted – a stallion's is three times that. Human sexuality held all the appeal of a polyp's budding. Every horse in west-central Arkansas was of his blood – and every mare was now full of mule, mule, his word for all that was foul and degenerate. He'd watched his daughters raped for profit with donkey sperm. Like breeding your wife or daughter to a chimpanzee and calling the monster an improvement on nature because it ate bananas and could swing on trees. He saw his magnificent apparatus for begetting future generations now treated as a joke – 'That thing's 'bout as useful as titties on a nun,' Lyle Coombs would joke, expecting me to laugh along with him.

'Wonder can they geld a stallion? Make a steer out of you and quiet you down some?'

I could feel the heat rising.

'Hey, I'm talking to you, old son.'

Penny Path reared up on his hind legs and in a blast of glory, turned black, white and gold. Tulip trees and magnolia blossomed, branches creaked, cotton bolls burst like popcorn, a roar of animal and insect pleasure deafened the yard. Flies and mosquitoes tumbled around us, too silly from lust even to bite, and the yard turned slimy with a million tiny frogs the size of bumblebees. He'd squeezed life from the soil and from the air.

To quiet Lyle Coombs forever, Penny Path reared up and sprayed us all in the chunky white mist of his immortality. I was drenched, Lyle Coombs swatted his arms in front of his face and raked the horse with his fork. One flick of a foreleg and the pitchfork was splintered and Coombs was left holding a shattered hand.

'Catfood!' he howled, and slithered away over the dying frogs.

I was five years old, in human time.

My father came to me that night. Lyle, with a bandaged hand and fire in his brain, had made sleep in the house impossible. I moved to the barn under cover of dark, scuffing my feet over dead, dry frogs.

'Your mother is scrub stock, a rampant hag,' said Panipat. 'I did it to hurt the donkey-man. She has not slept with him in six years without laughing.'

'He called the meat-processor,' I said.

'I'll be gone by then. It doesn't matter.'

'He'll hunt you down.'

'The cats are welcome to it,' he said. 'I've hunted tigers, cheetahs and desert lions. All things return to the soil. Whole forests bloom from my turds. Let the great Panipat quietly repose in kitty litter.'

'No, you won't,' I said.

I was a determined young man, even at an earthly five. In the revival tents of my childhood, the scariest story of them all, for a young boy, was Abraham's sacrifice of Isaac. My father may have looked more like Esau with his hairy arms, and he didn't have a people to lead or a land to find, but he was an Abraham, secure in his righteousness, founder of a line late in life with a wife who was ageing fast. If his god had told him to sacrifice me, he would have.

Is there a story in which Isaac sacrifices God?

We looked over the available equipment in the barn. There were some steel templates, worn pretty smooth and sharp, but we tested them on Panipat's neck and I couldn't draw blood. We rummaged around for a good blade and found only fragments of old implements that crumbled into rustflakes in my hand. By this time, Panipat was pretty excited about shedding his mortal coil. He planned to walk the earth a few years, on two feet, sacrificing real sex for the exercise of brute human power. Perhaps human beings had compensated for the lack of serious pleasure in their lives. The atomic bomb had just been dropped. The bomb, coupled with the war, had impressed him. He knew a long chapter in human history – the capturing, taming and exploiting of nature, the Age of the Horse – was drawing to a close. It was the chapter that had made him a deity.

We found only a roll of new, strong, baling wire.

He reared again on his hind legs, as he had that afternoon, and as I watched, the hind legs straightened, and the body transformed itself into a man perhaps nine or ten feet tall, with marble skin and glossy black curls, tall as a horse at full extension. It was the body, I know now, of Michelangelo's David, this time with his shoulder looped with wire instead of a slingshot. He paid no attention to me, but walked like Moloch himself to the loft-ladder and began to climb. Rungs burst as climbed, the loft planks creaked and cracked as he pulled himself over the edge. Then he stood, and looped the wire over the highest beam, and wrapped the other end tightly around his neck.

He stood, towering above me forty feet.

'Leave!' his human voice rang out.

As he dived to the floor, the body flashed through a hundred incarnations, the changing-room of his immortal soul, then resumed the familiar, equine dimensions. The middle beam cracked, the roof began to sway, and as I stood in the bare clay outside the door, I saw the giant horse, my father, swing twice before me, his legs out stiff, head relaxed at a terrible angle. The wire snapped, then came the thunderous, hundred-year crack of dry timber: down came the beam and loft and tons of hay, and to the screaming of the hogs and screeching of chickens, came the collapse of the barn, lying down and snapping, like cottonwoods in a tornado.

Had it not been for the flood, I might never have fulfilled my destiny. The Army Corps of Engineers, freed between the war and the Korean outbreak, turned its attention to a number of river projects in the South. No river that had ever overflowed its banks was safe, especially not with local congressmen, with thirty years' seniority, bobbing in the pork barrel.

We had good bottom land, but Lyle Coombs didn't fight it. He let the government buy us out, and took the profit to Little Rock and opened up a cotton brokerage. The house where all this happened and the ditch where Panipat is buried is now a harbour for bass, forty feet under water. We became middle-class and respectable. I graduated from Central High in the first integrated class, where I played absolutely no role of historic importance. That is not my scene. I am the dark shadow of Eros, the part that broke away.

In the way of these things, it was inevitable that I would find my way to Hollywood, the other place where gods mess with mortals and bloodlines get confused. I was going to school in Fayetteville, when some girls from a sorority asked if they could enter my picture in a look-alike contest. 'Who do I look like?' I asked, more puzzled than flattered, because that morning I had looked like a young Richard Nixon in my mirror.

'Oh, come on. You know,' they said. They were giggling. The one with the camera ran her finger down my nose and over my lips. 'Kennedy, of course. I think Bobby more than John, but that's okay.' I took her to bed that night and she called me Instant Replay.

Of course I won. Once my picture was in a Kennedy look-alike contest, it was bound to win. It would have won a Khrushchev or Harry Belafonte contest. What the producer had in mind was to cast the president of the United States in a sleazy porno film to be called *The Party of Your Choice.* I starred with the winners of the Jackie Kennedy, Pat Nixon and Mamie Eisenhower contests, doing things, I must confess, that any red-blooded American boy had fantasized about.

The producer was an upstate California lawyer, otherwise respectable. *The Party of Your Choice* was just the beginning. He had plans, once he saw my potential, to bring American classics explicitly to the screen. He loved Hawthorne. He'd studied witchcraft. He saw fresh ways of filming Henry James. He signed me up for *Tom and Becky Get Laid.* He planned a *Sister Carrie* with a quality cast of porno stars that would blow the socks off mid-America.

I should have recognized who he was.

The movies enjoyed a quiet success, even though 1961 was still the fifties. My acting name was Leo Libido. Forces were percolating through the system. They liked my versatility, the man with a thousand faces and a single rampant urge. No one could trace me – my identity was safe. I specialized in aged priests, teachers, judges and dentists – any role where the robes came off. I played hospitalized heroes jerking off (my Gipper's a classic). In *The Home Movies of J. Edgar Hoover* I played Martin Luther King, Jr and JFK again. Newspapers in Greenwich Village and Berkeley gave me awards. I had a following, in the sexualized underworld.

When my father was dying, I went back to Little Rock. He'd developed diabetes after my mother died, and he was a sorry sight, even enough for my sympathy. It was the week of the Kennedy assassination. He was blind, and reached out for my arm. 'I'm dying,' he said, 'so don't lie to me.'

He clutched my arm and he must have felt its smoothness, for his fingers jumped as though my flesh were coals.

'You know, I always suspected Elvie. She changed so much after you were born. You're not my son, are you?'

I could have brought him a deathbed satisfaction. When he squeezed my arm a second time he must have felt the Coombs-male fur. He was smiling. I sent him to the next world with something to think about.

'I am the son of the horse you knew as Penny Path,' I said.

I think he was speaking to me from the other side. He smiled and patted me once. 'Yes,' he said, 'I suspected as much. So much I missed.'

My rise to legitimacy coincided with Vietnam, the second wave of assassinations, with the acceptance by younger kids who seemed to have been born with attitudes I'd had to struggle for. I was losing my definition in the larger world of American decadence. I couldn't shovel my drugs fast enough into the veins of America. By now I'd given up acting and was writing, directing and producing my own brand of guerrilla cinema. Every Man a Stallion Productions. I produced in film, in photos, in songs and stories the fantasies my women told me. They didn't have to speak, I could read their minds as I passed them in the street.

My old producer came to see me again. He'd changed appearance. Now he was a dapper middle-aged lawyer with long blondish-grey sideburns, dressed in the Beach Boys florals of the late sixties. Dying in Arkansas, he confessed, was the smartest thing he'd ever done. Already he'd forgotten his centuries as a stallion. What he had as a man was quite satisfactory enough – it's not only women who fake their orgasms. It was a new age with new energies, and California men were at the controls.

'Well, Dad, I'm not in awe of you any more,' I said.

He was into hot tubs, computers, franchises, singles bars, drugs, disco music and electronics. He'd walked the streets of the Castro District, and liked what he'd seen. Clones of the Love God, he called them. First time in American history a community defined itself by sex. He saw a parallel economy to service a parallel sex.

'What happened to the God who died for love?' I asked. 'Everything I've done I've done in your name. Every Man a Stallion – I've dedicated my life to you.'

'I decided to stick around. Don't be a religious fanatic – what are you, Pentecostal after all? Sex was then. Money is now.'

'I guess I'm very then.'

'Then you're doomed, believe me.'

Who could believe sex was finished? It was the mid-seventies, everyone was leading a swinging life. My movies were almost respectable now, not quite mall-fare, but playing in the cities. Nixon was the president. Available women were losing their lustre. I'd helped sexualize the world, as part of a bargain. I sold my corporations, changed my face and address. Goodbye, Leo Libido. Farewell, Every Man a Stallion. For the sake of children, I decided to get married.

I took the name Elrod Stubbs and married the purest, sweetest woman I could find in Little Rock. She tells me I'm a handsome fellow in his late twenties, which suits me fine. My mirror still plays tricks; I know I'm in my late forties and given my avoidance of exercise, I can't be anything special. Her name is Daisy. We have three children, two boys and a girl. Their chromosomes are stable. They cannot coax bugs and birds and blossoms from the air. We live outside Atlanta. I am a media consultant.

I swear on all that's holy to me – the memory of my true, uncorrupted father who died that we all might lust more abundantly – that I did not intend the suffering I have unleashed. I'd made peace with both my fathers and only wished to be left alone.

That being said I must also confess even sons of the Love God know a mid-life crisis. My commercial life is full of models and provocative poses. Leo Libido remembers it all and can't always banish the urge. We were filming a Coca-Cola ad off the Florida Keys, a parody of *Treasure Island* where the pirate's chest is full of Diet Coke, and Friday is an exquisite blonde in a chartreuse bikini who gets left behind. I found her, alternately, meltingly then stabbingly beautiful. Her name was Felicia.

I was resting in a lawn chair. Felicia came over and crumpled down beside me. I felt the old urge coming on.

'I bet you don't lose out to Coke cans very often,' I said.

She whispered, 'I didn't lose, Leo Libido,' and kissed her fingers and trailed them down my nose and over my lips.

'You're too young to know about him.'

'Try me.'

'How do I look to you?'

'Short, squat and indifferent.'

'My chin?'

'Weak and wattled.'

In her trailer, she kept a sample of every designer drug known to modern chemistry. She changed her moods like hair colour. We fast-forwarded through a Stanislavskian afternoon: as Brando, Belmondo, De Niro, Nicholson. She popped her pills, snorted and shot, to match my changes. We called for instant replays.

On the drive into Key West she said, 'You will, of course, leave your wife.'

I was noncommittal. 'I'm happily married.'

'Say goodbye. I can make problems, you know.'

'What do you want?'

'Love,' she said. Then, quietly, 'Love's gotten too cheap. It needs an edge. I want real love. I want adoration.'

'Ever tried children?'

She snorted. 'Elrod Stubbs, or Leo Libido, or Travis T. Coombs, my boy, I wasn't even a woman till last year.'

I felt my genes collapsing, attacked in the core of my being. I felt a thick, black evil swirling in my veins. 'Father,' I said, 'you bastard.'

'It is the nature of the Love God to be loved. Do not despise me for what I am.'

She led me to a dockside street of dancehalls and restaurants. Jaws dropped, sailors couldn't pucker for a whistle. She was too close to their dreams. We paused outside a darkened, cedar-trimmed bistro called the Errant Knight. I could hear the Cole Porter medley inside: 'A New Kind of Love', 'It's All Right with Me.' Sing it, Judy.

I stood outside with Helen of Troy, Nefertiti, Mumtaz; I entered with my father's best and favourite, Michelangelo's David.

'They love me,' he said.

All heads swivelled. His arm was cold and deadly. He turned to me a final time before joining the men on the dance floor. He seemed to be laughing. 'Together, we'll bring back an age of corsets and cold showers. We'll make them pay, won't we, son?'

So, I said later that night to a high school teacher from Cleveland who'd been smiling at me brightly, admiring my profile with its stately Roman nose and lips, come here often?

Clark Blaise has taught in Montreal, Toronto, Saskatchewan and British Columbia, as well as at Skidmore College, Columbia University, Iowa, NYU, Sarah Lawrence and Emory. For several years he directed the International Writing Program at the University of Iowa. Among the most widely travelled of authors, he has taught or lectured in Japan, India, Singapore, Australia, Finland, Estonia, the Czech Republic, Holland, Germany, Haiti, and Mexico. He now lives in San Francisco with his wife, Bharati Mukherjee, and teaches at the University of California-Berkeley.